I0632223

Awakened by Grace

Awakened by Grace

Darlene West

RESOURCE *Publications* · Eugene, Oregon

AWAKENED BY GRACE

Copyright © 2020 Darlene West. All rights reserved. Except for brief quotations in critical publications or reviews, no part of this book may be reproduced in any manner without prior written permission from the publisher. Write: Permissions, Wipf and Stock Publishers, 199 W. 8th Ave., Suite 3, Eugene, OR 97401.

Resource Publications
An Imprint of Wipf and Stock Publishers
199 W. 8th Ave., Suite 3
Eugene, OR 97401

www.wipfandstock.com

PAPERBACK ISBN: 978-1-7252-5992-8
HARDCOVER ISBN: 978-1-7252-5993-5
EBOOK ISBN: 978-1-7252-5994-2

Manufactured in the U.S.A.   JANUARY 31, 2020

To my loving husband,
who is my best friend and encourager,
I adoringly dedicate this novel.

Table of Contents

CHAPTER 1

The Night of Maggie's Christmas Play

PROFESSOR FRANKLIN FRANKLYN WOULD have never been in church that night if it hadn't been for his granddaughter's Christmas play. He enjoyed spoiling his six-year-old princess, Maggie. When he and his wife, Katie, had arrived, the play had just begun.

At the entrance of the foyer, an older gentleman greeted them. Unbuckling her tan coat's belt with one hand, Katie took the program from the greeter, and thanked him. Franklin proceeded to unbutton his winter coat as they dashed toward the coat rack.

Franklin helped his wife with her coat. "I hope we didn't miss her dance."

"I don't think so." She glanced at her gold watch, "We're only seven minutes late. We didn't miss it."

As he shoved their coats into the packed cubby-space, Franklin felt someone bump his hip. He swiveled around. Looking around at his six-foot-four eye level, he didn't see anyone. That is, until he felt another bump against his hip.

Next to him was a thin woman hunched over with her body wobbling. Teetering, her red scarf swayed from her neck. Her red-furry hat covered most of her salt and pepper hair. Franklin leaned over a bit.

The woman was having difficulty. Her crooked fingers struggled to hang her coat on the hanger.

Franklin extended a hand toward her. "Young lady, may I help you with your coat?"

When she stood straight, she appeared shorter than he had perceived, but a bit taller than his petite wife.

"Young lady?" her broad smile exposed her large yellowish, crooked teeth. "I don't have to guess that you're a charmer. I am proud to say that I have eleven grand-children and five great-grandchildren, and one great-great-grandchild in the oven. I'm ninety-two years young."

Other than a few aging lines under her eyes and around her full lips, the smoothness of her light beige skin presented a much younger woman. "Ninety-two! Impossible! You look like you're in your fifties."

"Your charm won't get you anywhere with me, young man. But since you're a kind gentleman, I'll take you up on your offer."

"I'd be honored."

Katie assisted the woman with her scarf. "Mrs. McKinney, did you come alone?"

She must know the woman.

"Yes I did! I can drive myself though my family doesn't think so." She handed Katie her hat. "Timmy is narrating the play tonight."

"Yes I know. I saw him during dress rehearsal last night. He's very talented."

Katie touched her arm. "Mrs. McKinney, I'm sorry, I forgot to introduce you to my husband, Frank. Honey, I'd like you to meet Mrs. McKinney."

"This is Frank?" She appeared as ecstatic as a child who had caught Santa Claus with his bag of toys.

Franklin shook her cold and frail hand. "It's nice to meet you."

"I'm so happy to meet you. I've been praying for you."

Though he perceived prayer as a ridiculous ritual used to comfort religious people in times of need, he took no offense by her comment. Besides, he knew from experience that prayer neither helped nor hurt anyone.

"Katie, he's tall like my darling Grant was. I can't believe that it's been three months since he went home to be with the Lord."

A shiver jolted Franklin's body. "Mrs. McKinney, I'm so very sorry." He grabbed Katie's hand. Just the thought of losing her disturbed him.

The corners of Mrs. McKinney's lips turned upward. "Thank you. I know he's with Jesus and I'll see him soon, but I do miss him." Her drooping eyelids contrasted the divine contentment written in her face.

"Granny!" a young-bubbly blond screeched, "There you are!" the long-legged teen wrapped her arm around Mrs. McKinney's shoulders. "You should've let Daddy pick you up. We were worried about you."

"I'm not completely helpless."

The girl giggled. "But Granny—oh, never mind. Come on, we need to hurry," the girl led her away.

"Please don't move so fast. My knees aren't as young as yours."

"Where's your cane?"

"I don't need my cane!" Mrs. McKinney barked as they disappeared into the sanctuary.

Franklin chuckled, "She's quite feisty, isn't she? It appears that she has arthritis?"

"Yes she does. She has Rheumatoid. You won't believe this. She's a retired U.S. Marshal."

"Really? I can see it, but she doesn't look ninety-two."

"I know! God has blessed her with youth."

He placed his hand against her dark, wavy hair near the middle of Katie's back. "We better hurry before we miss Maggie."

A bald-headed usher escorted them to aisle seats five rows back from the front.

As Katie stepped toward the row of green chairs, she tripped. Franklin caught her arm and held onto it until she regained her balance.

"Baby, are you okay?"

"Yes, sweetheart."

When Franklin slipped into the aisle, he spotted several people gawking at them in the row ahead of them. *Christian rubberneckers!* He shot them a scowl. In sync, they jerked their heads forward.

Seated, he leaned near Katie and studied her heart-shaped face.

Stretching her neck, Katie scanned around the church. She tapped him on the leg. "Honey, look! Maggie's down there in the front row."

"Where?"

She pointed. "Down there, in the middle of the first row. Can you see her?"

He spotted her playing with her long dark hair. "Aww, I see her." She looked like a real angel with the snowy-white halo on top of her head. His chest rounded, he felt like shouting, "I'm her Grampy!"

Katie sat back. With her legs crossed, she pulled her red-flare skirt over her knee. She placed her bible on her lap, and she proceeded to read the program guide.

On stage, three children were performing a Christmas song. "I'm an Angel—ooh." They looked adorable in their shepherd costumes, holding staffs bigger than they were.

Franklin rested his arm across the back of Katie's chair, scoping out the people in the church. Then he glanced at Katie. He wondered how she could have ever gotten caught up with the Jesus freaks.

When they had married at eighteen, he never imagined that she would join the Holy Rollers club. Though he found Christianity difficult to live with, he respected her decision and learned how to deal with it.

Applause sounded. Maggie's group lined up in a single file and walked toward the staircase for the stage.

An older boy, about eleven or twelve, stood on the opposite side of the stage. In his white suit and white tie, he gave the appearance of a head angel in charge. The stage darkened and a spot light shined on the boy.

Speaking in a quiet tone, Katie pointed outward. "That's Timmy, Mrs. McKinney's great-grandson."

"He's a good looking boy."

Timmy bellowed through a hand-held microphone. "And suddenly there was with the angel a multitude of the heavenly host praising God and saying, 'Glory to God in the highest and on earth peace, goodwill toward men!'"

Background music sounded throughout the sanctuary melded with a professional children's choir, singing "Hark the Herald Angels Sing."

As the stage lights brightened, Maggie danced onto the stage along with six other charming little girls dressed as angels. She twirled and leaped offbeat like a clumsy ballerina. Still, his princess outshined all the other little girls.

Holding her arms outward, she spun around. Her hair whirled, knocking off her halo. When she stooped down to pick it up, Maggie bumped one child and the rest stumbled like a set of dominos.

Slumped in their seats, Franklin and Katie choked back their laughter.

After plopping her halo back on top of her head, Maggie repositioned her arms outward. As the female director raised her arms, Maggie's mouth fell open.

The other little performers resumed their dance. But Maggie hesitated, waving with both hands.

Katie shoved her elbow into Franklin's side. "Look, she sees us."

When they waved back, Maggie sprung back into her performance.

"She reminds me of you when you were her age," Franklin commented.

For a brief moment, he shut his eyes to recall that first day of kindergarten when he had met his beautiful wife. While he watched her walking down the aisle of that old school bus, he placed his hand over his heart. In the same way Alfalfa did whenever he had seen Darla in the classic "Our Gang" comedies. His wife's voice crashed his daydream.

"She's got my Irish genes. She's definitely an O'Toole."

Katie's grandparents had immigrated to Maine from Ireland in the early twentieth century. Since she was second generation born in the United States, she held her Irish heritage dear to her heart.

He placed his mouth to her ear. "Katherine Margaret O'Toole-Franklyn, she may be beautiful like you, but she'll never be as beautiful as you are."

She batted her eye-lashes and flashed him a smile. "Thank you."

Maggie leaped and stumbled sideways, catching herself before she bumped into the child next to her. She slid her hand across her forehead. As she restarted her dance, she stumbled again and fell to her knees. But she jumped right back up like a Kangaroo.

Katie whispered, "She's so adorable in her angel tutu?"

He tapped her on her turned-up freckled nose. "Like always, you did a great job on her costume."

"Thank you. I have fun working with the kids."

Since Katie had taught home economics at the local middle school, she had designed and made the costumes for the play. She also baked a few batches of cookies.

"I know you like to volunteer, but you should be paid for your expertise."

She pressed her side against his. "My darling Dr. Franklyn, you may equate your expertise with money, but I equate my expertise as a gift from God for blessing others."

"Then why do you accept your paycheck?"

Her lips tightened and her eyes bugged out.

Oh boy, I'm in trouble.

After drawing in a deep breath, her face relaxed. "Honey, that's my harvest. When you plant a blessing seed, God blesses you with a harvest to reciprocate more blessings. Just like, Professor, when you teach English, you're reciprocating your knowledge."

Franklin rubbed his hand along her arm. "I'm sorry, baby. That was rude. I get where you're coming from."

"Thank you."

Just then, Maggie's angel dance ended. The children took a bow, lined up, and walked toward the staircase.

Squirming in his chair, Franklin had no interest in watching the rest of the play.

"Honey look!" She had her finger pressed under Maggie's given name, Margaret K. Harris.

Their eyes met.

He waved a hand clockwise as he declared, "Katie my dear, next her name will be in lights on Broadway!"

"You're so funny." After a few seconds of scouring through her purse, she pulled out a pen.

"Well, you said that God wants us to dream big."

She grinned. "You do pay attention."

"Absolutely. All the time. Oh, don't look so cynical. Okay, I admit it. Sometimes I'm preoccupied."

Katie responded, "Thank you for your honesty, dear."

Children dressed in sheep, cow, and donkey costumes positioned themselves around the nativity scene on stage. They sang in chorus with a background band and a children's choir "What a Special Night."

Clicking her pen, Katie turned the program around. She jotted something on the backside.

Cramped in the row too narrow for his legs, Franklin stretched them out into the aisle, and crossed one foot over the other.

As he placed his hands behind his head, he spotted Katie yawning. *Yes. I'm out of here.* "Honey, would you like to go home?"

Katie cocked her head backward. "Huh? No. Why?"

"Baby, you seem so tired. If you're too tired to stay, I understand. I don't mind taking you home."

"Thank you, sweetheart. But I'm fine. Other than it's warm in here and it's making me a bit groggy."

"It is warm in here. It's making me groggy too, and we have a long drive home. Maybe we should go."

As he heard himself speak, it hit him. He had promised Maggie that he would go to her party after the play. "Um. . ."

"My dearest husband," she interrupted. "May I remind you, a little more than twenty miles up the highway is not that far, especially as fast as you drive. We'll be home in. . .," she froze, grasping her dress.

Alarmed, Franklin pulled in his legs and sat up. "What happened?"

Looking downward, she rubbed her thumb along her stomach.

"Honey, speak to me."

"The Holy Spirit is warning me about something."

"What do you mean warning?"

The man in front of them looked over his shoulder and shushed them.

"Shush Frank, you're getting loud."

"I'm getting loud? what?"

"Shh, you're embarrassing me." She turned her face downward and away.

"I'm—never mind. Please just tell me what's wrong."

Her brows furrowed. "We need to go home and forget . . ."

"Leave now? We can't just leave."

"I'm not suggesting that. I believe we need to skip the refreshments tonight and go straight home. The Spirit is tugging at my heart."

Applause sounded. The children on stage bowed.

"Katie," he spoke in a gentle tone, "sometimes when we're overtired our minds can play funny tricks on us, like hearing strange voices in our heads."

"I'm not hallucinating." She took his hand and placed it over her diaphragm. "The Holy Spirit is speaking to me from inside. That's one of the ways God speaks to us. His Spirit speaks to us through our spirit. It's a gut feeling, and it feels like something is not right—like a warning."

Sometimes her Christian rationale seemed rational. Nevertheless, Franklin based his beliefs on logic and tangible evidence. He always found an explanation for the unexplainable. Not that he was an atheist. He believed God existed, but not on the Jesus freak's level. But when she claimed God spoke to her through her stomach, he found that nonsensical, especially for her. He dismissed the warning.

"Baby, it's probably gas from the hot dogs and beans you had for supper. You know that Toot N Tell Em diner lives up to their name. I told you not to get the special, remember?"

"Why do you have to joke when you don't understand something? It isn't gas. It's the Holy Ghost."

"Baby, you believe he's telling you to go straight home?"

"Well, it feels like a warning."

Lights flooded the sanctuary. The pastor strolled across the stage.

It pained him to see worry etched into her face. The Christian's fear-mongering had burrowed into her very being like a Jellyfish's tentacles injecting toxin into their prey.

As the pastor discussed the meaning of the Christmas story, Franklin laid his hand on Katie's hand, and he wrapped his fingers around it. "Honey, if you feel that strongly about it, I'll take you home."

Her shoulders relaxed as in relief. "Thank you," she mouthed.

"Can we visit with Maggie for a few moments before we leave? Remember, we won't be able to see the kids as much after they move to Tulsa."

Kitty, their daughter, and Jake, her husband, had planned to move to Oklahoma for Bible College that following fall. But since Jake had landed a position near the training center as an accountant, the firm expected him to start by mid-January for tax season.

"It breaks my heart to think about it," Her eyes widened. "Frank, watch it! You're about to get. . ."

Before she could finish, Maggie jumped on Franklin's lap and threw her arms around his neck.

". . .a little girl on your lap." Katie slapped her hand against her mouth as she snorted.

The pastor's voice resonated ". . .bow your heads . . ."

"Bow your head, Grampy. The Pastor is going to pray."

With his head bowed and his eyes closed, it dawned on Franklin that he had no whole milk to make Maggie biscuits and gravy for breakfast when she spent the night the next day.

He opened one eye to peek around. *He's longer-winded than a stalled hurricane.*

The drawn-out prayer concluded with, ". . .and all the people said. . ." The entire church chorused a loud "Amen!"

Katie waved at someone. "Honey, there's Kitty!"

"Where?" Franklin looked around and into the crowd.

"She's over there," Katie continued waving, "I don't think she can see me. I'll go get her," she slid past Franklin.

Maggie pressed her freckled nose against Franklin's nose with her green eyes crossed. "I'm so happy to see you, Grampy. When I didn't see you, I got scared because I thought something bad happened to you and Nana."

"Princess, why would you think something like that?"

"I'm not sure," she pointed toward her chest, "it's just a feeling I got inside here."

This bad feeling nonsense had gotten out of hand. If it weren't for the law and his family, Franklin had the mind to knock their pastor's teeth out. He resolved their pastor had an insecurity problem and used fear to hold his congregation hostage.

Years ago, Franklin's grandparents had told him about an insecure pastor who had replaced their original pastor that had passed away. He had attempted to manipulate their congregation through fear to control them. But the townsmen in York, Maine, where he and Katie had grown up, didn't put up with it. They chased the phony out of town. At least the people in Maine were on to this guy, but how could he prove this to Katie.

"My little princes, feelings come and go," he poked her stomach.

She giggled like the Pillsbury Dough Boy.

"You're too precious," he kissed her on her baby-soft cheek.

"Well, praise the Lord you were here to see me dance. Did you like my dancing?"

"Oh, you danced like an angel princess."

"But, Grampy, I stumbled twice."

"We all stumble. It's what you do with it when you do stumble. Don't stay down. You pick yourself up and keep going." Tapping her on the nose, he added, "Just like you did tonight."

"Thank you, Grampy. I'll remember that."

"Good."

Katie had disappeared into the crowd. "We need to find Mommy and Nana." Franklin lifted Maggie off his lap and set her down on the floor. Holding Maggie's hand, he led the way into the aisle. "Did you see where your parents were sitting?"

Maggie pointed toward the front section of the church. "They're sitting over there. But I can't see them right now. There are too many people standing up," she wiggled her finger, "But they're somewhere near those children up front."

Franklin meandered their way through the crowded aisle.

Katie and Kitty emerged from a small group of people.

Wearing a toothy smile, Kitty hugged her father. "Daddy, I'm so happy you made it."

"Of course I made it." She seemed so tall, almost eye level with him. Franklin looked into her cobalt-blue eyes at almost eye-level. "I wouldn't have missed Maggie's play for anything."

"I know. But all that traffic at the mall exit must have been horrendous."

"The worse I have ever seen."

"Anyhow, this move, and everything is happening so fast, it's making me feel a bit nervous."

Hope sprang up in Franklin's heart. "You don't have to go to Tulsa. Nobody is forcing you to go."

She chortled, "Daddy, it's not that type of nervous. It's more like butterflies. I choose God's will for my life."

He refused to interfere with her choices like his overbearing father, Dr. Stewart Franklyn, had done to him.

She seemed much taller than her normal five foot-eight stature. "Why are you so tall?"

Looking downward, she twisted her ankle a bit. "I'm wearing stiletto heels. Do you like them?"

Franklin scratched the side of his face. "What, stiletto for stilts?"

Katie's eyes widened. "They're nice, but don't they hurt?"

"Your ankle is straight!"

"Actually, they're not the most comfortable shoes, but they're a perfect match for my new dress."

Kitty never ceased to amaze Franklin. "Not comfortable? You can break your neck in those things!"

"Daddy, please. You worry too much."

"Honey," Katie laid her hand on Franklin's forearm, "I helped her pick out the dress?"

"It looks beautiful on her, but I thought she didn't like pink because of her red hair?"

"Oh my goodness Daddy, it's not pink. It's champagne."

"It looks light pink to me."

With her thumb under her chin and her forefinger over her lips, Katie slid her eyes upward toward Franklin and waggled her eyebrows.

Maggie tugged on Franklin's hand. "Grampy, maybe it's a pink kind of champagne."

"You're absolutely right, Maggie," Franklin declared, "Its pink champagne."

"Mommy, I guessed it!"

As Kitty examined her dress, she snapped her fingers. "I forgot. I got some great news for you guys. I got a job at the college library."

"Honey, did you hear that? Kitty has a job."

Franklin chuckled, "Yes dear, I heard her. I'm standing right here."

"Mom, Daddy, this is better yet. Since I have a job too, we'll have the money to visit you guys in Alaska for two weeks instead of one this summer."

That previous summer Franklin and Katie had planned to open a seasonal diner near their vacation home in Fairbanks, Alaska, for the summer tourist season. He loved working with food and creating chef quality meals.

Maggie tugged on Franklin's sweater. "Grampy, can I work in your diner?"

"Absolutely." She reminded him of when he was a boy. Every chance he had, he helped Pappy with the family business.

From the time he was six, Franklin helped at Pappy's diner on the coast of Maine. That is, until Franklin had landed his faculty position at Scottsberry University in Tilton, New Hampshire. He had more in common with Pappy, a Michelin Star Chef, than he had with his father, an English professor like himself. Though made to feel guilty about walking in his father's footsteps, he preferred the restaurant business.

"Can I help you cook too, like we cook together in your house?"

"Absolutely, but when the diner is open, you'll have to work with Nana. That is, as long as your mother doesn't mind."

Both Franklin and Katie had agreed that while he created masterpieces in the back of the house, she would manage the front of the house and deal with the customers.

"Mommy, can I work with them, please."

"Yes, you can help out."

"I can? Yippy! I can't wait to tell Daddy."

That reminded Franklin. "Kitty, where's your husband?"

"He's already downstairs." She placed her purse under her arm. "Now that I'm thinking about it, he's probably wondering where we're at."

In a parade fashion, the rest followed.

Maggie tugged on Franklin's hand. "Grampy, Nana and I made Christmas cookies together for you."

"You made the cookies for me?"

"Uh huh. And we drew Christmas decorations on them with lots of frosting."

"Then let's hurry." Franklin lifted her up and sat her on his broad shoulders.

With her arms wrapped around his muscular neck, she clamped her hands together. "I love being up here. It makes me feel like a giant."

"Honey, hold on." Katie called out.

Startled by her voice, Franklin halted like a soldier obeying a drill sergeant's orders. "What's wrong?"

"Remember, we need to go home?"

Kitty halted and pivoted around. "What's going on?"

"Yes, I remember, but they're leaving in a few weeks and . . ."

"But you promised. You know this is important." Katie reminded.

"Mom, what did Daddy promise?"

Franklin had promised his little princess to attend her party. And up to then, he had never broken any of his promises. "Can we at least walk them downstairs?"

Maggie pleaded, "But Nana, I want Grampy to taste the cookies we made him. And—and if you leave, you'll miss the party. I want my friends to meet Grampy."

His stomach knotted to think he would disappoint her.

Kitty threw her hands upward. "Would someone please tell me what's going on!"

"Well, Honey, since you feel as though your gut was talking to you, you explain it to your daughter."

Tight-lipped, Katie bore her eyes toward him. "Kitty, I have this gut feeling inside. I'm not quite sure what it is, but I do know for sure that God wants us to go straight home."

"Oh! Then you better go home. If I had a feeling . . ."

"I had a feeling too." Maggie inserted.

Under his breath, Franklin muttered, "Oh brother."

"Daddy, I heard that! If Mom has a gut feeling that God is warning her to go home, then you need to take her home. I have a gut feeling too. That you think it's her imagination. Please think of it this way, you may be wrong. If you're wrong, you may regret it," she stepped closer to him, "As you taught me, it's better to be safe than sorry."

His daughter had a point. "You're right, Cinnamon Bun." Ever since the day she had eaten raw dough, when she was three, she had become his little cinnamon bun.

"Honey, I'm so sorry. I understand this is very real for you. Please forgive me. I'll take you home."

"Of course I forgive you, and thank you."

He reached for Maggie to set her down off his shoulders.

Maggie stayed on his shoulders. "But—but can I go home with you?"

Franklin hated to say no to her. "I would love to bring you home with us, but your nana is too tired tonight." *Uh-oh.*

"Nana, if you want to go to bed when we get home, I don't care. I just want to be with you and Grampy."

Katie shot a snare at Franklin. Then she responded to Maggie in a honey tone. "Oh, my little munchkin, I wish we could take you home. But there's only ten more days 'til Christmas. Grampy and I have to leave early tomorrow morning to finish our shopping. And besides, when you spend the night tomorrow night, Grampy and I have a surprise for you."

"Praise the Lord! I'm so excited!" Maggie pulled on Franklin's chin, turning his face upwards. She put her freckled face into his. "Grampy, you can put me down now. Jesus said you have to take Nana home."

She never ceased to amaze him by how intelligent she was. "Maggie, you understood that Nana feels like God is speaking to her?"

"Uh huh, I understand. Jesus is speaking to her spirit, inside," she poked at her stomach, "She has to listen to Him. I just wanted to be with you. But you and Nana are too busy right now, and I'm going to spend the night tomorrow night, and you have to get ready for my surprise. I don't want to ruin my surprise."

After Franklin set her down, Kitty took Maggie's hand. "Would you like to hold my purse?"

"Yes."

Katie and Franklin waited a moment, waving to them as Kitty and Maggie disappeared down the stairs.

"Katie, what's wrong, why the tears?"

"I'm so sad inside."

"Why? You'll see them tomorrow?"

"I don't know why, I just feel sad." She sighed, "Let's go."

He broke his promise to his little princess. He too felt sad, but he vowed to himself that he would make it up to her. "You've never been sad over something that was nothing. What's wrong?"

"I said, I don't know. It's as though, I'm never going to see them again."

"What? What did your pastor put in your mind?"

"Nothing. Where do you—never mind," she bit her lower lip, "Please, let's just go home."

It worried him to see her so troubled over some religious baloney. Though he had fallen for some of that stuff as a boy and even answered an altar call, he learned better about this Jesus stuff later on.

As he opened the car door for her, lighting flashed across the sky. He sniffed the air. *That's strange. It smells too cold for a thunderstorm.*

She stepped onto the running board and pointed up at the clouded sky. "This morning, the weather man said it was going to be clear tonight."

"When is the weather man ever right? Get in, baby, so I can get you home before it gets worse." Like always, he helped her in and shut her door.

All the way up the highway, she never said a word.

Too preoccupied with breaking a promise he had made with Maggie, he never considered the periodic rolls of thunder and lightning flashes.

As Franklin approached their exit, he remembered he needed the whole milk. At least he could make it up to Maggie by making her favorite breakfast. "Honey, I'm going to make a quick stop at the Red-Dot for a gallon of milk."

"Why? We have milk."

"We have skim milk. I need whole milk."

"What for? Why are you pulling into the parking lot? God said to go home."

"I want to make biscuits and gravy for Maggie."

"But she's not spending the night until tomorrow night."

Franklin pulled into a parking space. "I know, but we're going Christmas shopping all day tomorrow, and she'll be with us tomorrow night. I don't want to stop at the grocery store too."

"Why do you need to make biscuits and gravy? We're surprising her with a pizza and movie party tomorrow night. I thought we're taking her out to breakfast before I take her to church."

"Honey, they're leaving in a few weeks. She loves my biscuits and gravy. Besides, I missed her party."

"This is what this all about? You missed the refreshments, so you have to cook for her? When are you going to stop having guilt trips? Please, take me home!" Her voice dwindled, "God said to go home." She dropped her head against the head rest and pressed her lips together.

He shifted the Ford Expedition into park. "Honey, I'll only be a minute. I promise."

"We need to go home."

"Come on Baby, I missed her party to take you home. It's not going to kill you to wait a few extra moments. I'll be out in a flash. I promise, and I'll take you straight home." He kissed her on the cheek.

She leaned her head against the passenger window.

He hated to see her mope. But he wasn't about to become her enabler for that Christian nonsense.

With his hands in his coat pockets, Franklin hurried across the small section of the parking lot. A frigid drop of water hit his face. Slowing his pace a bit, he looked skyward into the starless sky. Another flash of lightening lit up the sky. Thunder roared in the distance as another cold droplet smacked him in the eye.

The moment he approached the old country store's glass door, he hesitated. *This is too much anxiety. I need to take her home.* He twisted around and peered over his shoulder.

Just as he was about to retreat, someone bumped into him.

"Excuse me, I'm sorry." The younger woman dressed in a heavy ski jacket apologized as she scurried passed him.

This is ridiculous. I'm here. After rushing in, he darted to the coolers, but it took him longer than he had anticipated. The checker, an elderly man, moved slowly and methodically, adding to Franklin's anxieties.

When he rushed out of the grocery store, Franklin slipped on the pavement. He caught himself from losing his footing. A bolt of lightning flashed across the sky. "Oh no, it's freezing rain!"

Franklin spotted a Toyota Tundra fishtail as it pulled out of the parking lot. The freezing rain felt like sharp needles against his face. "She must have had a premonition of this inclement weather."

With the gallon of milk in hand, he slid into the driver's seat. "Honey, are you okay?" he twisted around and placed the milk on the backseat floor, "Baby, please talk to me."

Sad-eyed, Katie pointed at the windshield. "It's freezing rain. There's ice everywhere! If you didn't believe God warned me, you could have at least humored me."

"I know, baby. I'm very sorry. I'm really sorry."

"I forgive you, but let's wait until it stops. I've got a bad feeling inside."

He laid his elbow against the tan steering wheel and grabbed his forehead; he exhaled. "Honey, the weather will only worsen. Trust me—I'll get you home safely. I always do, don't I?"

He started the car and turned on the defroster.

With her head tilted downward, she pinched her lower lip between her forefinger and her thumb.

While revving the engine a bit, he gazed at her. He wished he had taken her home. She was right, like always. The biscuits and gravy wasn't a priority. Katie was. How could he have been so thoughtless? His eyes welled up. "Baby, please buckle up." Without her, he had no life.

She nodded and pulled her seat belt around.

He heard her mumble. "What did you say?"

"I'm praying."

He snapped his seat belt and reached over and touched her face. "Good. You keep praying. I'll get you home where it's safe and warm."

As he pulled out of the parking lot, the light turned green at the intersection. He rushed to catch the light.

For a split second, he glanced at her beautiful silhouette. If he hadn't stopped, she would have been out of the weather and safe at home.

As he entered the intersection, he heard Katie utter, "Uh-oh."

A sudden bright flash—an instantaneous bang fused with a hard thrust. The sounds of metal ripping screeched in his ears. *What's happening!* Shattered glass flew toward him like a shower of large droplets. The SUV bounced and joggled. An abrupt stillness melded with loud music, inundating his vehicle.

Gasping for air caused a sharp pain in his right side. He sucked in a breath.

The front-end of a vehicle wedged into the side of the Expedition, bearing against Katie with her head hunched and off to the side. A large chunk of fiber glass had lodged into his forearm. With his blood soaked fingers, he reached for his bride.

She opened her eyes wide. "Jesus." Her head fell limp.

Trapped in a sea of crushed metal and shattered glass rendered him helpless. Once again, he tried to reach for her. "Katie," he wheezed. Everything spun as he faded into unconsciousness.

That night, Franklin died inside.

CHAPTER 2

The Second Anniversary of Katie's Death

IT WAS THE SECOND anniversary of the fatal accident that had crushed the life out of Katie. It happened the night Jack Rivers, the seventeen-year-old drunk driver, had T-boned them with his dully pick-up. The storm raging inside Franklin far exceeded the storm raging outside his two-story log home.

Squatted in front of his red wood stove in his family room, he placed another log onto the fire. Thunder rumbled, echoing through the loneliness of the dimly lit room.

Two years ago, while alone in his hospital room for more than three days, he had time to think. He had nobody else to blame but himself. Katie's death gave credence to her foreboding. But he had dismissed it, escorting her to her death.

Gripped by a crushing heartache, he glared into the fiery blaze. With the sweltering heat against his face, he wallowed in his self-contempt and pity. He killed his wife and destroyed his family, sentencing him to a life of unforgiving agony.

Unlike the lid on a pressure cooker, he had no valve for unleashing the emotional strain of his suffering. For him, the only emancipation from the vise-like grip of agonizing misery was suicide. But he was too much of a coward to do so. As he pushed the stove door shut, it clanged.

He locked the latch. A bright light glowed in the window for a brief second, followed by a crashing thunderous roll. Flashbacks of that night flared in his eyes.

The pounding beat of the drunkard's music blaring from Jack Rivers's pickup played along with flashing images of distorted faces hovering over him. *I'm sorry, your wife didn't make it!* Red and yellow roses blanketed her mahogany-wood coffin. Their feet crunched along the snow-covered cemetery ground. *I'm sorry, your wife didn't make it! Dad, she's in heaven.* Kitty sobbing into Jake's chest—six faceless pallbearers carried her to the gravesite. Franklin's flashbacks intensified, flinging him into more nightmarish recollections.

The muddled voices roared louder, fused with distorted pictures flashing through his mind. *Daddy, let us stay—help you, help you. I miss Nana—under the tree—her gifts, gifts, gifts. No, no—Grampy don't let me go! Katie's name on a tombstone—I killed her!* A sudden flash of Maggie's face weeping next to Katie's opened coffin frightened him back into real time.

"Noooooo!" He grabbed his head. "Stop!" He stood, yanked off his hearth gloves, and cast them down. His temples pounded. Breathing rapid breaths, his chest rose and fell. "I never deserved her!"

Franklin peered out into the darkness through the picture window. Katie's words, "The Holy Spirit is warning me," played in his mind like an old vinyl record skipping.

The black sky illuminated with bright flashes of lightning accompanied with the rumbling of thunder booming over his twenty-eight acres of pasture and woodland. The totality of it sounded melodic for him.

The violent squall thrashed rain against the house in the capacity of an orchestra of harmonious notes playing on the green metal roof and back deck. Each raindrop tapped to the melody. The entirety of the tempestuous weather created an elaborate musical composition.

It touched his soul and tears rolled down his cheeks. He raised his hands to conduct his imagined ensemble. As the thunder rolled, Franklin felt vibrations of drums and cymbals pounding throughout his auditorium, accompanied by Kitty's voice echoing in his ears, *Daddy, please let us come and visit you.*

"What shall I say, Cinnamon Bun, I killed your mother!" His shouts bellowed over the raging storm.

Crackling sounds from erratic bolts of lightning, crashing downward, amplified the acoustics, blasting out Katie's plea, *home now—now—now.* The ballad engulfed his body and gave rise to a more forceful execution of conducting his symphony.

He sang along with his imagined orchestra. "It's not going to kill you to wait a few extra moments. It's not going to kill you to wait a few extra moments," he directed the stormy weather faster and faster and faster,

"It's not going to kill you; It's not going to kill, kill you, kill, kill! KILL!" the fury brought him to his knees, weeping.

He examined his trembling hands before he placed them over his face. "Oh, God, what did I do? I hate myself! Baby, I'm so sorry." He grabbed his heart. It felt like he had a hole in it without anything to fill it. "Baby, I miss you. I miss you! I miss you, so much."

Sitting back on his heels, he shaped his hands into a steeple. It dawned on him. "There's no other explanation. God warned her." He pointed his long forefinger heavenward. "You let me live to torment me!" Arched over, he wept until he choked on his own saliva.

Coughing, he stood. Wiping his face with his handkerchief, he turned on the antler lamp nearest to the window by his brown recliner. The howling winds struck the double-paned windows with forcible blows. The chimney pipe of the woodstove knocked from the winter wind downdraft. It blew into the fire, sending the flames into a periodic chaotic dance.

When he looked toward the kitchen, the light from the canister ceiling lights blinded him. Rubbing his eyes, he moseyed in and took the red tea pot off his eight-burner gas range. Seeing Harry, his Siberian husky, fast asleep by the mudroom door eased his crushed spirit. He and the young husky were pals.

If he hadn't read the novel *Surviving the Alaskan Bush* earlier that year, he wouldn't have found Harry. The end of the story had inspired Franklin to get the dog.

When the protagonist, Grady, had been overcome by the lack of supplies and the frigid winter in the Alaskan bush, it tempted him to give up and die. But his responsibility to Kona, his husky, motivated him to not give up. "If I hadn't read that story, I would have never found you, buddy."

When he had found Harry on an animal rescue website, he had concluded that they both had a sad story. Harry's former owner had passed away after a sudden and short bout of leukemia and his wife died of a sudden and quick death. "Man, pal, you're still a good looking dog, but now you're a big fur ball."

At the sink, he filled the pot with his spring-fed well water. Still sniffling and grieving, he placed it on top of the back burner. As he clicked it on, Harry's claws tapped on the slate floor. Franklin grabbed a few paper towels from the roll that hung under the kitchen cabinet. He wiped his watering eyes and blew his nose, and then he tossed the towel into the trash can under the sink. With his back against the counter, he crossed his arms against his broad chest.

Harry sat with his nose pointed up toward Franklin, wagging his black and silver tail, thumping it against the floor. Franklin rolled up the sleeves of his flannel shirt and squatted to pet his husky.

He grabbed Harry's head, rubbing him behind his pointed ears. The whistling wind thrashed against the kitchen window over the sink. Franklin glanced over his shoulder. Straightway, the rain seemed fiercer as it hammered against the metal roof. He looked up.

Sliding his hand along the side of Harry's soft, silver-gray and white fur neck, he glanced into the husky's blue eye and brown eye. "Hear that Harry? Sounds like hail, not rain. Just think! I used to like that noise. Well, maybe it'll push that abnormal warm weather out of here. It should be snowing, not raining."

Without warning, Harry sneezed and sprayed mucous on Franklin's forearms. "Oh, great!" He stood and rushed over to the sink with Harry tagging along.

After he had washed up, he grabbed an old dishrag.

The teapot whistled and Harry woofed at the stove. With his ears pricked up and his muzzle raised, he sniffed the air.

After drying his hands, Franklin tossed the worn towel onto the wood-grain granite counter top. "You really don't like that noise, do you fella?" He grabbed the pot off the fire and set it down on the front burner. Harry coiled around Franklin's leg.

"Do you want a doggie biscuit?"

Scratching two steps backward, Harry yelped. He sat, pounding his tail against the floor, tilting his head, while he looked at Franklin with hopeful eyes.

As Franklin reached into the fire-hydrant cookie jar, Harry stood on all fours, panting. "Here you go fella." The young husky grabbed it with his mouth.

With the milk bone hanging from Harry's mouth, he leaped off to the mudroom door. Lying on the floor, he held the treat between his two paws and chomped on it.

After placing a teabag into a mug, Franklin poured the boiling water over it. As the tea steeped, he snatched a few cookies out of his cookie jar.

Franklin sat at head of his dining table. "Why do I sit at the head of this lonely table?" His eyes welled. "I miss my family."

Even though his heart ached for them, he had no choice but to let go of his family. He preferred they forget him than hate him for his crime.

Since his family still lived in Tulsa, it had made it easier for him to avoid them. But he had no plan for when they were done with school. While sipping on his tea, he pondered what he should do if they were to come back to New Hampshire.

As he drank his last swallow, the sounds of the storm stilled as if someone in the sky had used a lever to turn off the storm. A serene hush descended on the house and the wood crackling amplified the calm. He sucked-in the remaining droplets in the bottom of the cup.

Franklin rubbed his smooth thumbs over the raised design of a wilderness scene on the surface of the cup. It reminded him of the terrain surrounding his vacation home. He and Katie had bought the home on the Chena River in Alaska because of the great fishing.

Recalling the amazing vacation memories he had with his wife and his family pained him. Tears filled his eyes, yet again. He squeezed his forehead.

He cried, "I wish I could go back and change things. Katie, why didn't I listen to you?" He laid his head on top of his folded arms. "My life is so empty without you to hold in my arms." Burying his face in his arms, he wept until he nodded off.

The cordless phone in the family room rang. Franklin stood and lumbered toward the phone. "Now who's bothering me?" As he placed his hand on it, it stopped ringing. "Good. They'll leave me alone."

He sat down on his beige sectional. The annoying phone rang again. "Hello, who's calling me?"

"Frank, it's me."

"Johnny, I know who you are."

"Then why did you ask who was calling you?"

"Just state your business. It's late, and I'm tired."

Johnny expelled his breath into the phone. "I'd like to come by tomorrow around eleven. I need . . ."

"No."

"Frank, you're getting ridiculous! Now what's your problem?"

He kept his distance from his brother-in-law. Since Johnny and Katie were twins, seeing her reflection in him had proven too much for Franklin to bear.

"I'm a busy man."

"Doing what? Hiding in your house from your family and friends while you mope around in your self-imposed reclusive lifestyle, dwelling on the past?"

"My life is none of your business."

"You're right. It's between you and God. But tell me, why can't I come by tomorrow?"

"Mr. Holy Roller, if you must know, I have an oil change scheduled for my truck at eleven-thirty. Just talk to me on the phone."

"No, I need to talk to you in person."

Alarmed by that, Franklin imagined the worse. "Did anything happen to Kitty or Maggie?"

Johnny sighed, "No. But if you want to know if they're all right, I suggest you call them."

"Shut up! Kitty and Maggie are my business, not yours."

"Again, Frank, you're right. It's none of my business. Call me after you have your truck serviced and I'll come by."

After the rough night he was having, the last person Franklin wanted to face was his brother-in-law. "No. I'm too busy."

"You're impossible. Listen, I have a meeting tomorrow morning at the university. I'll be out by nine. Meet me in the museum's parking lot. And I'm not asking you, I'm telling you."

"Telling me? Who do you think you are? I'm not your child and I'm not going."

"You better be there or you'll regret it."

"Regret what?"

"If you're not there, you'll find out anyhow. And when you do, it'll be too late." Johnny warned. "I'll see you tomorrow at nine."

"What do you mean it'll be too late? What do you mean? I won't be there!" Franklin shouted into the phone, but Johnny had hung up.

"He just leaves me in suspense. Who does he think he is? Why should I go back to the university?"

After the accident, he had continued teaching class, but not by choice. While in the hospital, Franklin had decided to resign from both work and life. His doctor had insisted he go back to work for his mental well-being. But every day he returned home to his miserable nothingness, reminding him how rotten his life had become. So, he had given a covert resignation to the university a month earlier.

He threw the phone onto the sectional. It bounced off and crashed onto the hardwood floor, and blew apart. Franklin leaned over and picked up the several broken pieces, and held it in his hand. "It's unfixable, like me."

Sitting down, he laid the broken pieces on top of the end table next to the charger. After several minutes of sorting out and replaying his discussion with Johnny, it gave him a headache. "I better go see what he needs."

But at that moment, he regretted that he had helped Johnny solidify the Senior Collections Management position at Scottsberry's Museum of New England. He should have left him in Maine when the state laid him off due to funding.

While rubbing his head, he noticed a bright reflection in the picture window. "Is it snowing?"

With one hand on the arm of the sectional, he grunted as he pushed himself up.

Leaning into the window, he cuffed his hands around his face. "Oh, brother, look at it. It's coming down hard. Now I have to get up early to clear the driveway."

Franklin sat back down in his chair by the window. Harry moseyed in from the kitchen, and he laid down by Franklin's feet. After switching off the lamp by him, Franklin sat in the dark, listening to the ticking of his cuckoo clock. He glared at the fire inside the woodstove while he reflected on his misery.

CHAPTER 3

Franklin's Confrontations

FRANKLIN'S RED WAVY HAIR still felt damp from his morning shower as he poured his coffee. Taking a moment to gather his thoughts, he leaned against the edge of the counter and took a sip of the custom blended java. He glanced at Harry lying in his wicker doggie bed near the door to the daylight basement. Fast asleep, Harry's nose hung off the side of the bed. The four-slice toaster popped and Franklin spun around.

Standing over the counter, he removed the lid off his moose butter dish. As he slathered the toast with the softened butter, he came up with all types of scenario that Johnny had planned to talk to him about. Of course, each scenario worsened as he thought them up.

Whatever it was, Johnny's evasiveness agitated Franklin. "Stop over-thinking this. Shut-up brain! I'll deal with it when I meet him. I don't need a bellyache over it." He brought his breakfast over to his lonely dining table.

As he dunked his toast into the black coffee, Franklin relished the winter scenery outside his bay window. Under a sunny blue sky, his property was blanketed in a seasonal purity of the white snow.

"Oh boy! The barn's roof has about eight inches of snow on top of it. Perfect! I have to get up there and knock some of that snow off the roof. God, you put it there, You should take it away. What did you say? It's my job? Well, I didn't expect you to say anything less."

In spite of the work it may bring, Franklin loved the four distinct seasons. Though the splendor of fall that arrayed the land with hues of orange, red, yellow, and greens was his favorite time of year with the coziness of winter being a close second, he enjoyed witnessing life rejuvenated with the incoming of spring after a long, dark, and frozen wintry season. And yet, Franklin had always looked forward to the summer days with children and adults playing and frolicking under the long and bright summer skies. But he had nobody to share it with anymore.

Overnight, the temperature had plummeted from thirty-five degrees to a frigid fifteen degrees. The warmth and the smell of the burning apple wood enhanced the coziness in the family room. It reminded him of the romantic times he and Katie had toasting marshmallows in the living room fireplace. Even though loneliness and heartache overshadowed his life, the hominess of the warmth in his house juxtaposed against the wintery scenery outside soothed him.

Cupping his hands around the warm mug, he savored the serene moment. "One last sip of this coffee, then outside to shovel."

Just then, a sudden vroom of an engine blared through the tranquility of the moment.

"That sounds like that's on my property. What's going on?"

Franklin glanced at his dog. Harry's head popped up toward the direction of the noise. After he sniffed the air, he dropped his head and closed his eyes. "How can you sleep through that racket?"

Listening, he leaned his chair backward on two legs as he braced his fingers on the edge of the table. The pattern of the sound got louder and then faded out and got louder again. "That sounds like a snow blower. Somebody is on my property!"

Since the family room faced the pasture and garden area, he couldn't see a thing from his position. He moved forward and dropped the chair back onto all four legs. He lumbered out of the kitchen through the living room toward the front door. "Who's out there? Hey you, trespasser! It's Christmas time! Go on vacation!"

Fuming, he grabbed his red jacket from the coat rack. With one arm in the coat sleeve, Franklin turned the deadbolt and shoved his body against the storm door. It flew open, banged the side of the house, and swung back around pounding him on his arm. "Ouch!" With less force, he pushed it open again and he stomped outside onto the covered porch.

An average framed man, wearing a sheepskin jean jacket, was clearing Franklin's long driveway with a snow blower. Though he had seen him before that day, he had never met him. "Who is that guy? Bingo!" Franklin snapped his cold fingers, "That's the man who moved into the old Steinberg's place."

Joe and Rita Steinberg had lived across the street for more than fifty years. Jewish immigrants from Germany, they had bought the once working farm soon after they had earned their U.S. citizenship.

Franklin had avoided the intruder since he had moved in. He just wanted to be left alone.

"That house should have stayed in the family." The Steinbergs had found peace and safety there after they had escaped Hitler's death sentence.

Since the man's head hung downward, Franklin figured the man hadn't noticed him, so he hid behind the porch's thick log column and peeked around to spy on his neighbor.

"That's a nice Troy-built. It's a two-stager like mine, but noisier. Why can't people leave me alone? He better not think I'm paying for this. I'm not giving him a dime."

With half his body leaning around the column, a sudden gust of wind blew against his face. He popped back behind the column and zipped up his jacket. He glanced across the street. Though the Steinberg's son did a nice job on the new three-car garage, he missed the old barn. It felt more familiar, and Franklin liked familiar.

After the couple had passed away months apart from one another, their son, Joe Steinberg Jr., had left the old farmhouse empty for more than six months. Then the son decided to remodel the old place before he had placed it on the market with a loud-mouthed realtor. It had taken that realtor more than a year to sell the place. But Franklin had to admit Joe Jr. had done a nice job with the upgrades.

The once white house had been spruced up in light-lemon-chiffon yellow with alabaster trim. Without the shutters, the new round top windows created a more modern look to the more than a century old home. And the addition of the sandstone cobble driveway and the attached garage brought the home into the twenty-first century.

Though the changes were nice, that didn't alter the fact that Franklin had to like it. Because of it, he had to deal with a new neighbor. It appeared this transplant would become a nuisance. Nevertheless, Franklin liked the LUV, Little Utility Vehicle, parked inside the trespasser's garage, and he had admired it since the day the man had moved in.

The first time he had seen the LUV he almost inquired about the little pickup, but he didn't. However, since Franklin was a quintessential rubbernecker, once he had used his binoculars for a closer look through his living room's window.

"Boy, that thing is in mint condition. The paint-job is immaculate. I like that cream-color." He spotted a Christian fish symbol on the upper left corner of its tailgate, "He's a hypocritical Jesus freak?"

Scanning the man's property, he noticed a "Jesus Is the Reason for the Season" sign written in red on a white wooden sign on the hypocrite's front lawn.

As the man cleared off the last of the snow at the end of the driveway, Franklin realized that he better slip back into the house before being noticed. But he waited too long, being nosey and all. The man looked up toward his direction and waved before he turned off the blower.

Franklin froze. *He saw me! I finally agree with you, Dad. I'm stupid.* The last thing he wanted was to hear the Jesus freak preach to him. He prepared for battle of the fire and brimstone confrontation, proclaiming him a sinner going to hell without a get out of the fire for free card.

The neighbor's body twitched when he spotted Franklin standing straight and stiff like a British guard at Buckingham Palace, gloating.

With the blower in hand, the man hurried over to Franklin. "You startled me!" the hypocrite declared.

Franklin slipped his hands into the pockets of his down-feathered jacket as he readied himself to ward off the Holy Roller. "What do you think you did to me?" his deep voice croaked.

The man lowered his head. He wore the collar on his sheepskin-denim jacket turned up. His black stocking hat covered his hair. As he raised his head, he pushed his square-wire-framed glasses up and against the bridge of his nose. His work gloves were stained.

A sheepish facial expression appeared on his rugged face. Edging closer, the man apologized, "I'm so sorry. I feel so embarrassed. I didn't introduce myself."

Who wants you to introduce yourself? Just leave me alone. "I've never seen anything like this. Somebody going onto somebody else's property and start working," Weak-kneed, Franklin felt himself losing his composure, "Let me make this clear. I don't pay for work I didn't ask for!" *Just go away!*

The man stopped in his tracks. He had a blank stare in his deep-set eyes and his broad chin slackened a bit. "No!" He coughed and cleared his throat. He continued, "No. I'm not looking for payment. After I cleared my driveway, I just thought I'd give you a hand and do yours. I do apologize if I . . ."

Franklin felt his hand trembling. He grabbed it. *Leave me alone. I wasn't bothering you.*

"Please accept my apology. We recently moved across the street from the Northwest Montana area. I thought you could use a hand and . . ."

"I'm quite capable," Franklin bellowed.

"Oh, no, no, I didn't mean it that way. I was trying to be neighborly."

"Neighborly? That's pretty presumptuous of you assuming I'd allow a stranger to trespass on my property and clear my driveway without my permission!"

"Trespass? Wow!" He scratched the top of his head. "I—um, I do apologize, and I didn't mean to impose on you. I'm really sorry. We weren't properly introduced. I'm Mark Torkelson. We moved across the street three months ago. I did come by several times to meet you, but you were never home."

He had the mind to tell Mark that he had refused to answer the door, but he didn't. Mark's capability to repay his inflammatory remarks with a polite and cordial attitude puzzled Franklin.

"I'm sorry if I misconstrued my actions. I do apologize."

Stay away from me.

Franklin demanded, "Just get off my property."

Mark's jaw dropped.

What did I do?

"Sure. I'm very sorry for intruding. You have a blessed day." Mark headed back home.

"I just like to do things myself—I ahh!"

He watched for a moment as Mark crossed the street and mumbled, "What's that? John Deere 2520. Nice condition. At least he takes care of his equipment. Wait a minute. Am I seeing things? No way! He did! Who plows a hay lot? That's a strange one."

Franklin headed back into the house. "Have a blessed day. There's no such thing for me. Go plow your hay lot, fool. For all I care, you can plow the whole town. Besides, I don't socialize. Ah, just forget about it!" But he couldn't forget about it.

The Jesus freak had intruded on his miserable life. As he got ready for his meeting with Johnny, tears flooded his eyes. He released his frustrations by griping and slamming things around. He grabbed his keys, shoved them into his jacket pocket, and headed into the garage.

With his hand on the snow blower, the realization hit him. Mark cleared the driveway and he didn't have to do it. He dropped his head and sobbed. "Who's the fool now, idiot?"

He unplugged his truck's engine heater. As he stepped into his pick-up, he considered apologizing to Mark. He put the key into the ignition and started the truck.

"The man did me a favor. Maybe I should apologize," but he dismissed the idea, being concerned it might elicit a false impression of friendship, "Besides, he probably thinks I'm a monster. Just forget about it. I'm sure he'll never want to speak to me again. Good job, my man, Dr. Franklyn. You're great at embarrassing yourself."

He threw the stick-shift into reverse. As he stepped on the gas pedal he looked over his shoulder, "But why didn't he react to my insults?" He backed out of his driveway. After shifting into four-wheel-drive, he started down the road.

As he traveled down the old country road covered with packed snow, Franklin noticed the bratty neighborhood kids less than a block ahead of him.

The boy and the girl were throwing snow balls at each other on the side of the road in front of the light blue manufactured home. The house belonged to Bob Lapierre's tree farm about a mile up the road from Franklin's place.

For a brief moment, it reminded him of the days when he and Katie had bought their Christmas trees from the French Canadian couple, Bob and his wife, Annabelle. After Bob had his heart aneurysm, he no longer could manage the farm. His eldest son, Enzo Lapierre, had converted the place into a small commercial wholesale tree farm. Because of it, the Franklyns had switched to artificial trees.

Katie and Kitty loved cutting down their own tree. Thinking about how much they loved Christmas saddened him. "Why does everything have to change? Now I hate Christmas!"

As he passed the children, the boy threw a snowball at Franklin's truck, smashing it against the driver's window. He flinched and hit the brake.

Franklin opened the window. "You could have caused an accident." The kids stood staring at Franklin. "You kids have been nothing but trouble ever since you moved in last summer. Throwing rocks and watermelons in the road is not a game! It's dangerous!"

The boy darted toward their house with the little girl following close behind him.

"And you better not ride your bikes on my property ever again!" Franklin hollered.

The misbehaved boy turned his head and stuck his tongue out at Franklin, infuriating him further. "Where's your mother?"

At once, the boy grabbed the small girl's hand and bolted off with her around the back of the house.

Franklin had the mind to knock on their door. Though he had never met the parents, he assumed their bad behavior must have come from lack of discipline. He noticed their piece of junk red-Subaru Legacy-wagon parked under their carport. "Somebody must be home."

Since the house was so close to Bob's farmhouse, Franklin couldn't understand why Bob didn't do something about those pests. "It's not possible he doesn't know what's going on. Something's wrong here." If they were his tenants, Franklin would have evicted them long ago.

As he glared at the house trying to make up his mind what to do, a gust of icy wind hit him in the face. He shut the window and headed to the university.

"Forget about it. I need to find out what Johnny's up to, anyhow."

Franklin drove through the empty campus rather than the busy main road through town to get to the museum.

"There's Rufus," Johnny's 1974 vintage turquoise Ford F250. Several years prior, Franklin had helped Johnny restore that highboy to its pristine condition. At one time, restoring vehicles was their hobby. Something they did since they were in high school.

He pulled into the space next to Rufus. "Look at that! Johnny replaced the running lights with off-road spotlights. Nice. I like it."

Franklin glanced at his watch. "Five after nine! Where is he? Oh no, maybe he heard me say that I wasn't coming. That's why he hung up on me! He must be doing something else in there."

Just then, a side door for employees only swung open. Johnny emerged with another fellow holding a briefcase. "Who is that? Wow, he's tall! Maybe he's not as tall as he looks. He's walking with shrimp boat, hahaha! Anybody would look tall next to him." But then it hit him. The man's stature made Johnny look like a little boy. Franklin laughed so hard it hurt his stomach.

"Look at that!" The man's Russian-fur hat made the guy seem taller and Johnny even smaller, "What's that hat called again? I got it! It's an Ushanka."

Johnny and the man turned and started walking toward the parking lot. "Wait a minute! He better not bring him over here."

The two stopped and the man shook Johnny's hand and walked away in a different direction. Franklin sighed in relief. Johnny threw his hood over his head and zipped up his jacket as he proceeded to walk toward Franklin.

Though the walkway appeared slick, Johnny's gait, like always, was brisk. "Why in the world does he always have to walk like he's in hurry to get somewhere when he has nowhere to go?" Franklin chuckled.

With his truck still running, Franklin stepped out of it. While leaning against the hood, Franklin asked, "Mr. O'Toole, so tell me, what's so urgent that you had to drag me out here?"

"Mr. O'Toole, really?" Johnny smirked, "Shall I call you Benjamin?"

"Why would you call me that?"

"Why did you call me Mr. O'Toole?"

"I figured since you're the head honcho around here, that's your name around the museum."

With his hands on his hips, Johnny shot back, "And Benjamin is your real first name?"

Franklin had never used his birth name, Dr. B. Francis Franklyn, and nor had his parents. He only used the letter "B" when he had to sign legal documents. He preferred his nickname, Franklin.

On the first day of high school, while his coach did roll call, he had called out Franklin Franklyn. As a joke, Franklin answered to it. When he and his buddies had found it hilarious, it encouraged Franklin to adopt the nickname. But his parents had dubbed him Frank.

"Don't be ridiculous!" Franklin barked, "You know better than calling me that. Now you're being infantile."

Johnny turned his finger toward his chest and retorted, "I'm being infantile!" His hood slid off his head.

"Don't call me Benjamin. I hate that and you know it."

"And don't call me Mr. O'Toole, ever again! I'm your brother-in-law, not your boss!"

"Okay Johnny, touché."

Johnny shoved his hands in his pockets and he glared at Franklin. "Where did you go?"

"I was sitting in the truck waiting for you, but you were late."

He pointed his index finger at Franklin. "No! Where did you go? Frank, what happened to you?" Johnny stepped backward a few steps with his arms stretched out. "Who are you?"

"Dr. B. Francis Franklyn."

For a moment, Johnny's face froze with puckered lips and crinkled nose, as though he had smelled something bad. "I know you're still in there, somewhere. You've been avoiding me like the plague. And when I do see you, it's like you're in another world. And you haven't been in my house since the funeral. And lately, I can't talk to you without you barking at me! Most people heal over time, but you're worsening. If Katie saw what you've become, she wouldn't like you."

Incensed, he felt like a locomotive that had blown its stack with the whistle blasting. Images flashed before his eyes. Franklin imagined sitting at the controls with a precipice ahead and Johnny chained to the front, steaming full speed ahead.

"Frank, are you listening? Your eyes are glazed over."

He had the mind to punch the pipsqueak in the nose "You shut-up about Katie! You don't know what Katie liked or didn't like?"

Johnny's fair Irish complexion flushed fiery red and his veins popped out in his short neck. He stepped closer to Franklin, clenching his fists. His eyes sparked as he shot out his retort melded with spit. "She was my sister!"

"So what! She was my wife!"

"You were my best friend."

"Life's different now."

"What about Kitty?"

"Don't bring my daughter into this conversation, or I'll. . ." Franklin slammed his mouth shut, pressing his lips together, holding a fist up.

With his eyes fixed on Johnny's face, Franklin noticed that the scrawny boy he had grown up with had developed wrinkles on the sides of and under his emerald eyes. That point on his turned-up nose had turned downward. Silver and white hair weaved through the top and the temples of his backward-swept thick, wavy dark hair. *I hadn't I seen how much he's aged until now.*

Snorting through his nose like a bull that's about to charge a red cape, Johnny turned on his heels and stomped off.

"Where are you going?" Franklin shouted out.

Johnny stopped and dropped his head. Seconds later he spun around and rushed back. "Frank, I miss Katie too. As I'm sure you know, yesterday was the anniversary of the accident. Let's not fight, today. She was my sister. No, she is my sister."

"What do you mean? She's dead."

"No Frank. You died. She's alive in Heaven."

"Johnny, don't give me that heaven . . ."

He stuck his finger near Franklin's face. "Frank, stop! I will no longer participate in this confrontation with you!"

"You started it."

As he emphasized each word, Johnny pressed his finger against his chest. "I am not your punching bag."

When Franklin saw tears welling up in Johnny's eyes, he backed off. "Hey, man, just forget about it, okay?"

Johnny twisted his face into a grimace. After a brief moment, his brother-in-law relaxed his facial muscles. His eyes slid heavenward with one arm extended up. "Sweet Jesus, give me strength."

Since he prayed, Franklin figured he calmed down so he took the opportunity to find out what Johnny wanted in the first place. "By the way, what was on your mind when you called?"

He rubbed his freckled nose. "I need you to come over to my house tonight."

"Why couldn't you ask me that on the phone?"

"Because the last time I asked you, you said no and hung up on me."

Franklin turned his face away. "Well, my answer is still the same."

"Frank, look at me."

Franklin glanced over and slid his eyes downward.

"Listen, I'm not asking you. I'm telling you. I expect you to be at my house tonight at six."

"What? You're ordering me?"

"Yes. And if you're not there by six tonight, I'm going to your place and I'm dragging you out of there!"

"Ahhh—did you forget? I tower over you by almost a foot!" He placed his hands on his hips and smirked.

"Eleven inches to be exact. I've had enough of you afflicting pain on your family and yourself. Enough is enough, and today it stops!"

Franklin plunged his fist into the air. "You're just a pipsqueak. Try and make me."

"I'm so fed up with you and your self-pity party that if you don't show up I'll knock your door down with Rufus, yank you out of your two-story cocoon, and toss you into my truck. You're coming to my house tonight either way. We can do this the easy way or the hard way. You choose!"

Wow. The pipsqueak sounded serious, and serious enough that he could force Franklin out of the safety of his home. Even the very thought of it staggered him to such an extent his knees buckled. "But I eat at six."

"Mary's making supper. You better not make her labor for nothing."

"Supper? Tell her not to cook."

"Remember, be there at six and you better not be late!" Johnny spun around and stomped off to his truck.

"Hey," Franklin shouted, "You lied to me."

Johnny halted. With his keys in his hand, he looked over Rufus's hood. "What do you mean I lied to you?"

"You said if I didn't meet you I'd regret it when all you wanted to do was invite me to supper."

"I'm not inviting you to supper. All I said was Mary is making you supper. You better not make Mary labor for nothing."

He loved his sister-in-law, and he would never do anything to hurt her.

"You need to be at my house tonight or you will regret it! Do you understand me?"

"Yes."

Johnny leaped into his truck and slammed the door. He revved the engine and stormed out of the parking lot.

As Franklin slipped into his pickup, tears welled in his eyes. "His house must be all decked out for Christmas." He grabbed his head. "What's going on? What's he up to? I don't want to see Christmas."

He laid his forehead against the top of the steering wheel. "It's not a self pity-party, its reality. If I could only make Johnny understand the torment I'm going through." Blurry-eyed from his unstoppable tears, he drove home.

CHAPTER 4

Father and Daughter Reunion

JUST AS FRANKLIN HAD expected, Johnny's seventeenth-century colonial home was a Christmas spectacle in the midst of the New England snowy winter wonderland. Bedecked with dazzling lights and decorations, the entire house and its windows were outlined with red and white lights.

He stopped just short of the brick driveway. His grip on the steering wheel tightened. "I can't do this!" Franklin gazed at the Spruce tree's twinkling lights synchronized with music from Christmas Carolers placed in front of the tree. "I better do this." He turned into the driveway.

When he pulled in front of Johnny's attached garage, he glared at the closed door, visualizing Katie's brand new Ford explorer parked inside. Ever since that fatal Christmas, Johnny had it hid in his garage.

Franklin's eyes welled. "I hate to admit it. Johnny's right. But I don't want to sell it."

His heart galloped. He grabbed his chest. Was he having a heart attack? He took in several sharp short breaths. "Stop idiot!" He feared that he would hyperventilate. With his head rested against the headrest, he closed his eyes to calm himself, taking in deep and slow breaths.

After a few moments, Franklin pressed his finger against the artery in his neck to check his pulse. His heart rate slowed to normal.

He pulled back his coat sleeve and glanced at his watch. Almost six. It's time to go in and see what the little pipsqueak is up to.

As he stepped out of his truck, he hesitated eyeing the familiar decorations while the smoke flowing from the brick chimney emanated sweet aromas of apple wood. He debated with himself whether or not he should stay or leave.

He swallowed hard. "Okay, I better find out what I'm going to regret."

Lighted toy soldiers and candy canes illumed the stone walkway, brightening his dreaded path. The two angels suspended above the life-size nativity prompted the song "Hark the Herald Angel's Sing" to play in his mind. He grabbed his head and strained his neck. "Shut-up brain!" The music stopped. He broke into a sweat as he continued toward the decorated front porch.

Though Johnny's property had the appearance of a Norman Rock-well scene, nevertheless the sight of it inflamed Franklin's pain. He stepped up onto the first step of the wraparound porch. He glared at the oak Planked door. He plodded up the steps like a brave soldier being lead to an enemy's firing squad. He stood at the door.

As Franklin rattled the bells attached to the Christmas wreath, he spotted a little lobster ornament arranged in the midst of other orna-ments. It provoked a childhood memory of Pappy's Christmas Eve lob-ster stew. He touched the lobster and closed his eyes as he traveled back to a young lad of twelve. Franklin had never forgotten the tantalizing odors flowing from that ten quart aluminum pot filled with Pappy's stew.

That year, Pappy had allowed Franklin to make the Family's tradi-tional lobster stew with supervision. He loved listening to the old folk's historical stories of yesteryears as he stirred the stew.

After Franklin gave the stew a good stir, he reached for the lid near the bowl of the cooked lobster meat.

Pappy inquired, "Boy, did you taste that?"

Franklin snapped his head toward Pappy sitting with his three bud-dies around the old wooden dinette set.

As one of Pappy's friends dipped a chip into the French onion dip, the other two stared at Franklin, making him feel awkward. He wished he could run somewhere and hide. "Opps, I forgot. I'm sorry." He imagined himself a big idiot looking like a dorky dumb giant.

With Pappy's large hands folded on the table, he glanced around the table at his friends. Pappy stood and addressed them. "Carry on, gentle-men. I'm going to help my grandson who has the talent of becoming the next world renowned chef."

The men didn't dare question Pappy since he had bragging rights of being a Michelin star chef, himself. They all nodded and resumed with their conversations.

Pappy lifted the wooden spoon and stirred the stew . . .

"Frank, hello," he heard Mary's sweet and pleasant voice echo through his daydream. "Hello Frank. You in there? Hello."

He jolted backward. "Mary! How did you know I was at the door?"

"Usually when somebody does this," she reached outside and rang the doorbell as she continued, "it's a signal that somebody's at the door."

He was confused. No matter how hard he tried, he couldn't remember ringing it. "Very amusing, Mary. I don't remember ringing the doorbell."

She giggled, "And you admit to it? Frank you rang it just a few seconds ago." She laughed out loud.

"I'm glad you find me amusing."

"You can be." She waved her hand, motioning him to come in. "Well, are you going to come in or are you going to stand in the cold for the rest of the evening?"

"You're a barrel of laughs, ha ha." He stepped across the threshold.

"Frank, you know I'm teasing. I'm really glad to see you. It's been a while."

"Yes I know. I'm glad to see you too." He gave her a half of a hug.

He slipped his jacket and black trooper hat onto the coat rack. But Mary was all decked out in that shinning black and silver dress. "Why are you all fancied up? Are you having a party?"

"No, I'm not having a party. It's a special occasion."

Panicked, he imagined the worse. He barked, "What do you mean? What are you celebrating? I'm not celebrating anything. Are there other people coming? How many? I'm not staying!"

Mary jolted, hunched a bit, and grabbed her chest. Franklin had no doubt his bark had an adverse affect on her. Unlike the Franklins and the O'tooles, she had come from a family that had never raised their voices.

"Oh Mary, I'm so very sorry," he placed a hand on her petite shoulder, "I didn't mean to scare you. Really, I just panicked."

She straightened her petite frame. Mary's straight eyebrows appeared to freeze in their horizontal position. With her thin lips set in a hard line, she shut her round eyes. "It's okay," she raised a dismissive hand. "Don't worry. It's just that it's been a long time since I've heard you holler like that, but I don't think I can ever get use to it."

"I'm sorry."

"Frank you need to calm down. I know you've been through a lot and you're still going through a lot. I understand. But Frank, panicking is not going to help you."

"But I'm nervous. Your husband was evasive with me and that scares me."

He darted his eyes down the decorated foyer, looking for Johnny. "He's up to something. I know he is. Where is he?"

He stomped off down the foyer shouting, "Johnny! Where are you! Why is it so quiet in here? Johnny, what's going on?"

"Where did he go?" He stomped down the foyer.

Mary called out, "Frank."

Just as he reached the living room, he halted, eyeballing the area.

The tall lit Christmas tree glowed in the bay window, along with lighting from centerpieces on the coffee table, illuminated the living room. The dimmed crystal chandelier hung in the center of the room, casting its reflection on the hardwood floor. The warmth from the fire blazing in the stone fireplace augmented the Christmas ambiance throughout the room. The entirety of it created the perfect atmosphere for entertaining guests. But there were no people, not even Johnny.

Behind him, he heard Mary's heels tapping the floor. As he glanced over, she reached him. She swept her bangs from her eyes. Her short-sassy blond hair shimmered in the soft lightning.

"Mary, please talk to me. Are you having a party tonight? Are others coming? I don't want to be around a crowd. You and Johnny know better."

"No. Calm down, please."

"Then where's Johnny?"

Wearing a slight grin, she slipped her arm through his. "Please come with me. We have a surprise for you."

"I—I don't like surprises. He told me you were making supper."

"I did. I made a fantastic supper for you. But first let's go to Johnny's den."

"Oh! I get it. He wants to chew me out before we eat."

Mary slipped her arm out from his and placed her hands on her narrow hips. "Why would he want to do that? Frank, just follow me."

He could feel his heart beat pulsing in his temples as he walked down the hall. "What's wrong?"

"Nothing's wrong. Why would you think something like that?"

"Why do I have to meet him in his den? Who is he now? The Godfather."

She laughed out loud, "Don't be ridiculous."

"It's not funny."

She stopped in front of the den's door. "It is. Don't you think you're being a little ridiculous? Do you hear yourself? What do you think we're going to do, put you in a cement bucket and throw you into the Webster Lake? Besides, the lake is frozen." She snapped her fingers, "Shucks, too bad. Oh well, there goes our plans."

"Very amusing."

"Frank, just go inside."

"You want me to go in alone?"

She kept on walking without acknowledging him.

After she was out of sight, he wondered if he could slip out without being noticed. But being too curious, he dropped the escape idea.

Reaching for the doorknob, his hand trembled. When he opened the door, Kitty appeared before his eyes, standing in front of Johnny's desk like a timid little girl, tugging on her green sweater over her jeans.

He resisted the overwhelming urge to take her in his arms. Standing in the presence of his sweet and guileless daughter embarrassed him. He refused to touch her with his murderous hands.

A momentary silence. His heart sunk. "Um."

"Hello, Daddy," her voice quivered.

He had no right to be there. He was an unfit father. The more he thought about it, it infuriated him that Johnny had the gall to shame him this way. And yet, he had no doubt that if he hadn't come, he would have regretted it. Just like Johnny had told him.

He whispered, "Kitty, it's you."

Kitty edged closer to him, "It's me. But why are you looking at me like you've seen a ghost?"

"You cut off your beautiful hair."

"I did. But it's still below my shoulders. See!" she turned her head, "Do you like it?"

Though Franklin liked the way it flowed around her face like a picture frame, it dawned on him how he had missed so much over the past two years. Even her makeup seemed different. It felt as though he had awoken from a deep sleep, and life had marched forward without him. Nevertheless, he had nobody else to blame but himself. "It's nice, but you look different."

Tears welled in her eyes. "I like your flannel shirt. I like the different shades of green in that plaid." Her chin trembled. "You look good."

Seeing the heart-shaped pendant around her neck pained Franklin. He and Katie had bought it for her sixteenth birthday. It reminded him of his bygone joyous family life.

"Daddy, say something."

Confused, he blurted, "It's been two years."

"We tried to come home to see you, but you wouldn't allow it. Remember, Daddy? You weren't celebrating the holidays. And last summer and the summer before, you said that you were too busy teaching summer classes for you to travel, or for us to come for a visit. Daddy, you made up a lot of excuses to not see me."

"They weren't excuses!" He forced back tears.

"Oh Yes they were. I can't believe you!"

"What can't you believe?"

"I'm your daughter. You haven't seen me in two years and you're so cold! Why?"

I don't want her to know. You'll hate me for what I've done. He took in a deep breath, keeping his composure.

She cried out, "Daddy, look at me. Stop avoiding eye contact with me."

His heart pounded so much that he thought it would explode out of his chest.

She pushed her hand against his shoulder. "Look at me!"

He slid his eyes upward.

"We told you that we would cancel our plans so we could be with you. But you told us we needed to move on with our lives and go to Oklahoma! Remember Daddy?

Several times you insisted that's what Mom would have wanted us to do. You said move on.

And ever since, you've been pushing me away. Why have you avoided me? What did I do to make you hate me?" Her mascara melted into her tears running down her cheeks.

"That's ridiculous! I could never hate you." His eyes watered. "But you needed to move on with your life."

"Did you mean without you?"

Speechless, he stood motionless with his jaw slacked. "No. I, ah."

"Why did you push me away? Why? I love you! Why don't you love me anymore?"

Franklin grabbed her and held her tight in his arms. "I love you, Cinnamon Bun."

"I want my father back. Please Daddy, come back to me." Sobbing, she pressed her face into his chest bopping her fists against him.

All along, he had known it would be difficult for her, but witnessing her suffering tore at his heart.

He rubbed her back. "Shh, shh, I'm so sorry."

She raised her head. With her forehead creased and her eyebrows puckered, tears streamed from the corners of her half-shut eyes. Her chin quivered. Sucking in quick short breaths, she sniffled, "I was—I was Daddy's little girl—remember?" She dropped her face back against his chest.

Those words stabbed him in the heart like a dagger. Uncontrollable tears streamed from his eyes. "That has never changed. You'll always be Daddy's little girl."

Holding onto his arm, she raised her head. "Daddy, I love you. Please, don't push me away ever again. Please, Daddy, please, please . . ."

He opened his mouth, but he couldn't speak as though something had grabbed his throat, choking him.

Within a few seconds, his voice came to him. "I won't. I . . . .." His voice cracked. He stopped speaking.

"Promise me you won't push me away ever again."

If only he could tell her that he had lived in torment without her to protect her. He doubted if he could fulfill such a promise. However, the thought of losing her again posed too harrowing for him. "I promise."

"You promise?"

Franklin held her tight. "Yes. I'll never let you go ever again." He removed the handkerchief from his jean's pocket and wiped her sweet, soaked face. Then he handed her his handkerchief to blow her reddened nose.

Still sniffling and wiping her nose, she remarked, "Daddy, Mom's death was an accident. I hope you're not blaming yourself for what happened."

"I don't want to discuss it."

Kitty stepped back. "But, Daddy, if you would reach out to Jesus . . ."

As she preached, his daughter's voice faded. Bits and pieces of images of the accident flashed in his mind. The more vivid they were, the more Kitty's voice faded like an echo dwindling through a long tunnel.

"God said to go home." Katie's pleas sounded through the snap-shots of the accident tormenting him like he had found himself in the midst of a horror movie trailer. He reached his hand toward his dying wife—her head slouched over with a blank stare in her motionless eyes.

"Daddy!" Kitty shrieked.

Startling him. "Huh!"

"You were staring without blinking. Are you okay?"

"Ahh. . ."

"Where were you? You scared me."

"I'm sorry. I was thinking about something."

She closed her eyes, expelling a sigh. "Daddy, all you need to do is seek Jesus and you'll find that He's a loving and merciful God. Please, at least think it over."

Murderers like him had no mercy. Besides, God had refused to stop him that night so why should he even speak to that so called loving God?

He barked, "This discussion is over!"

Kitty jolted. "Okay, it's over." Her lower lip trembled.

He changed the subject. "Where are Maggie and Jake?"

"Jake is with her at the hotel."

"The hotel? Why didn't they come with you?"

"Well, Daddy, I wanted to talk to you alone. Is that okay?"

"Yes, of course it's okay."

Gazing at him with tearful eyes, her lips quivered.

As he looked into her pitiful face, his heart broke. "I—ah mean, I'm glad you did come alone."

A smile popped on her face. "I would like to fix things between you and me."

I'm as unfixable as my broken cordless phone.

He gazed into her glinting eyes and wondered if he had done more harm than good by protecting her from his guilt-ridden miserable life.

"We're good."

"We're good? What does that mean?"

"I need time to process—You're right! We need to talk." *What a jerk, you jerk.* "I mean, I'm happy you came. Things will get better now."

She appeared puzzled, nerving him.

"Cinnamon Bun, I'm very sorry. But I've been so confused and broken, I love you, and I always will."

She hugged him. "I understand. I love you too."

That easy? What. Shut-up. Go with it. He kissed her on top of her head. "Hey, can I see Maggie?"

"Yes, of course you can, and there's something I'd like to talk to you about."

Here it comes. "What's that?"

"I have some news and I need a favor. Please Daddy, sit down."

Franklin watched his daughter as she walked around the desk. "A favor? What kind of favor?"

When she sat across from him, she gestured him to sit down. "Daddy, please sit down."

As he sat in the leather chair, he braced himself.

She folded her hands in front of her on the desktop. "Jake and I are graduating this coming May."

"I figured that."

"Daddy, we're going to be ordained pastors in May."

I get it. She wants me to attend her ceremony. "Congratulations! I'm happy for you."

"Thank you. We're starting to prepare for after graduation. We've been praying about what God wants us to do next. Now, Daddy, before I tell you, please keep in mind we're still praying about this and we haven't decided anything yet."

He readied himself for the worst. "What haven't you decided?"

"Daddy it's so exciting, brace yourself."

"Believe me, I'm bracing myself. Just spit it out."

"We applied for a youth pastor position in Thailand. They've just planted the church. They've been looking for a couple, and they've contacted us for an interview."

"Thailand? Why Thailand?" There it was. The bad news he had expected. In that instant, Franklin figured it all out. She stopped by to say good-by before she took Maggie off to some foreign land and he wouldn't see her again until she turned, at the least, twenty-one.

Her smile faded, and she bit her lower lip. "A while back, we had told you and Mom we were praying about working in the mission field. Remember?"

"No."

Tilting her head, she squeezed her lips together. "You don't remember? Jake and I had several conversations with you and Mom, and you don't remember a single one of these conversations."

"Come to think of it, I have a vague recollection about something like that."

"Vague? You thought it was a great idea! And you said so."

Ah-oh! "Kitty, I don't remember you ever saying anything about Thailand."

"What? We never did discuss Thailand . . ."

If he had only paid attention to their Christian plans, he would have at least tried to put some sense into her head about the cons of living in a foreign country, especially with a little girl.

"Um, Thailand is a long way from here. The culture and the language are different. Maggie's eight now and she'll experience culture shock."

"Daddy, I understand this. But . . ."

By the time Maggie turned twenty-one she may no longer speak English and then he wouldn't be able to communicate with his own flesh and blood granddaughter. *Now I'm being ridiculous.*

". . . and we need to go to Phoenix for five days to meet with the missionaries. And we'd like to. . ."

"It's hot in Arizona." *You fool, Maggie won't forget English.*

"Not this time of year. Anyhow, where was I?" She glanced downward.

"Arizona is famous for rattle snakes," Franklin declared.

Kitty hit the edge of the desk. "So is Oklahoma. But they're not roaming around in Tulsa looking for us, so just by chance they can bite us." Resting her elbow on the desk, she slammed her hand on side of her head. "I don't believe this."

It wasn't his intent to frustrate her. But he had reason for his concern. "Thailand has typhoons, tsunamis, and malaria carrying mosquitoes, and Maggie's a defenseless little girl."

"Oh my sweet Jesus, help me." She folded her hands in front of her. "I'm trying to ask you if we can leave Maggie with you for five days."

He could have leaped with excitement about having her alone for five days. But at the same time, he wondered if she'd guess he had helped kill her nana. That Thailand thing concerned him too much to let it go. "How long?"

"I just told you five days, and we'll be back mid-morning on Wednesday."

"No. How long will you be in Thailand?"

"If we go, I believe we'll be there for two years." She added, "Maggie's excited to see you."

"Why do you believe it's for two years? Can it be longer?"

"No, I don't believe so. Daddy I don't have all the details."

"But I don't understand, why?"

"What do you mean, why?"

"Why do you have to go to Arizona for five days when they live in Thailand?"

She grabbed her head. "Oh my sweet Jesus. Please, stop having two different conversations with me. You're confusing me. Okay, the Arizona part. The missionaries' home church is in Phoenix, and they're having a revival this week. They're the guest speakers."

Though Katie had attended many of those revivals, Franklin had never figured out why she needed reviving when she had done all the Christian requirements, like going to church and reading the bible.

"Daddy, am I bothering you?"

"What? You're not bothering me. I love you, and I'm excited about having Maggie."

Just then, from his peripheral vision, Franklin spotted a buffet platter of different foods.

"You got a funny way of showing it."

Eyeing the platter, he crossed his hands behind his head. "You've got to give me a chance to process all this. Do you think she forgot me?" *I'm starving.*

"Oh my goodness, it's only been two years. She's never forgotten you. She's excited to see you."

"Really?"

"Yes, really. She can't wait to see her Grampy. That's all she's been talking about for the past several days. Jake and I will bring her over in the morning. Okay?"

"Sure. What time?"

"Around ten. Is that okay?"

"Yes."

She smiled. "Thank you, Daddy. I love you."

"Cinnamon bun, I love you, and I'm happy you're here."

"So am I!" she grinned, pursing her lips.

His stomach growled as he mulled over the platter of finger sandwiches, grapes, and sugar cookies with a pitcher of fruit punch. "What's this? I thought we were having supper with Johnny and Mary."

"No we're not. They went to a celebration party at the museum, but Mary made the food for us."

"What are they celebrating?" He stood and picked a purple grape from it's stem.

"Well, Johnny got a promotion. He's now the executive director of the museum. So tonight they're having a promotional party for him."

"Executive? Really? Where was he when I got here?"

"He was in the garage waiting for Mary to bring you in here. The plan was after you were in here with me, they'd take off."

That confirmed it. Johnny did have a covert plan that involved Kitty. "It's great news. Let's eat and catch up."

A wide-mouthed smile appeared across Kitty's face. "Now that's something I would love to do!"

"What's in the Crockpot?" He lifted the lid.

She responded, "Its Mary's famous navy bean and ham soup."

"It sure is. She can make a great pot of soup. I'm hungry, how about you?" he asked, placing the platter of the scrumptious edibles on the desk between them.

"Yes, I'm starving."

"You were born starving."

While examining the contents in the chicken salad sandwich, he inquired, "By the way, why didn't you stay with Johnny? He has plenty of room. You didn't need to stay at a hotel."

"Are you serious? Is this one of those gotcha questions?"

And that it was. "What do you mean?"

She set a roast beef sandwich onto her plate. "Think about it. If I had stayed here, I wouldn't have heard the end of it. Besides, I would have rather been home than here. But I wasn't about to show up in your dooryard unannounced. You would've had a tizzy fit or fainted."

She's my Cinnamon Bun. "Maybe I would have been a little stunned, but I wouldn't have fainted. Let's eat."

"Not before we pray."

"Pray, why?"

"Bow your head, Daddy. I'll do the praying."

As she prayed, it brought back memories when Katie insisted on saying grace before they ate.

After she said her amen, he poured punch into the crystal glasses. "By the way, how are you getting back to the hotel?"

"Johnny's taking me back."

"No. I'm your father. I'll take you back. Is it in Tilton?"

"Uh huh. Jealous, Daddy?"

"Of the pipsqueak? Never."

As they dined, Kitty shared stories about her adventures in Oklahoma and about Maggie, and Franklin paid attention to every word. The two exchanged a few laughs over childhood memories and shed tears over fond memories of Katie. They stayed in Johnny's den for a few hours. Together, they cleaned up the dishes and put away the leftovers.

Kitty wiped her hands dry with a dish towel and placed it on the counter top. "I'm so happy we had this time together. I feel so much better now."

"So do I. But we better get out of here before Johnny and Mary get back. I'm tired, and I'm sure they'll be tired too."

She nodded. "I'm tired too. It's been a long day."

Franklin dropped Kitty off at the hotel. Though she walked like an elegant woman through the doors of the hotel lobby, he pictured her in pigtails, skipping into her preschool classroom. Encouraged by their meeting, he had to admit that he could never let her go again. And yet, he realized his life would become more complicated from now on. But what would happen if she found out that he had killed her mother? That was his biggest worry.

CHAPTER 5

Dina's Donut House

THE NEXT MORNING AFTER a sleepless night, Franklin headed out to Dina's Donut House to pickup some fresh doughnuts and muffins for Maggie. Since he left before sunrise, he drove along a lonesome dark road. In his mind, he conducted a scenario analysis of the worst outcomes that might transpire by allowing his family back into his tortured life.

The worst of possible consequence would be if his family figured out the truth about him, and hate him for it. And yet, they may not. Nevertheless, it felt strange for him to resume the role of a father and grandfather without his wife, and he had nobody to blame but himself.

The full moon lit the way into the shopping center's parking lot. "Like Pappy use to say, 'All the nuts come out during the full moon.'" He stopped the truck in the middle of the lot, let down the window, stuck his head out, and shouted, "Here I am moon! The biggest nut of all!"

With the cold air pouring into the opened window, he scanned the shopping center through the windshield. All the storefronts were dark with the exception of Dina's, which would account for the lack of parked cars. There were about a dozen vehicles parked in front of and near the doughnut shop. As he had expected, the locals' gathering spot for gossip was as busy as an anthill at six in the morning.

"Boy, it's freezing out there." He shut the window and raised the heater fan.

In spite of the fact that he hadn't patronized that doughnut shop since Katie died, nothing had changed. It was obvious that Taki Papadakos, the owner, loved his Greek heritage. As always, the blue and white Christmas lights with two men in Greek-costumes decorated the storefront window. But the "O" in the blue neon "Open for Business" sign had burnt out since he had been there last.

Franklin gazed through the windshield with his elbow resting on the steering wheel. He rubbed the stubble on his unshaven chin and wondered if he could slip in and out without being noticed. "What are my options: being seen or the best pastries in town?" Since they were for Maggie, Franklin took the chance and pulled into a parking space a few storefronts down from Dina's.

The door bong sounded as Franklin entered the decades-old dough-nut shop. The blue and white décor throughout the bakery matched the colors of the Greek flag that hung behind the register. When he passed the Christmas tree near the entrance, he noticed most of the nine tables were occupied.

Three men stood in line at the register. A younger woman rang up orders. Several customers stood in front of the bakery case. Two other middle-aged women scurried behind the case filling white-doughnut boxes with various baked goods, as a young man served the customers seated at the tables.

He scanned the bakery, looking for Uncle Taki, but Franklin didn't see him. Taki must have been in the kitchen baking his delectable Greek and American pastries.

Even over the noisy chatter throughout the bakery, Franklin heard the door bong sound off two more times while he stood in line.

With his hands in his winter jacket's pockets, he eyed the apple blue-berry muffins on top of the bakery case. Then Uncle Taki appeared from the back, carrying a tray of his famous Loukoumades. He had forgotten about those luscious little doughnut holes soaked in honey, and sprinkled with cinnamon and chopped walnuts.

Oh boy, Taki is looking my way. Did he see me? Maybe not. "He's too busy," Franklin muttered. He surmised it might be better if he just left and buy the doughnuts at the grocery store up the road, but his mouth watered for those Loukoumades.

From behind the bakery case, Taki slid the tray into the upper back case. He announced, "I got the Greek doughnuts, and this is the last batch for today."

The girl at the register hollered, "I need an order of those Greek doughnuts!"

Oh brother, the Loukoumades are selling out.

Then Taki turned around and looked out into the dinning area, Franklin looked away for a few moments. Trying not to look conspicuous, he pretended to be admiring the decked out Christmas tree near the front entrance. He peeked over his shoulder.

Taki moved closer to the kitchen entrance as he talked to a customer. He stopped and he folded his hands on top of the bakery case, and he continued talking with the customer.

The sound of chairs scraping against the concrete floor startled him. He twisted around. Seven men, all local farmers, were dragging two tables together. Although he knew all of them, he had forgotten about them. For numerous years, every Friday morning, they had met at Dina's for breakfast. And more times than not, Franklin had joined them to mingle and catch the local gossip.

He looked away, hoping nobody would see him. *This is too nerve-wracking. I need to get out of here before someone sees me.*

But before he could leave, Franklin felt someone tap on his shoulder. Stunned, he flinched and pivoted around.

"Bob Lapierre." It was the tree farmer up the road from Franklin's place, wearing a broad smile, exposing his crooked yellowish teeth.

Speaking in a distinctive French accent, Bob commented, "Frank! I thought my eyes were playing tricks on me. I said to myself, self, is that my good friend Frank? You know, the professor who likes to go off-roading in the woods and restore old trucks? Then I answered myself, why yes, yes it is!"

For a short and thin man, Bob's laughter roared deep like a tuba, and it was contagious. Franklin cracked-up. He hadn't laughed like that since the fatal accident. Somehow, Bob's sunny and jovial personality could always brighten a gloomy day for Franklin.

As Bob reached out his hand, he asked, "How've you been, my good man?"

Still chuckling, Franklin replied, "I'm alive!" He shook Bob's hand.

Bob wiped his forehead with the back of his hand. "Phew! Good thing! I thought you were a ghost. Besides, any day above ground is a good day." He laughed out a belly laugh, cracking up Franklin, yet again.

It amazed Franklin how spry Bob was. He seemed more like a man in his forties rather than in his mid-eighties. The heart aneurysm never slowed him down. Franklin agreed with Bob. If Bob had his way, he'd still be working the tree farm. But his family did what they thought best for him.

"It's been almost two years, yes?"

Franklin chortled, "Yes, it's been a while."

"I see you pass by the farm, but you don't stop by and say hi, no?"

Franklin wished he could crawl under the table. "I'm sorry. But it's been difficult for me without Katie."

Bob unzipped his black jacket, leaving it opened over his dark blue coveralls. It seemed as though those coveralls were all he had ever wore. "I did not stop by your place because I had a hunch. You don't feel so much like socializing. I knew you'd come around when you were ready. "

"You were right. Thank you for understanding."

"I understand, but you got to stop moping. My Annabelle," Bob's wife, "she nagged, 'Go see Frank. See if he's okay.' I'd tell her he'll come around when he's ready. He needs mending time, yes?"

At times, it seemed as though Bob knew what he was thinking almost as well as Pappy had known. "Yes."

"Come on, I'll buy you a cup of coffee. Let's sit over there." Bob pointed toward a small table in the far corner, "It won't be as cold when people come in and out."

Franklin froze. The thought of being noticed caused his heart to palpitate. The loudness of the noisy room increased his anxiety. With every sounding of the door bong, his face tightened.

Bob shouted across the room, "Uncle Taki!"

In that instant, the room spun. *I'm going to pass out!*

"What!" Taki shouted back and moved in front of the counter near the register.

Wearing a wide-mouthed smile, Bob joked, "Why do you just stand there? Get to work and bring me two coffees and two orders of those nasty Greek Doughnuts."

All heads snapped in Franklin's direction. *Stop looking at me!*

Wiping his hands on his white apron, Taki countered, "Hey, don't bother me! I'm busy!"

"But you're not too busy to take my money," Bob hollered back.

Uncle Taki's loud laughter jiggled his pot belly. "Ah, just sit down you trouble maker."

Bob slapped Franklin on the back. "Come on, let's go sit down."

"Bob, I can't—I can't stay."

"Why not?"

"Kitty and Jake are in town, and they're bringing Maggie over. It's getting late—and I—ahh. . ."

"That's good news, yes?"

"Yes, it's very good news."

"What time do you expect them?"

"Ten."

Bob glanced at his wristwatch. "You got almost four hours. You got plenty time to shoot breeze with an old man. Come and sit down. Relax. Believe me, you have plenty of time."

Feeling wobbly, Franklin hesitated.

"Come on! It's not every day you get a cheap Frenchman like me to buy you a cheap breakfast with bad coffee."

Feeling his tension melt, Franklin burst out laughing. "Okay."

As the two sat down, Uncle Taki's gravelly voice boomed through the bakery. "Hey Frank, is that you?"

"Why did you call him by his name if you didn't know it was him?" Bob hollered back.

All eyes were on Franklin. He wished he could float away or find a hole to hide in.

Taki shouted, "You ugly Frenchman, sit still. I'll be right over."

Several men from that group of the seven men came over to Franklin said hello, shook his hand, and chit-chatted a bit with him, while the others shouted salutations and waved from their seats.

They seem sincere about missing me. That comforted him.

After the men reassembled at their tables, Uncle Taki brought over a pot of coffee with a large plate of his Loukoumades. "No charge."

Bob flinched. "No charge? For me? No! What happened? Did you loose your mind?"

"No. Not for you." Taki's bushy mustache wiggled as he talked, "I don't treat cheap Frenchman."

Laughing, Taki grabbed Bob's shoulder and squeezed it. Then he pulled a chair over from another table, turned it around, and straddled it. "Franklin, how've you been?"

Actually, I've been suffering. "I'm okay."

The large dark bags under Uncle Taki's eyes were like a monument of the long hard hours he had put into his business for the past three decades. "Just okay? Why?" he drummed his fingers against the back of the chair.

"Well, life's been tough without Katie."

Uncle Taki nodded his head, "I understand. It was tough for the wife and me when we lost our beautiful Kaldona."

At the same time, Bob and Taki gestured the sign of the cross. Though Uncle Taki attended the Greek Orthodox Church and Bob attended the Roman Catholic Church, their religious beliefs paralleled each other.

From under Taki's white uniform shirt, he slid out his gold chain and kissed the crucifix medallion. "I know how difficult it is."

Though it had been five years when Kaldona had passed from spinal meningitis, Franklin had never forgotten how much Katie cried over losing one of her best friends. He would have never thought the gravesite next to Kaldona's would be for his Katie three years later. The memory of it pained him.

Uncle Taki tapped his thick and long index finger on the back of the chair. "It still hurts today." Nodding his head toward Bob, he added, "But Bob helped me a lot," he placed his hand over his heart and patted, "He has a big heart."

Bobbing his head, tears welled up in Bob's eyes. "Annabelle and me, we loved her too."

The two of them stared at one another with tears in their eyes. And yet again, the two gestured the sign of the cross.

With one hand over his chair, Taki pointed his forefinger toward Franklin. "But my friend, you have to keep living. Understand?"

Bob concurred, "Yes, you have to keep living. My priest would tell you, you need to rejoice for her life."

Uncle Taki's eyes lit up. "Bob! My priest would say the same thing. See, Greek Orthodox and Catholic, we are the same faith."

"Yes, we are."

"Franklin, do you understand?" Uncle Taki added, "You have to keep living, and Katie would agree."

His friends were right. "I understand."

Nevertheless, they didn't understand that without Katie by his side, it was as though he had an unmendable hole in his heart. How can he go on without her?

"Good. I have to go back to work." Uncle Taki stood, flipped the chair around, and shoved it back under the other table. "Don't be a stranger, okay?"

"Okay."

Since he had Bob alone, Franklin seized the opportunity to find out about the bratty kids in the rental on the tree farm. "The kids that are in your rental property . . ."

Bob flashed a dismissive wave at Franklin. "I know the kids have been out of hand. They have given you trouble, yes?"

"Yes."

"And they give others trouble too. I know, I know. So many complaints. I'll explain." Bob wrapped his hands around the cream-colored coffee mug. "You know my Emily."

"Yes, Emily your granddaughter."

"She's a social worker in Minneapolis area."

"I remember you telling me something about that," Franklin replied.

Talking with his hands, Bob explained, "She worked with the children's grandmother. Her name is Sue Hamilton. I believe she was receptionist when she worked with Emily. Anyhow, last spring her daughter, kids' mother, went to prison for armed robbery. She and her boyfriend try to rob a convenient store, but they got caught. And Emily, she's good friends with Sue."

"Because of Sue, she helped Emily find an apartment, and she helped her with other things. When her daughter went to the prison, Sue was sick inside." He padded himself against his chest. "You know, it broke her heart. And she has no husband to help her. Very sad."

"I can't imagine living with that kind of burden," Franklin inserted.

"Yes, but when Emily found out that my rental was available, she recommended that Sue come here so she could see new surroundings and meet new people. Now she's raising her grandchildren in a new town. It's best for all. I think that it was a good idea. I'm sure you do too."

Franklin had chomped down on a doughnut as he nodded yes. In Franklin's opinion, the kids' story sounded somewhat similar to Jake, his son-in-law's, story.

Though Jake was born in Mississippi, he had grown up in Florida with his grandparents. When his mother, Evelyn, had learned she was pregnant of Jake, his father divorced her and disappeared. A few months after Jake's third birthday, his mother's doctor had discovered she had four-stage leukemia. Six weeks later, she passed away. But before she died, she had arranged for her parents to adopt Jake.

Franklin reached for a napkin from the napkin holder. He swallowed his food down hard. As he wiped the sticky honey from his fingers, he asked, "What about their father?"

With his lips pressed together, Bob swayed his head back and forth. "No. It's not father, it is called fathers. They're two years apart and each kid has a different father. And Frank, their fathers have nothing to do with them. I think, it's Lucas's—No—maybe it's Mackenzie's—oh well, I know it's one of their fathers. He went to prison for, I think for drug trafficking, I don't remember exactly. But that don't matter. He's in prison too. The other father, nobody knows."

Franklin sat back resting his elbows on the arms of the chair. "Wow!"

"Yes wow. And they're only seven and nine. They're still babies and they've been through so much."

Franklin shook his head. "Those poor kids. I'm so sorry."

"Yes. Poor kids. I'm feeling bad for them."

Franklin took a swig of coffee. "I know it must be difficult for her raising her grandchildren, but can't their grandmother control them?"

By the look of surprise on Bob's face, Franklin realized he may not have been aware of the incident from the day before.

"Yes, she does. You must be thinking about last summer when they were throwing things in the street, yes?

But Sue's doing a wonderful job with them. At first they were quite a handful for her, but now she has—what do you call it? Oh yes, a handle on them. They needed love. The kids love her very much. I think the last time we've had a problem with them was when they threw the watermelons in the street. It was just before they went back to school. And I don't think they'll be throwing things anymore. Sue doesn't have much money."

While listening, Franklin kept his mouth shut about his run in with them the day before. It occurred to him that the kids had some commonality with him. "That's a shame."

They had nobody but their grandmother. And Pappy had been more of a father figure to him than his own domineering father. But unlike Franklin, those kids had barely started their lives and they had been through a lifetime of sorrows. Franklin wasn't about to add to their misery by complaining about them.

Bob added, "Yes it's a shame. But Annabelle watches them sometimes to help out. Like yesterday they had a snow day and Sue had to go to work. Sometimes she sees them off to their school bus. The kids like my wife very much. She bakes with them and takes them places."

Franklin asked, "Where does Sue work?"

"She works at the hospital cafeteria. But Sue is home when the kids get off the school bus."

The waiter stopped by with a pot of coffee. Franklin placed his hand over the top of the mug. "No thank you. I've got to get going."

The young man offered Bob more coffee too. Bob responded, "No, no. I had enough too. Thank you anyways."

As the waiter scurried off, Franklin glanced at his watch. "Bob, I have to go."

"I understand. You're nervous because you're excited they are coming. Like butterflies in your stomach."

"Yes, you're correct. I am."

"How long are they staying?"

"Kitty and Jake aren't staying long. They're leaving Maggie with me for five days. Actually, they'll return on the sixth day. They have business in Arizona."

"Ah ha! I see why you're nervous. You're going to take care of Maggie alone, yes?"

"Yes. And this is the first time I've ever had her alone without Katie."

"You'll do just fine."

"I hope so." The chair skidded back as Franklin stood.

Bob stood too. He looked upward with his long and thin nose pointing skyward at Franklin. "You going to bring home some doughnuts for your family, yes?"

"That's the plan."

"Good. You should bring Maggie by to meet Sue's children. I'm sure they'll be happy to meet her, and I know Annabelle would love to see her."

Franklin had to think long and hard about that one. "We'll see how things go."

"Well, young man, stop by sometime, okay! I'm not getting any younger."

The remark hit Franklin like a prize fighter had punched him in the face. Those words were the same last words he had heard Pappy say the last time Franklin had visited him in Maine. Two days later Pappy had passed away in his sleep. Though Franklin had visited him as much as he could, Pappy had uttered those dreadful words because of his age; he had just turned ninety-nine.

"Bob, I'm so very sorry. I promise I'll stop by and I would like you to feel free to stop by my place anytime."

"I will. But now, you better get out of here so you can get ready for Maggie."

Before Franklin left, he ordered the doughnuts and muffins. While he paid the bill, Uncle Taki came out with a small pink box and stood next to him. Franklin shoved his wallet in his back pocket.

As Taki handed him the box, he whispered, "Baklava for your family."

"Why thank you, but how did you know they're in town?"

"Oh, it might have been an ugly Frenchman." Uncle Taki winked.

Franklin chuckled, "Of course. Thank you."

"No problem. I know they're Kitty's favorite."

"They are."

"I'll see you soon, right?" Uncle Taki offered his hand.

"Absolutely." Franklin took his hand and shook it.

On the way out to his truck, Franklin realized visiting with old friends wasn't as bad has he had imagined it would be. In spite of the fact he had concluded that he could never function in society or socialize without Katie, he somewhat had a good time.

He placed the boxes of pastries on the passenger seat. "In fact, I feel a bit invigorated by it." He shut the passenger door. "Huh, I never realized how much I missed Bob and Uncle Taki. But what's happening to my life?"

What if everyone expected him to socialize? Why did he take the risk of going to Dina's in the first place? "I can't socialize anymore."

To worsen things, he had promised Bob he'd stop by, and he even invited him to stop by his place. His father's famous words for him jetted through his mind, "What an idiot!" Being bombarded with family and friends all at once crashed down on him. He reached his hand behind his neck, rubbing the throbbing pain. With his eyes blurred with tears, he drove home.

CHAPTER 6

Maggie Arrives at Grampy's House

WHEN FRANKLIN STEPPED INTO the mud room from the garage, it dawned on him that the cheery feeling he had from visiting with his good friend wouldn't last long, not for him.

After he had shaved and lit a fire in the living room's fire place, he arranged the pastries onto a platter, and placed it onto the coffee table.

Back in the kitchen, he whipped up Maggie's favorite recipe for hot cocoa, made with chocolate chips melted in half and half and with a touch of vanilla bean. He grabbed a plastic spoon to taste it. "It's perfect."

Harry curled himself around Franklin's legs.

He squatted and rubbed him behind his ears. "Harry I want you to meet my family, but I'm not sure how things are going to go. They may decide not to leave Maggie with me after all, or Maggie may not want to stay with me. I don't know, because anything could happen. I'll get you some treats and you can wait in the mudroom. When I'm sure all is well, I'll let you meet them." After he had tended to Harry, he proceeded with his preparations.

While pouring the hot cocoa into a thermal pot, his hands trembled. "But suppose she doesn't like my recipe anymore." He couldn't steady his hands. He spilled some. "What a mess." He wiped off the counter.

Reaching in the cupboard for mugs, he spotted the mug he and Katie had bought Maggie for her sixth birthday. They had bought it on Valentine's Day, a few weeks before her birthday.

As he removed it off the shelf, silent tears rolled down his checks. If he had only known that would be their last Valentine's together, he would have never let her out of his arms. He turned around and leaned against the counter with one foot across the other. With his lips puckered, he closed his eyes and he imagined leaning in to kiss his deceased wife as he had often done. "Why do I keep tormenting myself like this?"

Franklin slid his finger over the gray wolf paw prints that spelled out Maggie's name on the mug. That Valentine's, the candle light flickered on Katie's face as she sat across from him at their favorite Italian restaurant. Forevermore, he no longer could hold her in his arms and kiss her good-night. "I must be a masochist. Just shut up brain."

Thinking how Maggie had named the mug Wolfuss, brought comfort to his heart. Her very presence brought joy into his life.

He placed Wolfuss down on the counter and dropped mini-marsh-mallows into the bottom of the cup, one by one. Then he cried out, "Baby, how can I keep Maggie without you? I'm lost without you! It's like I have a hollow pain deep within my heart. I miss you so much! I don't know how to live anymore!" he sobbed in his dish towel until there were no more tears to cry.

Franklin glanced at the kitchen clock. "Uh-oh, it's five to ten." He wiped his face and grabbed the pot of hot chocolate along with the mugs, and rushed into the living room. With care, he arranged them next to the pastries.

"It's ten. Where are they?"

Through the living room window, he peered down the street. "Of course there's no sign of them. Why should they be here on time? Hold on! Did Kitty say around or at ten?" Though he tried, he couldn't remember.

While pacing, every so often he stopped and peeked out the window. He grabbed his head and shouted out, "Their tardiness is driving me crazy! Where are they?"

To keep his mind off of the time, he rummaged through the magazine slot on his end table. "Huh, Hunting Illustrated. I forgot I had this edition. Who cares?" He shoved it back into the slot and resumed pacing.

When he looked out the window for about the tenth time, he noticed some activity across the street at Mark's place. With a large sign mounted on a post, Mark treaded through his snow-covered front lawn with his wife, who held a sledgehammer up against her shoulder.

"That's strange. I wonder what they're up too."

When they reached the edge of their property, she pointed downward as though marking the spot. They hammered the U-channel sign-post into the snowy ground.

Franklin tried to read it without being obvious so he hid behind one of the white stanza panels, which framed the grand-window. Pulling it back a bit, he spied on them.

"Move out of the way long-legged lady. I can't read it with you in the way. Move over. You Christian lame brain."

The woman moved as if she heard him. "Now that's hilarious!"

Before he could read their sign, an SUV pulled up and blocked his view.

Who were they, and why were they parking there?

The passenger door swung open and Kitty emerged from the vehicle. "Uh-oh!" He hurried to his chair, hoping they didn't see him peeking behind the curtains.

Franklin listened as their footsteps thumped up the wooden steps and onto the porch. The doorbell rang. Before it quit ringing, his freckled faced Maggie appeared in the window for a second and jumped out of sight. The suddenness of it startled him. He trembled so much that he feared his skin might fall off his body.

He struggled out of the chair. His legs and ankles felt heavy, like there was something weighting them down. But somehow, he managed to move his feet.

The doorbell rang again, and several knocks followed.

"Daddy, come on! It's cold out here!" Kitty shouted.

When Franklin opened the door, Maggie hollered, "Grampy!" She ran into him, and held him around his waist.

Stunned by her enthusiasm to see him, Franklin held out his arms.

Exposing her adult front teeth like bugs bunny, her emerald eyes twinkled as much as a gemstone. "I'm so glad to see you. I missed you so much."

He placed his hands around her and lifted her up.

She wrapped her hands around his neck and kissed him on the cheek. "Grampy, I love you"

Overwhelmed with emotion, he placed his hand behind her head and held her tight against his shoulder. "You've grown so much."

"I'm four-foot-two now. But did you hear what I said."

"What's that, princess?"

She placed her nose against his. "I said I love you."

With her face in his, his voice cracked, "I love you too."

Her growth had added weight on her. He kissed her on her face and set her down. As he did, Franklin noticed that Maggie was wearing a wolf hat and mittens shaped like wolf paws. It thrilled him that she still liked wolves.

"Daddy, can we come in, please? We're freezing?"

"Then why don't you come into the house, instead of standing out there in the freezing weather?"

"Daddy, can you please step aside so Jake and I can get passed you."

"Oh, I'm sorry. I wasn't thinking. It's so good to have all of you home." He stood aside and Maggie moved aside. Kitty and Jake hurried through the door.

Kitty chuckled, "Thank you for letting us in, Daddy."

Just then, he spotted Kitty's fingers turning blue. "Where are your gloves? What were you thinking? It's not summer out there. Do you want your fingers to turn black and fall off like your little friend Conner?"

"Ew," Maggie screeched. "Mom, you never told me you had a friend whose fingers fell off. That's scary! Can my fingers turn black and fall off too?"

Kitty barked, "Daddy! Look what you did!"

Confused, Franklin asked, "What did I do?"

"You scared her."

"Not on purpose."

"Maggie, Conner had frostbite. They didn't fall off. They were surgically removed," Kitty explained.

Kitty had gone to grade school with Conner. But after he had the horrific accident of falling through the ice on Webster Lake, his family had decided to move to the west coast of Florida.

"Mom that visual hurts my fingers."

Jake gave Franklin a half hug. "Dad, it's good to see you."

"It's good to see you too, son. Franklin chuckled, "Jake, it got cold last night, but I didn't think it got that cold. You should start taking off some of those layers of clothes so you can get done before sundown."

"Well Dad, it's down right cold in this neck of the woods. Besides, I'm a southerner all the way to the bone."

"But the North Pole is not in our door yard, it's in the man's door yard across the street."

Kitty rubbed her hands near the fire.

"Kitty, why didn't you put your hands in your pockets? They would have been warmer."

"Daddy, please."

That confirmed it. Without a doubt, he didn't know how to act like a father without Katie.

"Daddy, why do you look so worried? Are you okay?"

He wasn't, but he didn't want her to know that. "Actually, I'm fine. I'm just concerned about you out there in that subfreezing weather."

"Daddy, that's so sweet, but I'm fine too. I still have all my fingers too."

Before he could close the door, Maggie ran back outside. "Why did you go back outside?"

"I want to see the North Pole across the street."

Franklin chortled, "It's not across the street. I was joking with your father. Come on inside."

She turned around, pointing behind her. "There's a sign there. I want to read it."

"Just get inside before you catch your death."

Maggie hurried past him, and she declared, "I don't catch death! I tell death it has no power over me."

"What does that mean?" There was no response. Baffled, he figured they were all too busy removing their outerwear to have heard him.

Kitty turned away from the coat rack. She hugged Franklin again.

"Where's your gloves?"

She yanked off her bucket hat and ruffled her hair. "If you must know, I packed them in my suitcase."

"Now that sounds like a brilliant plan."

Kitty rubbed her hands along her arms. "Daddy, what's gotten into you?"

"What do you mean?"

"You're being condescending."

Lost for words, he stared at her. "Um . . ."

"Daddy, if you must know, I was moving too fast because we were running late. And, I was excited about seeing you."

His heart sank. "I'm sorry, I ah . . ."

"Daddy, that's okay. I love you."

If he messed up like that as a father, how would he do as a grandfather alone with Maggie?

Maggie handed her jacket, hat, and mittens to her mother, and then set her boots down next to her mother's and father's boots on the shoe rack. By the time Maggie and Kitty were in their stocking feet, Jake hung the last layer of his Antarctica type of outerwear on a brass hook.

Jake's shoulder-length blond hair was flat and tangled against his head. He looked into the mirror and fluffed his hair. When he finished, his straight bangs hung just above his thick eyebrows.

Ever since Kitty had married him, Jake had worn his hair in a high and tight Marine Corps type haircut. It seemed strange that Jake had grown his hair long.

Kitty stood in front of the fire place. "Oh, this feels so good."

"Ayuh, it's real nice in here when I'm alone."

"Daddy you said 'Ayuh!' I haven't heard you say that forever."

"I'm from Maine. It slips out some . . ." He spotted Maggie acting a bit strange.

A frown appeared on her face. She walked past him, and she moseyed over to the red plaid sofa. She dropped her backpack on the floor before she plopped down on the sofa. With her head titled downward, she played with one of her pigtails.

Franklin and Jake glanced at each other, exchanging puzzled looks.

Kitty darted her eyes toward her husband. With her forehead creased, it appeared she communicated with her husband via facial expressions.

After watching Maggie for a moment or two, Franklin sat in his chair. "Maggie, are you okay?"

She shrugged her shoulders.

Her reaction alarmed Franklin. He ran it through his mind, searching for anything that he had said or did to upset her. Beads of sweat dripped down his temples.

Jake hurried over to Maggie. When he sat down, he placed his arm around her shoulders. She didn't move a muscle.

"Hey, honey bunch, what's wrong?"

"Nothing."

"Maggie," he placed his finger under her chin and lifted it, "would you please look at me and tell me the truth?"

She tilted her head upward and grabbed onto his arm. "Daddy, you're embarrassing me."

With Kitty's eyes wide, she looked at Franklin. She mouthed, "I'm sorry."

Franklin mouthed back, "She'll be fine." But he didn't believe that himself. His worst fear had manifested. Maggie wouldn't stay with him and he had to come to terms with it.

Jake responded, "Maggie I'm sorry if I'm embarrassing you, but . . ."

Maggie slammed her hand against her forehead tilting her head downward.

" . . .what caused your mood to change? Just a few seconds ago, you were happy and now," Jake animated a frown, "you're so sad."

Under her breath, Maggie replied, "I want to stay with Grampy, but I don't think he wants me to stay with him."

Shocked by what she had said, Franklin interceded, "Why would you think something like that?"

Without hesitation, Kitty sat down next to her. "Yes, why would you think something like that?" Kitty removed a thread off of Maggie's sweater.

Leaning into Jake's arm with her lips pursed, she rolled her eyes. Red faced, she explained, "Yesterday when I was in the bathroom and Uncle Johnny was in our hotel room, I heard him say that Grampy would rather be left alone these days and that he's a recluse."

She turned her head toward Franklin. "Mom, I think a recluse is some kind of animal from the Amazon jungle, but Grampy doesn't look like a strange animal. I'm learning about the Amazon in school."

"Uncle Johnny!" Franklin snarled.

Livid that Johnny had become a hypercritical Christian gossiper like all the other sanctimonious saints he had been in contact with. They walk around with their holier-than-thou noses up while lambasting others for their sins. He visualized punching Johnny in the nose.

Kitty's face flushed red. "Daddy, I ah . . ."

Pointing his finger, Franklin interrupted her, "Kitty, this has nothing to do with you."

Upset, he sat at the edge of his chair with his hands dangling between his legs. "Maggie, would you please come over here."

She glanced over toward her mother and then her father.

Jake placed his arm around Maggie's shoulders. "Honey bunch, I'm sure Grampy never said that he didn't want you. Grampy loves you."

With her eyes peeled on her father, Maggie slid off the couch. She slid her fingers across a small section of the coffee table. As she climbed around her mother's feet, she tripped a little, but she caught herself. When she stepped in front of Franklin, she hung her head with her eyes skyward. "Am I in trouble?"

Speaking in a gentle and tender tone, Franklin reassured her. "Absolutely not. You're my little princess. Did you forget?"

She raised her head and made eye contact with him. In a loud whisper, she answered, "No."

"Maggie, it's been a long time since you visited me. I've missed you. Please stay with me. I'd really like that."

Wide-eyed, she responded, "Really?"

"Oh yes, really. And we'll have lots of fun together like we use too."

Her lower lip quivered and it curled inward.

He fought back the tears. That is until he saw her eyes well up. Just then, she reached for him.

Franklin reached out and grabbed her. "I love you, and I've missed you very much."

Tears dropped off her eyelids. Gasping her breath, she cried, "I love you too, and I missed you very much too." Crying, she buried her face against his shoulder.

While he patted her back, he glanced over to Kitty. Seeing her eyes red and swollen with tears flowing along the sides of her heartfelt smile, Franklin could no longer force back his tears.

When Franklin reached deep into his jean's pocket for his handkerchief, he caught a glimpse at Jake wiping his eyes with his forefinger. At that moment with all of them in tears, it reminded him of the last time they had all cried when he had taken them to the airport; the day they had moved to Tulsa.

That day, Franklin had Maggie in his arms while rushing through the airport. She had her legs latched around his waist. When they had arrived at the security checkpoint, Jake reached for her.

Maggie clenched Franklin's jacket, screaming, "No, no, Daddy. I want to stay with Grampy. No, no, Daddy."

The more Jake tugged her, the louder her pitiful screams blasted throughout the terminal. It took all three of them to pry her off of Franklin. They all shed tears and huddled together for a group hug.

As they walked through the security lines, Franklin waited there watching them with silent tears falling from his eyes. He stayed in that spot until he could no longer hear Maggie's cries. Out in the airport parking lot, he sat in his truck and wept.

Franklin used his handkerchief to wipe Maggie's soaked face. "Princess, I love you. Don't worry your little head over what Uncle Johnny had said. Sometimes his mouth runs ahead of his brain."

"Then he lied?"

"No. He was mistaken. Johnny would never lie, but he has a habit of saying things without thinking."

"Oh, he made a mistake."

"Yes, it was a mistake." Though he decided he would deal with Johnny's big mouth later when he could get him alone, Franklin would never encourage her to disrespect her uncle.

"Thank you, Grampy for helping me understand Uncle Johnny better." She pushed herself upward and kissed Franklin on the cheek.

"I bought some fresh doughnuts and muffins, and I made some hot chocolate. I'm sure hungry for a snack, how about you?"

"Grampy, I'm starving."

Franklin chuckled, "You sound like your mother."

Maggie hopped over to the goodies on the coffee table. "Daddy, Mom, is it okay if I have a doughnut and hot chocolate?"

While Kitty scanned the goodies in front of her, she responded, "Of course you can. Pick out what you want."

Kitty's eyes popped and her mouth dropped. "Daddy, that's baklava! As she grabbed a napkin, she asked, "Is it Uncle Taki's baklava?"

"Yes it is. And they're a present from him to you."

"Wow! What a blessing. Daddy, please thank him for me."

Standing in front of the table, Maggie eyeballed the little Greek pastry. "Mom, I didn't know you had an Uncle Taki."

"He's not my uncle," Kitty replied.

"Honey," Jake leaned toward Kitty waggling his eyebrows, "you're not going to hog all the baklava, are you?"

"Then why did you call him Uncle Taki?" Maggie interrupted.

"Because everybody calls him that. That's just his nickname." Kitty glanced over to Jake batting her eyes. "Maybe I can save one little morsel just for you."

Maggie spun around. "Grampy, is Uncle Taki your friend?"

"You don't remember?"

As she answered, "No," she shook her head.

"He's the owner of Dina's Donut House. Remember, Nana and I use to take you there? And he's friends with most everybody in town."

Her whole face lit up like recognition had dawned on her face. "I remember! He's that Greek man. He makes the best Apple muffins and the best jelly doughnuts in the world."

"And the best baklava in the world," Kitty added.

Maggie plopped down on the tweeted throw rug, and she stretched her legs under the coffee table. "Look!" she grabbed the wolf mug and raised it above her head, "Grampy found Wolfuss!"

Kitty looked toward Franklin. "Daddy, that's so sweet of you to put it out for her. You do think of everything, don't you?"

Though thrilled that he had delighted Maggie with the mug and he had gotten an attaboy from his daughter, he regarded himself undeserving of their praise. He stood and strolled over to the buffet of doughnuts and muffins. "Well, I don't think of everything, but I try."

While hugging the mug in her arms, Maggie's lustrous smile and twinkling eyes melted Franklin's heart. She declared, "You're the best Grampy in the whole wide world. Did you forget that?"

Franklin chuckled out loud. "Touché, you little munchkin." But he wished he could fulfill that for her. "Maggie if you set the mug down, I'll fill it with hot cocoa."

"Look! There are mini-marshmallows on the bottom of Wolfuss." She tilted the mug, "We always use whipped cream. I don't remember ever having marshmallows with hot chocolate. You do think of everything, Grampy."

"Hey Princess, take your little fingers out of the cup, so I can pour the hot chocolate over them. Unless you want some fingers with your hot cocoa."

"Grampy, you're so funny. Just like I remembered you."

He poured the hot chocolate over the marshmallows.

Maggie exclaimed, "They're floating to the top! Why do they do that?"

"They're light and fluffy because they have a lot of air in them, and the air is less dense than the cocoa," Franklin explained.

"Makes sense." She rolled one in her cup, "Very interesting. Thank you."

"You're welcome." After he had taken a few of the baked goods, Franklin returned to his chair.

As Jake placed a piece of baklava on a plate, Kitty took a bite of hers and Franklin had his teeth in an apple muffin.

"My love," Jake addressed Kitty, "I think we should pray for this blessing before we eat."

"Opps! I was so excited I forgot!"

With the muffin in his teeth, Franklin watched his family bow their heads. Feeling guilty, he bowed his head too. *Why does he have so many things to thank God about? Jake, just pray for the food.*

They all said "Amen," with the exception of Franklin.

An hour later and after a wonderful fellowship with his family, Kitty and Jake left to catch their evening flight out of Manchester. When they did, Franklin and Maggie walked them outside. Before they left, Franklin grabbed them all for a group hug.

As Kitty was about to step down the stairs, she ran back over to Franklin and gave him another hug. "I love you so much," she whispered.

"I love you too, my little Cinnamon Bun." He patted her on the back.

She stepped down the stairs, waving at them.

Maggie leaned over the banister, waving back to her mother. "Don't forget to call me, Mom."

"I won't," Kitty shouted back.

Though excited about having Maggie, Franklin feared that everything that could go wrong would go wrong for him.

CHAPTER 7

It's Time for Christmas' Return

MAGGIE STOOD ON THE porch with Franklin as Kitty and Jake drove away. When Kitty's rental vehicle disappeared into the horizon down the road, it saddened Franklin. At that moment, he realized he had to prepare himself for the inevitable that he won't see her but one more time before she moved to Thailand. And the worst of it, if he were to die before she returned from Thailand, he would never see her again. Anything that happened good for him never lasted.

Franklin sniffed the air and announced, "It smells like snow."

Maggie crinkled her nose up and down like a bunny rabbit. "You smell snow?"

"Yes, I do," he pointed toward the sky, "Look. Dark clouds are rolling our way from the northeast. That's a sure indication . . ."

Pointing skyward, she interrupted, "Those are Nimbostratus clouds! I learned about them in school."

"Yes, you're correct."

"But Grampy, I can't smell snow." With her turned-up nose crinkled and her forehead knitted together, she asked, "What kind of smell is it?"

"It's an icy and crisp dampness. It's as though it's more a feeling than an actual smell. You can feel it in your senses."

"I smell icy. It makes the inside of my nose cold, but I don't smell that crisp dampness. I don't know what it's supposed to smell like."

"After a while, if you come around more often, you'll acquire the skill." Why would Franklin encourage her like that? Once she moves to Thailand, he'll most likely never see his granddaughter again.

She hopped off the railing. "It snowed once in Tulsa last year. . ."

While listening, Franklin watched the storm brewing.

". . .but it was gone before we ate lunch that day. But when we went to Aspen for Christmas last year, it snowed a lot there. Daddy says he can take it or leave it, but he'd rather leave it."

"I bet he would."

"But I love snow. I like playing in it and making snow angels with my mom. Daddy made a snow angel with me and Mom twice when we were in Aspen. It was my mom that taught me how to ski, but Daddy stayed in the cabin reading and stuff like that. And, and, I like to ice skate. We had so much fun. We got to stay at my friend's cabin for free. Well, actually Mr. Bryon is my parents' friend . . ."

It made him happy to hear her ramble, once again. It was as though they had never been separated for the past two years. He couldn't help but wonder if he had never lost his little princess in the first place. *Don't be too hasty to hope such a thing.*

"But Grampy, I don't ever remember it smelling like snow when we were there either. And when we were there, the snow—what does my mom call it?" She tilted her head with her finger pressed on her temple. "Yes, when the snow flies, is that correct?"

"Yes. But in your case, it flew." He chuckled.

She giggled, "You're funny. You laugh at your own jokes."

"I thought it was a bit humorous."

"Yes you're right, it was a bit humorous. But as I was saying, I don't remember it smelling like anything."

A sudden gust of icy wind whirled over Franklin's property and blasted through the porch. It whipped across his face. He noticed the trees bending back and forth as the ominous clouds rolled in across the darkening sky. Without hesitation, he brought Maggie inside within the safety of his home.

Since Maggie was much shorter than most girls her age, she couldn't reach the hooks on the coat rack. Franklin offered to assist her with her jacket, but she insisted on hanging it herself. Her independence made him proud.

Maggie leaped and tossed it on the coat rack. "There, I did it! I told you I could."

"Yes you did and you did a great job."

"My head and ears are cold," she announced as she rubbed the top of her head.

"Your ears and nose are bright red too. From now on, you need to put on a hat before you go outside."

"Okay, but I didn't know we were going to stay out there that long."

"You're right, neither did I think so. But you should never go out without your hat and gloves in the winter. No matter how long. . ."

"But Grampy, you didn't have your hat and gloves on. Why don't you follow your own advice?"

Shamefaced, he had no answer. She was eight and he was the adult. Since he should have led through example, he had no choice but to humble himself. "You're right. I'm sorry."

"That's okay. But from now on we both need to put on our hats and gloves before we go outside. And if one forgets, we remind the other. Deal?"

"That's a deal."

She offered her hand. "Let's shake on it."

He took her delicate little hand by his fingertips. "Okay, we'll remind each other."

"I like that."

Feeling groggy, Franklin yawned as he browsed through the mail from the day before that he had left on the table by his entrance way. Though it wasn't quite one, he was tired. That day, he started it earlier than normal after a long sleepless night. With the Scottsberry University's News Monitor in hand, he tossed the unnecessary spam advertisements into the fireplace. He wished he could go upstairs and take a nap, but he had Maggie and he couldn't leave her alone.

Plopping down on the sofa, Maggie rubbed her hand along the cushion. "Grampy, what are we going to do?"

"I'm not sure," he responded as he moseyed over to his chair.

"Look Grampy, the beige in the couch's red plaid matches the color on yours and Nana's chairs!"

"Yes it does." He sat down. "Ahh, that feels so good."

"Grampy, why do you have that woodstove all the way down there by the stairs when you have a fireplace right here?"

Flipping through the pages of the Monitor, he crossed one leg over the other. "The fireplace looses heat, but it keeps things cozy. The woodstove heats the house."

"But Grampy, how do you keep the woodstove burning when your not home?"

As he looked up, he pushed his reading glasses up. "I don't. I have a combination of an oil-wood boiler for back-up heat for when I'm away, but I haven't used oil for a long time."

Even though he had inherited most of his wealth from Pappy, he refused to squander his fortune on ridiculous oil brokers and traders who had manipulated crude oil prices.

"Hello Grampy!"

Peeking over his paper, he answered, "Yes."

"Where were you?"

"Reading the paper and thinking. Why?"

"I called you three times to ask you a question, but you didn't answer me."

"I'm sorry. What would you like to know?

"What's an oil-wood boiler?"

"It's a furnace that runs on either oil or wood. The wood or oil heats the water for steam heat, and it comes out of the radiators around the house." He pointed at the wall by the fireplace, as he continued, "Like that one over there."

"Where's the boiler?"

"It's in a little room in the far side of the back of the garage, near the outside door that opens near the wood shed." He rattled the paper and resumed reading.

The coziness of his chair along with the crackling sounds of the wood burning in the fireplace, made him groggier. While Maggie continued chattering, he halfway listened to her. But her rambling did help him stay awake.

"Grampy, where's your TV? I can't remember."

"It's in the family room."

The last thing he had heard her say was, "Oh yes, I remember. I use to lie on the big brown couch and watch TV in that room next to the kitchen."

An article grabbed his attention. It surprised him that there were two other professors retiring at the end of the spring. He muttered, "Now, they'll have to replace three . . .,"

"What kind of grandfather are you?" Maggie bellowed.

"Ahh," Franklin's baritone short scream emitted from deep in his chest.

Maggie busted out laughing with her entire body jiggling.

"You startled me!"

"You scream funny!"

"Okay, it's not that funny."

"Oh yes it is. I never heard a man scream before. You sounded like a big toad croaking."

"Now that's a first! I've been told that I laugh like Herman Munster and my voice is deep like Darth Vader's, but I have never been compared to a Toad."

She fell down on her knees. Hysterical, her body rocked back and forth as it shook.

He too cracked up. Franklin loved her chipmunk type of giggle. After several moments, their hysterics waned down to sporadic chuckles.

Maggie declared, "You're a funny Grampy."

"Yes, I'm hilarious. A barrel of laughs," he replied, while thinking about his miserable life. "By the way, what were you saying about a grandfather?"

"I asked you what kind of grandfather are you?"

"What do you mean by what kind of grandfather am I?"

"Hello, I'm eight. Trust me, watching you read that paper has no entertainment value for someone like," she turned her finger toward her chest, "me."

"I thought we were going to relax for a while."

"Where did you get that idea? Did you discuss that with me?"

"I didn't think I had to."

"Remember? You're no longer alone," she raised two fingers, "It's two of us now. And usually, when there are two or more people involved, we should agree on what we would like to do."

Whoa, I got a live one. Franklin placed the paper down on his end table. "You're right. I'm sorry."

But before he could ask her what she would like to do, she placed her hands on her hips and pressed her lips together. Tapping her foot, she stared down her nose at him like a mother disappointed with her child. "By the way, where's your Christmas tree?"

"There are a few doughnuts left; would you like one?"

"Don't change the subject, please." She crossed her arms across her chest.

"What do you mean?"

"It's the middle of December."

"So what?"

"You have no tree and you don't even have," as she held her forefinger near her thumb, she continued, "one little itsy-bitsy Christmas decoration. My mom and Daddy have our tree up and the entire house decorated by Thanksgiving, every year!"

"Lah-di-dah-di-dah." He couldn't believe how petulant he had sounded, especially toward his granddaughter.

Her eyes popped and her mouth dropped. She gaped at him like he was a rotting piece of meat besieged by flies and maggots.

Only one word shot out of his mouth. "Uh-oh."

His big fat trap had been stricken by an incurable case of turista.

Yet again, she placed her hands on her hips. "And what was that all about?"

Embarrassed, he wished he had a hole to crawl up in.

While leaving one hand on her hip, Maggie pressed her finger on her tight-lipped mouth, and tapped it.

In a soft tone, he responded, "Maggie, I'm so vey sorry. My behavior was rude. Please forgive me."

"I forgive you. But what do you have against Christmas?"

"Nothing! I just don't celebrate it any longer?" *You liar! You hate the thought of it.*

In a slow methodical fashion, Maggie folded her arms and she shook her head in arcs of disbelief. "Why don't you celebrate Jesus' birthday?"

"I heard it's a pagan holiday because Jesus wasn't born on December twenty-fifth."

A scowl materialized on her face and she pointed her finger above her head. "Oh! You're one of those!"

"What? One of those? What do you mean one of those?"

"You're one of those who hates Christmas."

Since Katie's death, he had vowed that he would never celebrate Christmas or any other holiday ever again. He had nothing left to celebrate without Katie.

"No, I don't hate it. It's just that—it's complicated. I don't want to discuss it any longer. And young lady, we will change the subject."

Her lips sucked inward and her eyes rolled upward.

What is she doing?

After a few seconds, she popped her lips out and raised her eyebrows like a light bulb had lit in her head. "Okay, I won't ask you about your Christmas decorations, but will you play the question and answer game with me?"

"That's a wonderful idea! How do you play it?"

"One asks a question and the other answers truthfully, but I get to start."

"Okay, that sounds like fun." He would have done anything to change the subject.

"So, do you agree with the terms?"

"Terms?" Franklin busted out a hearty laugh, visualizing her marking an x next to a signature line on a legal sized contract like a loan officer at a bank. "Maybe I should read the small print first."

She pushed up her upper lip. "Huh? What's that?"

"Nothing," he waved his hand, "Yes, I agree."

"Thank you. Placing her hand on the armrest of his chair, she asked, "May I sit here?"

"Absolutely." He helped her up.

She scooted her knees to her chest and wrapped her arms around her legs. "Why don't you celebrate Jesus' birthday?"

"I thought we weren't going to discuss this any longer."

"But Grampy, I said I wouldn't discuss your Christmas decorations. This is about Jesus' birthday. Besides, you agreed with the terms."

Her cuteness melted his heart. "Excuse me, my little princess. I forgot that we had a verbal contract. But I would rather not discuss anything about Christmas."

She blew out a long breath. "Grampy, would you please humor me?"

"Humor you?" Her vocabulary tickled his funny bone. "Okay I'll humor you."

"So, why don't you want to celebrate Christmas?"

"I didn't say I didn't want to celebrate Christmas."

With her palms turned upward, she tilted her head. "Then why don't you celebrate it?"

"I'm all alone," but Franklin didn't end it there. He heard his mouth blurt out, "Besides, we don't know His real birthday."

She turned her lips inward.

I'll never learn to shut my big mouth. "It's the truth. I live alone."

"Yes, you live alone. But why do you insist that Christmas is not the reason for celebrating Jesus' birthday?"

He sat up in his chair. "Maggie, nobody knows his exact birth date. But I have heard biblical scholars believe it might have been in the month of September. It's because the Roman Empire collected taxes in the fall. Now, like I said, I heard about it, but I'm not sure if it's true or not. Nana thought it sounded reasonable."

She lowered her head, closed her eyes, and muttered something. Within a few seconds, she looked heavenward, smiled, and clapped her hands. "Yes! Thank you Jesus."

"Hold on! Were you praying?"

"Yes, why do you have something against prayer?"

"No, praying is good. I was just wondering."

Wearing an askance expression, she stared at him for a brief moment. "My mom told me you gave her a dog. His name was Scout. Do you remember?"

"Yes, Scout. I remember him. He was a mixed terrier and a good looking dog. He was all tan with a white spot on his nose. Your mother loved him."

"Do you remember what you gave him?"

"What do you mean? A bone?"

"No! Not a bone, think."

After a quick outburst, Franklin choked back the laughter. "Now that's a trick! Consider an answer to an ambiguous question."

"Huh! Grampy, what does that mean."

"Give me a quick second. Let's see! We gave Scout a good home and a lot of things. Why do you ask?"

"When you gave my mother Scout, you told her that he was about six months old. Do you remember telling her that?"

"Well, he was about five or six months old. Scout was a stray dog. A friend of mine was the dog warden and gave him to me. Your mother had been asking for a puppy, so I took him for her. I really liked that dog. He was adorable. Scout loved squeaky toys. Whenever I went to a pet shop, I'd bring him home a new toy.

Once, I brought him a toy that looked like T-bone steak. Oh, he loved that one. I miss that cute little fella. He never grew very big." He extended his hand forward near the arm of the chair. "He didn't grow any taller than this."

She rolled her eyes and folded her arms across her chest.

"What's wrong? What did I do now?"

"Can you please stay focused on the questions?"

Amused, Franklin replied, "I'm sorry. I'll try."

"My mom said you gave him a birthday, do you remember?"

"Oh yes, Nana and I helped her count back on the calendar, and we landed on October. But your mother chose the tenth of the month because that year it fell on a Saturday. She wanted to be home from school to celebrate his first birthday."

"Did Scout like the celebration?"

"I suppose. He loved the attention."

"Grampy, I have one more question?"

"Shoot princess, I'm all ears."

"Well, it was okay for you to set a day aside to celebrate your dog's birthday, but why not for your Savior's birthday?"

She stung him like a bee.

He couldn't argue with that. "You're absolutely correct."

"Thank you, Grampy. Mom once told me, it takes a good man to admit when he's wrong."

"You're mother has a lot of wisdom."

"Thank you. When you set a day aside to make it holy unto the Lord to worship Him, then God honors it, and it is holy unto Him. If you don't believe me, you can read it in Romans 14:6. Nana taught me that?"

"Nana taught you that?" He held back his composure. After all, he had no doubt in his heart that there would be more stuff brought up to remind him of Katie. Though difficult, he had to stay strong for his little princess.

"Yes. Would you like me to read the scripture to you? My bible is in my backpack."

Oh brother, not the bible. "You don't have to read it to me, sweetie pie. I believe you." He noticed Maggie's demeanor had changed.

With her upper eyelids turned downward and her upper lip curved down, she had become quiet and subdued.

That troubled Franklin. He placed his hand on her arm. "Hey little princess, are you okay?"

"Grampy, why didn't you call us?"

His heart pounded inside his chest. He could hear his blood swooshing in his ear. "What made you think of that?"

"I've been thinking about it ever since we got on the plane yesterday. My mom cried a lot because you didn't call us."

Confronted by the outcome of his recklessness, hit Franklin like a dull dagger had pierced into his heart. Salty drops streamed from the back corners of his eyes. While lost in his self-imposed exile, he had become too self-absorbed in his own pain to consider his daughter's. He had failed his daughter. What kind of father had he become?

Franklin wiped his face with his handkerchief.

"Grampy, are you okay."

After inhaling a few deep breaths, he answered, "Maggie, I'm so very sorry for hurting you and your mother. It's been hard for me without your Nana. But I promise you, I will work hard to never hurt you or your Mother again."

"You promise?"

"Yes I promise. I got an idea! Let's decorate the living room for Christmas."

"Yippy!" she jumped off the armrest. "Can we decorate a tree too?"

"By all means, we have to have a tree."

"Can we decorate today?"

"Absolutely!"

Her mouth widened like a hippopotamus. "Can we start right now?"

It hit him like a hammer. He had just agreed to decorate for Christmas. "Ahh, yes. Um, sure." But Franklin refused to squirm out of it for Maggie's sake.

She tugged on his hand. "Let's go get them. Where are the decorations?"

Stunned by the reality of the pain he had caused his family, he pointed downward toward the basement.

Her jaw dropped. She fired questions at him like a machine gun. "Did you bury the Christmas decorations? And did you put a head stone on their grave? Does it say, in the memory of Christmas? Or in the memory of Jesus' birthday? Or here lies Christmas?"

"Whoa! Calm down. They're stored downstairs."

"You didn't bury them?"

"No."

She slid her hand across her forehead. "Phew, that's a relief!"

"What made you think I buried the decorations?"

"I don't know why. The thought just flew into my head when you pointed downward."

"You're a funny little girl."

She yanked on a few of his fingers. "Come on Grampy, let's go get them. I'll follow you."

But Maggie didn't follow him. Instead, she walked backwards in front of him narrating descriptive stories of how the Harris family decorated their home.

As they approached the basement door, he froze. He hadn't been down there since the day before the accident. Family members had packed the ornaments and had stored them in the basement's utility room, before Franklin had come home from the hospital.

While he stood there staring at the door, he remembered. "Whoa! Harry!

"Who's Harry?"

"I forgot all about him!"

"Who's Harry?"

He glanced at his watch and spun around and marched toward the mudroom. "Boy I'm brilliant! That poor fella has been in there for more than four hours. I'm sure he's not a happy camper."

She put her arm out like a cop stopping traffic. "Wait, pleeease!"

He halted, just short of the mudroom door. "What's wrong?"

Maggie's voice quavered. "Is there a stranger behind that door?"

"What?"

"Who's behind that door? I don't like strangers," she declared.

"No, there's no stranger behind that door."

"Then who's this Harry that you have camping in your house?"

"What? Camping? Maggie, what are you talking about?"

"You said that man behind that door is not a happy camper."

He busted out laughing. "You never heard that saying before? He's not a happy camper—by the look on your face, I assume it is no."

She swayed her head. "No."

"Fear not my little pretty. You'll like what's in here." As he opened the door, he announced, "Introducing, Harry!" The Husky galloped out, howling in excitement.

Maggie's face lit up bright like a display of the Northern Lights illuminating a winter's sky.

"He's so cute. I love Huskies." She knelt down in front of him and wrapped her arms around his furry neck. "He's so soft and warm, but why does he have one blue eye and one brown eye?"

"Some do. That's normal in the breed."

Harry licked her face. "I wish you were my doggie. But my parents said we have to move into our own home before we can get a puppy."

Harry yanked his head away from her. Whining and yelping, he ran around in circles.

Maggie sprung to her feet. "Is he okay?"

"He's got to wash-up."

"Oh! I get it. He needs to go to the bathroom."

"Exactly!"

Harry curled around Franklin's legs, whining. "Come on, fella."

Before he could open the back door all the way, Harry squeezed through, leaped off the deck, and ran around the snow covered pasture. Franklin watched a moment as Harry sniffed for the perfect spot to do his duty.

While they waited for Harry to finish his business and stretch his legs, Maggie helped Franklin clean up the mess from earlier. She chatted about their Christmas tree back home in Oklahoma, but Franklin didn't pay much attention.

He dreaded the thought of having to go down stairs to his daylight basement because he hadn't been down there since he had escorted Katie into the fatal accident. If it weren't for Maggie, he wouldn't have even considered going back down there.

CHAPTER 8

Down in the Daylight Basement

FOLLOWING HARRY, MAGGIE SCURRIED down the stairs. But Franklin took each step slow and methodical like the beat in a downtempo musical arrangement. His granddaughter and his dog darted through the basement apartment investigating the area. But he lingered on the last step observing the space.

The room looked the same, but it no longer felt like part of his house. Though familiar, somehow it seemed unfamiliar. He stepped off the staircase onto the sandstone carpet. It seemed as though he had stepped into a stranger's home filled with an eerie emptiness.

The warmth that once emanated from the woodstove had become as cold as the river rocks surrounding it. Joyous sounds of chatter and laughter from family and friends had silenced. Many of the Franklyn family's fondest memories were a distant past collection of reminisces narrated by an unknown author. His tight-nit family that once had surrounded him had fractured by his one ill-fated decision. That one misstep had altered his life forever.

His granddaughter's voice interrupted his woeful thoughts.

"Grampy! I remember the last time I was in this little kitchen," she hollered from one of the two swivel stools at the counter. "I was with Nana."

Wagging his tail, Harry stretched his paws outward with his hind quarter raised. He yapped at Maggie, as he hopped backward.

"I remember I was sitting right here," she turned the stool toward the other stool. Pointing, she added, "And Nana sat right here on the other stool."

While she narrated her story, Franklin moved toward her.

She continued, "We were decorating the sugar cookies for the party that night."

She spun the stool toward the counter and placed her hands on the counter top. Franklin sat on the other stool.

"I remember there were bowls here," she tapped her finger on the counter, "of red and green and white frosting. Oh yes, there were red and green sprinkles and M&M's too. The M&M's were the red and green ones for Christmas, but they called them holiday M&M's. We didn't like that."

She glanced at Franklin with watery eyes. "And she let me pipe the frosting onto the cookies, but she held her hand over mine." Her chin trembled. "She made me think that I decorated the cookies by praising me for doing such a good job. "Tears fell off her eyelids. "Grampy, I miss her." She reached for him. "I miss her too much. I want her back."

He swept her into his arms and held her tight. "Shh, shh, my little princess, I know. Shhhh, I know baby doll. I miss her too and I want her back too."

She pressed her face against his chest. "I miss Nana," she repeated several times.

Salty droplets flowed down his cheeks into the corners of his lips. Her sorrowful cries broke his heart. *Katie, how would you help her?*

Maggie pulled back. "I made you cry. I'm sorry." She tilted her head and hung it.

He grabbed an old napkin off the counter top and wiped her soaked face. "Baby doll, I'm sorry that this made you sad."

"Grampy, I haven't cried for a long time. I don't know why I'm crying today."

He grabbed a few more napkins. "It's okay. Around here, there's a lot to remind you of her, and it's perfectly fine to cry. It helps wash away your sadness."

"Thank you, Grampy. It does help." She grabbed a few napkins too, and reached to wipe Franklin's face.

That gesture melted Franklin's heart. He took the napkins, but the more he wiped his face the more the tears poured out. The grieving had to stop for Maggie's sake. At her young age, she shouldn't have been subjected to it in the first place.

With his forefinger, he wiped a tear drop off her cheek. "Look, the last drop of sadness just fell out of your eye."

"Grampy, you're so funny. You always make me feel better."

Seeing a smile on her face delighted him.

"Did you know that you're brilliant like Daddy? He makes me laugh when I'm crying too."

Franklin had always known that Jake was an outstanding husband and father for his daughter and granddaughter. "So, I'm brilliant like Daddy? That's a good thing."

"Yes it is."

He squeezed her. "Hey, let's get those decorations and bring Christmas to this house, once again."

She clapped her hands. "Yes, let's do that." Afterwards, she rubbed her red swollen eyes, leaped off his lap, and she skipped several steps away from the kitchen before she stopped. She looked over her shoulder. "Where am I going?"

"I was wondering the same thing." Franklin slid off the stool. "Come on, silly, follow me."

She bowed and waved her hand. "The best Grampy ever lead the way!"

"You're a funny little girl."

"Not like my daddy and you. Oh I forgot to ask. Can we decorate the outside too?"

"No. It's too late."

"How about tomorrow?"

After her parents returned from Arizona, he would have enough work taking down the tree, and he didn't need any more work than that. "Maggie, it's only you and me. That's a lot of work for us."

"Alright, but do you have a wreath?"

"I have several. Why?"

"Can we hang one outside on the front door, please?"

Dazzled by her exaggerated pleading face, he replied, "Yes, you little rascal."

"Yes." She skipped alongside him to the utility room.

Inside the utility room, there were several boxes and a few dozen containers of indoor and outdoor decorations near a concrete wall.

"I remember this room. I was never allowed in here before."

"Then, how do you remember it?"

"I went in once." She raised her finger, "Only once, because I had to know."

"You just had to know why you weren't allowed in here."

"Most certainly, Moe."

He snapped his head toward her. "How do you know the "Three Stooges?"

"I watched them on YouTube."

"Of course."

He found the three trees leaning against the far end of the wall with tarps thrown over them. It appeared odd to him that they weren't taken apart and stored into the Christmas tree containers, but he couldn't complain. At least his family was kind enough to take care of the trees and decorations for him, while in the hospital recovering from his injuries.

When he removed the tarp off the tallest tree, it thrilled him to see the lights were still hooked to the branches. He slipped his fingers into his back pockets thinking on how to get the tree upstairs with just a little girl to help him.

"Grampy, look over here. Under these tarps, there are two more trees."

"Yes there are. One is for the family room and the other one is for down here, but the nine-footer goes in the living room."

"Oh yes, I remember now, and we use to help you and Nana decorate them all. Can we decorate all three?"

"Nice try, kiddo."

"How about the big one?"

"That's the plan."

With her hand formed into a fist, she yanked down her arm. "Yes!"

As he examined the lights, he remarked, "And they left the tree stand on it too. Sweet."

"Who are they?"

Still preoccupied, he mentioned, "Your Uncle Johnny's kids."

"Oh yeah, Mommy's cousins. But Grampy." She tugged on his shirt.

Focused on how he could manage getting that large tree upstairs, he answered, "Yes."

"Why didn't you put your Christmas trees away yourself?"

He dropped his head and closed his eyes. "I couldn't."

"I'm sorry. I just remembered that you were in the hospital. Mom's cousins were at Uncle Johnny's house the day after your acci. . ."

He twisted a loose vintage C-7 Christmas tree light bulb before he had realized she stopped talking. He looked over his shoulder, and then twisted around.

Rubbing her lips together with her eyes narrowed and casted downward, she appeared deep in thought.

"Hey you." Franklin called out.

Biting her lower lip, she looked up at him. "Grampy, I understand now."

"Understand what?"

"You no longer celebrate Christmas because you lost Nana at Christmas time. I'm so sorry Grampy. If it hurts you too much to decorate, we don't have too.

When you and Nana had the accident, nobody wanted to celebrate Christmas, not even me. And it was hard to celebrate the next Christmas because it didn't seem the same without you and Nana.

But last year, when Daddy took us to Aspen, it made things better, because we had a lot of fun. Mom said Nana would want us to celebrate her life because Nana is not in our past. She's in our future."

Oh boy, now, she sounds like Johnny.

He squatted and held her shoulders. "Maggie, look at me."

Sniffling, she rubbed her eyes.

"We're not going to do this anymore. There's been enough sadness in this house. Since you've come to visit, there's a lot of joy in this house, and I want to keep it that way. No more tears, please."

"But Grampy, happy tears replaced my sad tears."

"Now you're crying happy tears?"

"Yes. Though I miss her now, Nana is in our future." Maggie looked heavenward and raised her arms. She spun on her heals as she declared, "We'll spend all of eternity with her!"

Katie had died, period. That Jesus stuff gave her hope. Though it seemed too unrealistic and delusional for him, she found it real. He kept his mouth shut. He refused to steal her joy.

"Okay. Let's have some fun and decorate the tree. Do you think you're strong enough to help me carry the big one upstairs?"

"Oh yes, Grampy. I'm really strong. I belong to the swimming and gymnastic team at the YMCA. I do that for physical education."

"You do gymnastics?"

"Yep. My favorites are the unparallel bars, the balance beam, and tumbling. Watch me flip."

Before he could say no, she flipped. "That was fantastic, but you shouldn't do that in the house."

"I know. I can get hurt. I'm sorry, but I just wanted you to see me do it."

"Thank you, but don't do it again. I think this tree might be too heavy. Maybe we should use the smaller one."

With her arms spread out wide, she declared, "Grampy, I can do all things through Christ, who strengthens me. We have to have the big one."

Though he hadn't read the bible since his Mammy and Pappy read it with him, he attempted to interpret it for her. "I believe that particular scripture is telling us that Jesus will give you the inner strength when you feel sad inside."

Her eyes rolled skyward. "Oh, my goodness! All means everything. I think we need to do a word study on all."

"You want to give me a word study to understand the word all?"

"Yes, but I don't want to do it right now. We're having too much fun."

For her to say she wanted to teach him the definition of the word "all" was rib-tickling.

"What's so funny!"

"I'm sorry princess, but you are so adorable. You don't need to teach me about the word all."

"Grampy, this is a serious matter. It's very important for you to understand what God is saying to you."

He quelled the laughter. "I'm sorry. You're correct. It's a serious matter."

"Okay. You're forgiven. We'll deal with this later."

"Oh, we will?"

"Yes, but let's get the tree upstairs so we can decorate it."

"Okay. Let me take a look at this first and see how we can do this." Franklin stood back with his hand on his chin. He snapped his fingers. "I got it! I'll lay it down and we'll lift it up the stairs. You take the top end and I'll take the bottom end."

"Grampy, great idea."

He laid the tree on the floor. "Okay, get ready."

Maggie stretched her arms with legs extended. "I'm ready."

"Okay, as I tilt it, you place her hands under the top."

Scooping her arms under the tree, she helped lift it as she declared, "I can do all things through Christ, who strengthens me."

"Okay," he exhaled, "let's go straight up the stairs with it."

The two carried it up the stairs, through the kitchen, and into the living room without much incident with the exception of breaking three light bulbs. They set it up in the corner near the fireplace and adjusted the branches.

Franklin and Maggie stood back.

"It's perfect," Maggie declared.

He rubbed his chin. "Would you prefer regular Christmas ornaments or replicas and miniatures or both?"

"What do you mean replicas and miniatures?"

"Instead of balls and bell shapes, they're shaped like miniature structures such as trains, trucks, cartoon characters, and other stuff like that. Nana liked using those for the tree in the living room. Nana called it our Toyland tree."

Her face lit up like a firefly casting its light in the darkness of the night. "Grampy, I remember. I would love a Toyland tree."

"Then let's go back downstairs and get them."

"Okay. This is going to be the most special Christmas tree ever."

Nothing could be perfect or special without his Katie. She's the one that made Christmas perfect for him and the family. He missed her gingerbread cookies. Nevertheless, he could try and make everything as nice as possible for Maggie, even though she wouldn't be with him for Christmas.

CHAPTER 9

Family Stories over Pizza

AFTER THEY HAD HUNG all but one ornament on the tree, Franklin handed Maggie a little crystal horse-drawn sled. "Here, you do the honors and hang the last one?"

"Thank you. I get to do the last decoration." She walked around the tree, touching and moving a few of the branches. "Right here, Grampy. I think this is the perfect spot. How 'bout you?"

"Let me see." He stood back a bit and examined the spot she had chosen. "Yes it's perfect. By gosh, it is."

As she slid it onto a branch, she heralded, "Ta-dah! Announcing the last ornament is being placed onto the most magnificent Christmas tree in the world. Drum roll please!"

Indulging her, Franklin boomed deep sounds of a beating drum. "Bum, brrum, brrum, bum, bum, bum."

Twirling around in her stocking feet, she clapped her hands. "Hooray! We did it."

"Yes we did, and it's magnificent, but it needs one more thing." He dug into the box for his red and gold garland. "Here it is."

"That's the garland. Shouldn't we have done that before the decorations? That's how we do it at our place, so we don't hide any of the ornaments."

He stood there with the garland in hand. "Um, yes. I'm a putz. You are correct. I forgot about the garland."

"I forgot too, so we're both putzes."

He chortled, "But I believe we can make it work if we do this carefully."

As the two wrapped the last of garland, the motion light lit on the porch and the doorbell rang.

"Wow, great timing. That must be our pizza," Franklin added, "and I'm starving. How about you?"

Maggie grabbed her stomach. "I'm so starving."

He opened the front door, looking behind him at Maggie. "There's no doubt you're your mother's daughter."

Just as Franklin pushed open the storm door, in monotone, the short and stubby teenager uttered, "That will be twenty-two dollars and seventy-five cents."

Franklin took offense. "What's your problem? You could have at least said hello before discussing the money."

"Okay. Hello. That will be twenty-two dollars and seventy-five cents."

Franklin yanked twenty-six dollars from his wallet. "If you keep this up, you will loose your job."

"I hate this job, and I'm quitting tonight."

Aldo, the owner of Donati's Italian Palace, had the best pizza around. In Franklin's opinion, even New York pizza had competition with Donati's. Aldo had a reputation of hiring the most friendly and efficient personnel. This young man's attitude confused him.

Franklin handed the man the money. "So your new job must not require good customer service skills."

The young man smirked, "There is no new job. I've worked long enough to collect unemployment."

Franklin disliked lazy people more than Christians. "So you can stay home and do nothing, and so you can live off of the taxpayers?"

"No. So I can become a professional video gamer." After the delivery boy had handed Franklin change and the pizza, the young man held out his hand.

Maggie appeared by Franklin's side. "Grampy, it's snowing like you said it would, and he's covered in snow too. That's so funny. He looks like a snowman."

Too aggravated by the audacity of that young man, Franklin couldn't respond to Maggie. He growled, "You want a tip? Get a job! Franklin slammed the door. He grumbled, "Most people work while they're training for a profession."

"Uh-oh, that man is in big trouble. What did he do?"

"Come on, forget about it. Let's enjoy our meal."

He salivated over the aroma flowing out of the box. "Come on, princess. Let's go get some plates and a couple cans of Coke."

When the two returned from the kitchen, Maggie popped open the Coke cans. Afterwards, she sat down on the sofa waiting for Franklin to light up the tree.

He squatted by the electric outlet as he doubled checked that everything was plugged in, correctly.

"Grampy hurry, turn them on!"

"Okay, I'm almost done." He stood near the switches that controlled the outlets.

"Come on, Grampy, please just turn them on!"

"Okay, one, two, three." The entire living room went dark. The flames from the fireplace flickered like a campfire glowing under an overcastted night sky. Straightway, the room gleamed with red, green, and white lights illuminating the ornaments that adorned the branches.

Clapping her hands Maggie shouted, "Yes! I think it's the most beautiful tree in the world."

"You're right. It is a beautiful tree."

Franklin sat down. She scooted closer to him and she crossed her legs Indian style. Even though his mouth watered for a bite of that pizza, he gave Maggie the first slice.

As he slid out a slice for himself, Franklin could almost taste the pie. But as the pizza hit his lips, Maggie screeched, "Wait!"

"Why? What happened? Are you okay?"

"Yes, I'm fine. But aren't you going to pray for the pizza?"

"What? Why? What's wrong with the pizza?"

"Oh my goodness, Grampy. You're supposed to thank the Lord for your food and ask Him to bless it before you eat it."

"Pray?"

Maggie responded, "And why are you looking at me like I have two heads?"

With his stomach growling and the pizza a mere two millimeters from his mouth, it took a lot of brute force for Franklin to put it on the plate in front of him.

"I'm sorry. I'm starving and I wasn't thinking."

She shrugged her shoulders. "That's okay. I understand. I've done that before. But Mommy or. . ."

Because of the rumbling pain in his empty stomach, he wished she would stop rattling on and just pray.

". . .Okay Grampy, go ahead."

"Go ahead and do what?"

"Pray." She bowed her head. "I'm waiting."

For all he cared, she could wait until dooms day. He refused to pray.

"Opps, I forgot you're not saved yet." She placed her hand on his arm. "I'm sorry Grampy, I'll pray."

Yet? What did she mean by yet?

She raised her hands heavenward. With her face glowing in the glittering lights. "Father, in the name of Jesus. . ."

No Jesus freak is going to hijack me with their holy spook nonsense. Not even my granddaughter.

". . .for this wonderful pizza, and we ask you to bless it. Since Grampy is starving, we'll say amen here. Amen."

By the time he took his first bite, she had chomped away half of her slice.

"This is yummy. I never had a meatball pizza before. I think this will be my favorite kind from now on."

"Meatball pizza is my favorite too."

Pointing toward the ceiling beam over the tree, she swallowed hard. "Grampy, look the angel top is making a shadow on the ceiling. Why is your ceiling so high?"

Franklin had no interest in the tree-top or the ceiling. He was eating. He didn't want to be bothered by any shadow.

"Grampy, did you hear me?"

He wiped his mouth. "Yes, I heard you, but I'm busy eating right now."

"You're busy eating? Can't you eat and look at the same time? Or is that too complicated for you?" She giggled. Tiny bits of food flew out of her mouth.

"Okay, that's enough laughing at your Grampy."

"I bet you can't chew gum and walk at the same time."

"Yes I can, and I see the angel's shadow. It's high because it's a cathedral ceiling." He wiped her mouth with a napkin. "Maggie, stop laughing. You're drooling food down your chin."

She leaned her head on his shoulder. "You're a funny grandfather."

"Bingo! So that's the kind of grandfather I am. You little monkey."

After that comment, she giggled harder.

When her laughter waned, she asked, "Did you know we all have an angel watching over us?"

Franklin slid another slice out of the box. "I heard about that."

That reminded him of one of the times Pappy and Mammy had taken him to their church. He had learned about the angels in the children's Sunday school.

"Did you ever wonder what your angel looks like? I do. I believe mine has gold hair."

"Nope, I never thought about it." He took a gulp of coke.

"Why not Grampy?"

"I don't know. I just haven't thought about it for a long time." But he had his reasons why he no longer thought about angels or anything else about God.

Once, he had played an angel in an Easter play at Pappy's church. Since Mammy asked him to play the part, he did if for her. But that night, Mammy had a stroke; it left her wheelchair bound. Franklin had prayed for her to walk again, but God never answered that prayer. Instead, she passed away a mere three months after her first stroke and after three other strokes. He had never forgotten it.

When Franklin swallowed his last bite, he caught a glimpse of Maggie gazing at the tree. "Princess, you really like the tree, don't you?"

"Yes. I was thinking we got the most beautiful Toyland tree in the world. Now all it needs is Christmas presents under it to make it perfect."

"Presents? Why presents?"

"Because Christmas trees have Christmas presents under them. And it makes Jesus happy when we give presents to our loved ones, especially to those who can't afford much."

Since he'd be alone for Christmas, decorating the tree was good enough.

Her eyes glittered in the soft lights. "Can we please go Christmas shopping tomorrow?"

"Christmas shopping? For what? What do you mean?"

"Christmas shopping means we go and buy Christmas gifts. They're gifts wrapped in Christmas paper, and you put them under the tree for your family to give them on Christmas morning."

"I know what they are."

She waggled her eyebrows. "Then why did you ask."

"You're a smarty pants."

Though he loved her humorous personality, and he loved her more than his own life, he refused to shop for Christmas. "Tomorrow is Saturday and it will be very, very crowded. You don't want to fight all those crowds, now do you?"

"Oh yes I do. I love crowds. It makes it feel more like Christmas, and I got seventy-eight dollars I need to spend. I have to buy Mom and Daddy presents, and I can't buy their presents in front of them."

"You have seventy-eight dollars? Where did you get that kind of money?"

Wearing a closed mouth grin, again she waggled her eyebrows. "I worked for it."

"Worked for it? You can't work, you're only eight."

"Oh I did work for it, and I worked hard. Mrs. Nunn, our neighbor, she's very old. She's a hundred and five. She pays me to help her around her house, and she tells me stories of the old days. I love old days' stories."

"She's a hundred and five? Wow! That is old. She must have some longevity in her family, and a lot of great old time stories for you."

"Uh-huh! Did you ever hear of that famous ship Titanic?"

"Yes. It sank on tax day, April fifteenth."

"Grampy you're funny, tax day." She placed a small bite of pizza onto her plate. "Well, her cousin was on it when it sank, and she survived."

"That's interesting."

"Yes it is. Oh, oh, yes. She grew up in the house next door to Henry Ford's home. She actually knew the man who invented the car."

"No, he invented the assembly line to build cars so middle-class people could afford them."

"I remember that now. That's what she said. And she drives, and Daddy says she drives better than my mom." Maggie started laughing so hard that her face turned bright red.

"Are you okay? You got some serious giggles, young lady."

With her mouth wide-open, drool dripped off her tongue. She opened her mouth, but nothing came out. After several attempts, she managed to speak. "When Mom broke somebody's side mirror at the grocery store, Daddy told her that Mrs. Nunn drives better than her." Hysterical, Maggie threw her head downward and held her stomach.

Franklin guffawed with tears. "Maggie, I haven't laughed this hard in years, but I think your daddy was teasing your mother."

"Daddy does that a lot."

Before he closed the lid on the empty pizza box, he threw his napkin into it. "That reminds me of a story when your mother had her first driving lesson."

Wide-eyed, Maggie popped the last pizza morsel in her mouth. "Did she crash that time too?"

As he tried to tell her the story, he cracked up. "Your mother's first driving lesson—she hit an old Buick—slam—bang— the door—I don't know how—the Buick's door handle was on top of the hood on Nana's Bronco. And she stopped in the middle of. . ." He couldn't contain himself long enough to finish.

For several moments they roared before their hysteria had turned into out burst of occasional chuckles.

"Grampy, I saved up my money for almost three months. I really want to spend it on Christmas for my parents. Please Grampy, take me Christmas shopping tomorrow."

She had worked hard for the money, unlike that lazy delivery man. Franklin answered, "Okay, we can go shopping tomorrow, but we have to leave early."

"Yes!" With one hand on the back of the couch, Maggie pulled herself up toward his face, and gave him a kiss on the cheek. "I love you."

He wrapped an arm around her and gave her a squeeze. "I love you too."

"You're the best Grampy ever."

"And you're the best granddaughter ever. If you clean up and put your pajamas on, we can watch a Christmas movie."

"Yes." She hopped off the couch. As she started hurrying off, she stopped in her tracks. "My mom let me bring my favorite Christmas DVD. It's called Born on Christmas. It's about a girl who was born on Christmas morning and she's not happy about sharing her birthday with Jesus, but an angel visits her and changes her mind. At the end, she gives the angel a birthday present for Jesus. Can we see that one?"

"Now that you have told me the beginning, middle, and the end, of course we can see it."

While running up the stairs, she hollered back, "Don't worry. We can do our prayers and devotion after the movie."

"Oh boy," he muttered. But after he thought about it, he had nothing to worry about. She'll fall asleep before it ends.

During the opening credits, Maggie fell asleep. He carried her upstairs and pulled back the covers on Kitty's old bed. He pulled the bedding over her shoulders. It amazed him by how much he saw Katie's likeness in her. It was as though Maggie was a little effigy of her grandmother.

Pushing the hair from her face, he kissed her on the forehead. He turned off the night lamp. She stirred a bit. He walked softly out of the room.

Downstairs, he enjoyed his quiet and lone time. While poking at a log in the fireplace, he attempted to rationalize why he had told her that he would take her shopping. Even before Katie had passed away, he hated going to the mall. How did she talk him into taking her? There wouldn't be any Christmas celebration at his house once she left. At least, they'll have an adventure together.

Franklin placed another log onto the fire. One flame flickered more than the others. It seemed to dance to the sounds of the crackling wood like a ballerina. The more he studied it, the more furious the dance became. As the temptation to entertain the image began overtaking him, his family flashed into his mind. He pushed back on the phantom.

Closing his eyes and opening them again didn't work. The ballet continued. He fought it, but the image fought back.

He dropped the poker and shut the screen. He stood. Trembling, he hit the wall switch and flooded the room with light. "There! Illusions, stop bothering me."

CHAPTER 10

Biscuits and Gravy

THE NEXT MORNING, FRANKLIN's kitchen smelled like the apple wood burning in the woodstove. While he sat at the dining table sipping his coffee, he debated whether or not to make biscuits and gravy for Maggie. Ever since that fatal night, he promised himself he would never make it again. Glaring through the bay window at the snow covered landscape, he thought hard on what to do.

"Oh forget about it! The biscuits and gravy didn't kill Katie. Just make it for her you oversized idiot." Besides, he had a craving for it too. With that, he stood and marched to his walk-in food pantry. "Shut-up brain! I'm not going to think about it any longer." He gathered all the ingredients he needed.

Just as Franklin pulled the biscuits out of the oven, Maggie walked in.

"Grampy, what smells so good?"

"Come and get it. It's biscuits and gravy that will warm up the inners." He announced hunched over the sheet pan while placing the hot biscuits onto a plate.

She hurried over to him and touched one of the biscuits with her forefinger. "Ouch! That's hot."

With the towel in one hand and the other hand on his hip, he watched for a brief second as she blew on her finger. "They had just come out of a four hundred degree oven. What did you expect?"

"I don't know. They looked good."

He filled a cup with ice from the refrigerator's automatic ice maker. "Come over here."

"My finger turned red, look."

"Here, stick it in the ice."

"Ouch! That's cold." She pulled it out.

"Put it back in the ice before you get a blister."

After a few moments, he pulled it out of the ice and examined it. "I think you'll survive."

"Thank you, Grampy. Daddy put ice on my finger when I touched the hot burner on the camp stove."

"Why would you do that?"

"I didn't do it on purpose. That one was an accident."

"Wow, that must have hurt."

"It did," she concurred.

"Let's get the biscuits and gravy on the table."

"Okay." She skipped over to the stove, and she reached for the lid on the sauté pan of the scalding gravy.

Like a rattlesnake striking its prey, he seized her hand. "You think those biscuit were hot. That will scorch your hand. And then, we'll be going to the hospital instead of the mall."

Maggie flinched. Wide-eyed, she sucked her lower lip inward. "Yikes. I'm sorry."

"What were you trying to do?"

"Get the gravy for you."

"Thank you, but would you please sit down before we have a terrible accident?"

While he placed the gravy and biscuits in the middle of the table, she stood by the dining chair.

Franklin placed the serving spoon into the gravy. "Why don't you sit down?"

"I'm sorry. I'm just excited. I know better about the hot stuff. I've been cooking by myself ever since I was six. Don't you remember we use to cook together, forever? You called me your little sous chef, remember?"

The seriousness on her little freckled face augmented her cuteness. It tickled him. "Of course I remember. But you've been cooking alone ever since you were six? Now that's interesting. Do you like to cook?"

"Oh yes, I love to cook."

That answer elated him. "Well, I think you should sit down, so I can serve up breakfast."

"That's a good idea."

As he helped her scoot in, Franklin asked, "By the way, what encouraged you to continue cooking?"

"You. When I cook, it reminded me of all the good times we had together in the kitchen."

That crushed him, but he had no one to blame but himself.

"And your biscuits and gravy were always my favorite. Before I leave, can you teach me how you make them?"

How could he have broken his little princess's heart? To add to her misery, he did it when she had lost her nana. What kind of selfish monster had he become?

"Hello Grampy."

He couldn't deny it. He had become an epitome of a selfish human being.

"Grampy! Are you in there?"

He gazed at her innocent face. "I'm so sorry princess."

"You scared me. Where did you go?"

How could he answer her? "I—ahh—I ah—I was just thinking about something."

"Please don't do that again."

He forced a grin. "I'm sorry. Let's eat this hot food before we head out in the cold."

"How cold is it?"

"It's ten degrees." He grabbed the gallon of milk. "Up to a few days ago, the weather had been warmer than usual for this time of year. I never thought we'd see snowfall this year. Before the other day, it's been raining on and off since October."

"I'm glad it snowed too. It would have been boring without snow for Christmas like in Oklahoma."

"Princess, I have to agree with you there." He poured the milk into the tumblers, and sat down. "How many biscuits do you want, one or two?"

She held up three fingers.

"Three? That's too many for a little stomach like yours."

"Oh no it's not. Trust me, I'm starving. I think I have a fast metabolism."

"Why would you think that?"

"I looked it up on the internet." She leaned over her plate and smelled the food, "This smells so delicious." She placed her napkin on her lap.

"The internet confirmed it, okay." He scooped up a forkful of food.

Maggie hollered, "Grampy, don't!"

"What's the problem?"

"Don't eat that. We have to pray first."

"Pray?"

"Yes pray. I'll do the praying until you get saved. Bow your head please."

Her persistence that in the future he'll become a Jesus freak annoyed him more than the constant demand for prayer. "Before you pray, I got an idea."

She titled her head. "What's your idea?"

"Let's pray for all the meals we're going to eat today. That way, we'll be good for the rest of the day."

With her lips pressed together, she rolled them. "I don't believe we can do that."

"Why not? Nana use to pray for our safety in the morning, and I believe the prayer was good for the day. If you can pray for your safety once a day, why can't you pray for a full days worth of meals?"

She let out a loud sigh. "I would have to check on that one before we chance it. So, Grampy please bow your head. I'd like to pray so we can eat." She took his hand.

Though he bowed his head while she prayed, he couldn't stop thinking about what he had done to her.

In the name of Jesus, I say amen." She raised her head. "Grampy, you can eat now."

"Thank you for your permission."

"You're very welcome." ,

Before he could finish with his second bite, she had started on her second biscuit. With her cheeks bulging, she attempted to stuff her mouth with more food.

"Maggie, stop shoveling your food in your mouth. You can choke."

She flashed him a thumbs up. Then she swallowed hard. She grabbed her throat. "That hurt."

"I bet it did. You need to slow down."

"I know, but I'm starving. I haven't had biscuits and gravy this good since the last time you made them for me."

"I understand, but you don't just open your mouth up, and shovel the food down you're your throat like a farmer shoveling manure into a manure spreader."

"Ew, manure," she shook her hands, "Ew. I'm eating. Grampy please don't give me that kind of visual. That's disgusting."

"Maggie, just eat."

"Okay, but how did you learn how to cook like this?"

"My grandfather taught me how to cook."

"Your grandfather? My great-great grandfather? He could cook too?"

Franklin missed those days when he had worked with Pappy at his restaurant. Cooking with him had been some of the best times of his childhood. But the best of the best times was when Pappy had taken him fishing and hunting.

Sometimes, Pappy would take him to his hunting cabin in the woods up north for an entire week. The daily menu depended on what they had shot or fished out of the river. He could never forget those bygone days.

"Yes, he could. He was a professional chef. Before I was born, he was an executive chef at a Michelin star restaurant."

Her eyes lit up as a huge smile appeared across her face. "Your grandfather was an executive chef at a Michelin star restaurant? Really! Like Chef Watson?"

"You know Chef Watson?"

"Oh yes. I watch him on TV all the time. He's the best and funniest chef of all. What restaurant did your grandfather work at?"

"It was the historical Parker House in Boston, Massachusetts."

Her brows popped up. "Is the restaurant still there?"

"Yes, but I'm sure it's under new management by now, or even new ownership. Anyhow, I apprenticed under Pappy before I became a professor."

"What's an apprentice?"

"Well, it's someone who works under a professional to learn a trade or business."

She took a gulp of milk. "Oh. Didn't you like being a chef?

"I loved it."

"So, why did you become a professor?"

He scraped his fork across his plate. "It's complicated."

"Complicated, how? Do you like being a professor better?"

"Not really. But like I said it's complicated."

In hopes of earning his father's approval, Franklin had followed in his father's footsteps as an English professor. After his father had died of a massive heart attack at fifty-eight, Franklin realized he could never have lived up to his father's expectations no matter what he had done.

"Was your grandfather's food real good like yours?"

"Far better. I think I miss his cooking almost as much as I miss him. His specialty was Lobster Stew. It was so creamy with lobster in every spoonful."

"Grampy you're making me hungry for it. Can you make it for me?"

"Now that's a great idea. I'll do it one night for supper?"

"Can I help you?"

"Absolutely."

"Yee haw! Thank you."

But how did she know about lobster? She lived in beef country. "Maggie, have you ever had lobster?"

"I had lobster one time. It was last year at a wedding. After the wedding, we went to a huge room at a hotel in Fort Worth. We had it as an app—what do you call it? Um, I got it! An appitisser."

"A what?"

"Grampy, I don't remember the name. It's a little meal before the meal."

"Oh, you mean an appetizer."

"That's it, an appetizer. But they served it with little bowls of melted butter to dunk the lobster in."

"You're so cute. It's called drawn butter."

"Drawn? Grampy, they didn't draw it, they melted it."

He busted out laughing.

"What's so funny?"

"Princess the word drawn is the term for clarified butter. In other words, the butter is melted and then cooled. After it's cooled, the hard fat on top is removed."

Franklin glanced at his watch. "Oh wonderful, it's almost eight. We need to get moving. We have a long drive ahead of us, and I'd like to get there before the parking lot fills up." He drank down the rest of his milk. "Come on, help me clean up."

After they finished with the dishes, Franklin settled Harry in for the day. Maggie waited for him near the mudroom door.

Digging deep into his pocket for his keys, he asked, "You ready to go shopping?"

"Yes I . . ." She tilted her head skyward, "Wait! We can't go yet."

Franklin's heart hammered inside his chest. "Why? What's wrong?"

"Jesus said, 'Wait.'"

"Wait for what?"

"I don't know. Jesus said for us to wait. That's all I know. We need to listen to Him."

His hands shook. "Okay. Let's sit at the table and wait."

She sat down. But Franklin paced around in circles.

CHAPTER 11

Unexpected Visitors

THE FRONT DOOR BELL rang. Franklin jolted. "Who's that?"

Maggie extended her arm toward the living room. "You won't know unless you answer the door."

He patted his jacket pockets and spun on his heels a few times. "The door—yes—I'll answer the door." He stomped off through the house toward the front entrance.

"Grampy wait for me. I got little legs. I can't walk that fast."

He heard Maggie holler behind him, but he kept marching on. *God if you're there, don't let Kitty be hurt too. I can't loose her. It can't be the cops. I don't want bad news.* He felt tears well up in his eyes, and his hair stood on the back of his neck. He rubbed it.

When he touched the door knob, his hands were sweaty. His heart felt like it was about to explode out of his chest.

He opened the door. "Bob Lapierre?"

With a huge gleeful grin on his face, Bob waved like someone waving to a baby.

He had the mind to punch Bob in his big French nose, but all he could do was laugh. Bob could make a British Castle Guard of Buckingham Palace crack-up.

Maggie squeezed through the small space between the door and Franklin. "I remember him. He's the nice man with the tree farm."

As Franklin unlocked the storm door, he noticed an average sized woman with short blond hair, standing behind Bob. Just then, he caught a glimpse of the two bratty kids that had thrown the snowballs at his truck.

Wondering why Bob brought them to his home, Franklin observed the crowd on his front porch.

With his head cocked forward and his eyes squinted, Bob stared into Franklin's face. "How are you, my friend?"

"I ah. . ."

"Good, I break the ice. Now can we come in out of the cold? Yes?"

"Absolutely." Franklin stepped aside.

After Bob and the other three had filed into the living room, Maggie inquired, "Mr. Bob, do you remember me? I'm Maggie. I live in Oklahoma now."

Bob hunched over and tapped her nose. "Of course I remember you. How can I forget your beautiful face with all those adorable freckles?"

Meanwhile, the woman stood with her arms crossed over her chest with her large purse dangling from her hand. The two children stayed close to her with their eyes peeled on Franklin.

"What's under that foil?" Maggie asked, as she pointed at a platter in Bob's hand.

Franklin found it amazing how different the children's characteristics were for a sister and a brother. The boy had a dark complexion, dark brown hair, and gray-blue eyes. On the other hand, his sister had a light complexion, strawberry blond hair, and crystal blue eyes.

"Well little missy, let me introduce everyone. Then I will tell you what's under the foil, okay?"

Maggie affirmed, "Okay."

Bob rubbed his nose. "Frank, I would like you to meet my tenant. This is Sue Hamilton, and these here are her two grandchildren, Lucas and Mackenzie." He pointed at Franklin. "And this is my good friend, Professor Franklyn. He works at the university."

The girl turned away, and hid her face in her grandmother's jacket sleeve.

Like a dead fish, Sue gave Franklin a limp handshake. "It's nice to meet you," she said with a raspy voice. For some reason, she avoided eye contact.

The intrusion felt uncomfortable. But he surmised Sue appeared far more uncomfortable around him than he was with her in his home. "It's nice to meet you too." Franklin took a few steps backward. "Please have a seat."

Why would he do something that stupid? He didn't want any guest in his home, especially uninvited ones.

Bob interrupted, "No thank you, my friend. We can't stay long, and you and Maggie are dressed like you were heading out. Yes?"

Franklin got a glimpse of Lucas. The poor boy appeared scared. "Well—yes, but it's fine. It's nothing that can't wait."

With a hand on each child's shoulders, Sue prodded the kids to move in front of her. She kept her eyes on her grandchildren. "The other day when Annabelle was watching them, she told me that she saw my grandchildren throwing snowballs at your truck. I'd like to apologize for their misbehavior, and they have something to say to you. Don't you kids?"

Lucas and Mackenzie stepped in front of Franklin, but Mackenzie stayed behind her brother, holding onto him.

Gazing down, Lucas's voice quivered. "I'm—I'm, I'm sorry."

With Mackenzie's lower lip over her top lip, she started crying.

Lucas stood in front of her. "It wasn't her fault. I made her do it."

That melted Franklin's heart. He wished he hadn't been mean to them the other day. They were just small children, and he growled at them without taking into consideration what they were going through.

Franklin squatted down in front of Lucas. "Hey, I'm not angry at you or your sister."

Mackenzie peeped around her brother. "You're not mad at me."

He wished he could hold them both in his arms and comfort them, but he had no authority to do so. "No, not at all. You both made a mistake."

Rubbing her eyes, Mackenzie moved out from behind her brother.

Franklin continued, "Everybody makes mistakes. But you need to learn from your mistakes."

With his face downward and his eyeballs rolled nearly behind his head, Lucas answered in a brittle tone. "I learned from my mistake."

And Mackenzie parroted, "I learned too."

"Good, but I need you both to promise me that you won't ever throw anything out in the street, ever again, because it can cause a serious accident."

"We promise," Lucas put his hand on Mackenzie's shoulder, "don't we Mackenzie?"

McKenzie nodded her head, and she sniffled, "Yes, I promise."

Franklin glanced up toward Sue.

Teary-eyed, she mouthed, "Thank you."

Franklin mouthed back, "Sure."

Sue turned her face away.

When Franklin stood, Maggie pressed in. "Hi, I'm Maggie. I'm his granddaughter."

"I'm Lucas," he grabbed his sister's arm, "and this is my sister, Mackenzie."

With her shoulders lifted, Sue's eyes smiled affectionately at her grandchildren.

Maggie continued, "I'm here visiting. But whenever I'm here, would you like to come over and play with me?"

"Oh boy, yes. We'd love to come over and play." Lucas pulled McKenzie next to him. "Won't we, McKenzie?"

"Uh-huh," McKenzie nodded.

"See Frank, my friend," Bob interjected, "the children are friends now. So Maggie, would you like me to show you and your new friends what's on this platter?"

Maggie pulled her arm down, and exclaimed, "Yes."

"All of you come over here and watch." Bob removed the foil. "It's Annabelle's fresh homemade gingerbread people. Maggie, would you like to share them with your new friends? Yes?"

"Yes, sir. I think that's a fantastic idea."

After he handed her the platter, Maggie showed the cookies to Lucas and McKenzie. "Look, there are both girls and boys. Mackenzie, you can choose first since you're the smallest."

"I can?" Mackenzie reached for one of the gingerbread girls. With her hand hovering over the cookie, she froze. She looked over her shoulder. "Grandma, can I have one?"

With her arched brows raised a bit, a gentle smile appeared across Sue's face. "Yes you can, baby doll."

Lucas's face lit up. "Me too, Grandma?"

"Yes, of course you too."

"Oh boy!" Lucas took one of the gingerbread boys.

Maggie took hers, and she slid her eyes up toward Franklin. "Grampy, may I have one?"

"Absolutely."

Without wasting a minute, Maggie bit into hers. "Mr. Lapierre, please tell Mrs. Lapierre that these are delicious. Aren't they Lucas and McKenzie?"

With their mouths filled with cookies, the two confirmed yes in concert.

"Frank, this was a good visit, yes, but we must go and no longer keep you."

Franklin shook Bob's hand. "Yes, it was a good visit. Thank you, my friend, for bringing the children. Please tell Annabelle thank you for the cookies. I do appreciate everything you both do for us."

Swallowing hard, Maggie added, "Yes, thank you Mr. Lapierre. Please tell Mrs. Lapierre thank you for me too."

Lucas chorused, "And thanks for me and McKenzie too."

"Sure son, my Annabelle and me, we always glad to make happy faces."

Franklin glanced at his watch. "Well my friend, we do need to get going. You have a good day."

"You too my friend."

After they left, Franklin couldn't stop thinking about Sue's grand-children. His eyes watered. He fought back the tears. He didn't want Maggie to see them.

"Princess, are you ready to go?"

"I'm ready. Let's go shopping!"

Franklin started toward the garage door. He stopped short of the door. "Wait a minute. How did you know they were coming here?"

"Remember, I said God told me to wait, but I didn't know why. When God speaks, we need to obey. It's for our own good to listen to Him because He knows what's best for us."

He didn't want that explanation. "Okay, let's get going."

She walked passed him as he held the door open for her. "This is going to be so exciting. Do you realize this is our very first mall outing together?"

"Yes." Though Franklin didn't want to admit it, he too looked forward in taking her shopping, even on the busy mall.

CHAPTER 12

The Church Across the Street

IN THE GARAGE, FRANKLIN unplugged the engine heater on his truck.

"Grampy, what's that cord?"

"It's an engine heater. It helps keep the engine warm in the winter, so it will start on the cold mornings."

"Daddy has a diesel engine in his truck too, but he doesn't need that. I think it's because it's a lot warmer down in Tulsa."

"Yes, you're correct. Come on, let's hop in the truck so we can go."

While Franklin warmed the truck, his mind wandered off. It baffled Franklin on how Maggie could have known that Bob was coming over. There had to have been an explanation for it. She may have thought God spoke to her, but he found that hard to believe. If God spoke to her, why wouldn't He speak to Franklin? Then Franklin toyed with the idea that she had a special gift for premonitions. Or maybe, she just had a fine tuned woman's intuition.

He heard Maggie say something. He responded with a safe answer. "No."

"Why not?"

"What? Why not what?"

"Why can't we go to church tomorrow? It's Sunday."

"Church? No!" He'd do most anything for her, but not church.

"But why not?"

"It's too far." Though true, nevertheless, an excuse.

"How far is too far for you?"

Franklin put the truck into reverse. "It's more than twenty miles one way."

Maggie bowed her head and mumbled.

"What did you say?"

"I was praying."

He pressed on the brake. "Praying?"

"Yes."

"Why are you praying?"

"In all my ways, I acknowledge him. You will too when you get saved." Wiggling her feet, she tilted her head downward. "Please, let me finish."

Her confidence annoyed him. If he were on his death bed, he wouldn't join the Jesus freak movement. "What do you mean by when I get saved?"

"Grampy please, I'm listening."

That spooked him. He braced himself for another one of her predictions.

After a few seconds, she lifted her head. "Grampy you can go now."

Relieved that she had no other predictions, he relaxed. "Thank you for your permission, madam."

"You're very welcome, Grampy sir," she replied, looking out the passenger window.

He started in reverse. "Are you ready to go shopping?"

"Oh yes, I'm so very excited." She clapped her feet together. "This is going to be so much fun."

"Well young lady, I'm not happy about fighting the crowds, but I'm glad we're going on an adventure together."

"That's okay. I promise you, you'll survive the crowds. Just follow my lead. I'm experienced at this."

Franklin chuckled, "I bet you are."

"I can't believe that I'm actually going Christmas shopping with my Grampy. In my entire life, I never thought we'd go shopping for Christmas together."

"I never thought so either," he remarked, and then he continued, "So, this day has been long coming for you."

"Oh yes, and we're going to have so much fun."

"And, I agree."

While watching behind him in his two spotter mirrors, he backed the truck onto the old-country road, plastered with ruts and potholes.

Maggie taped her finger on the passenger's window. "Stop! Look!"

He hit the brake. "What happened?"

"Look a church. Praise the Lord! Hallelujah! There's a church." She twisted around toward him. "Grampy, look at that sign."

"Maggie, please move your head. I can't see."

She pressed her body back against the seat. "Can you see it, now?"

"Yes, let me read this. Living Faith Church, Sunday Service at 10 a.m.

What? Mark's a pastor?"

Franklin's eyes blurred and his ears deafened. His thoughts spun around in his head like they were spinning on a Round-up amusement park ride. Since he had given Maggie a lame excuse, she would expect the distance issue resolved. How could he take her to that church, after he had harassed that man? He felt a sudden tug on his arm.

"Grampy, what's wrong? Why do you have such a funny look on your face?"

He shook his head, and reread the sign.

"Hello, Grampy. Are you in there?"

"Um—yes, princess. I'm just surprised."

"Is it a happy surprise, right? You don't have to drive a long ways. All we have to do is walk across the street."

Leaning his head against the head rest, he closed his eyes.

"Grampy, can we please go?"

Offhand, he had no more excuses. "How can I say no to a face like that?"

"Does that mean, yes?"

Under protest, he surrendered. "I suppose."

Maggie covered her wide-mouthed smile with her hand. "Yes, we're going to church."

"Hold on. Did God tell you there was a church across the street?"

"No. He told me to look out the window. But I didn't know I was going to see that church sign. Now that's something to shout about." She sunk back into her seat, beaming.

He would shout alright, but from the agony of being humbled by attending Mark's church. He started down the street. His stomach felt sick. Placing his foot on the gas, his head pounded.

"Wait!" she shrieked.

He jammed on the break, and grabbed his heart. The truck joggled. "What happened?"

"Why didn't you know your neighbor was a pastor, but you knew his name?"

"Maggie, I love you, but you need to think before you sound off like you're being killed. You could have caused an accident or scared me into a heart attack."

She reached over and laid her finger tips on his arm. "I'm sorry I scared you."

"Okay princess." He closed his eyes and took in a few slow breaths. "Let's get going."

"But Grampy. Why didn't know he had a church across the street? Don't you look out your window?"

"Um," he rubbed his nose, "they just moved in a little while ago. And, I—um—Grampy is a busy man. I met him once. One day I—ah, happened to be outside and he said, 'howdy neighbor' and I said 'howdy back.' We shook hands and introduced ourselves. But he never told me he was a pastor. I was on my way to work, and I—ah, I never gave him a chance to tell me. And that's the extent of it." *You liar!*

"But you didn't see the sign?" She tapped her finger on the window. "It's right there, and it's in big orange painted letters too on a board."

"No I didn't. Yesterday, I saw him hammer it in the ground. Before I could read it, your parents drove up and blocked the sign."

"Oh, I get it. The car obstructed your view. Can we go now?"

"Where?"

"Hello Grampy, we're going shopping. Did you forget?"

"Yes, of course I did."

"You're so funny, Grampy. You always make me laugh."

While driving down the highway, Maggie's chattering helped Franklin keep his mind off the anticipated humiliation awaiting him at Mark's church. But when he pulled behind the long line of cars waiting to get into the mall's parking lot, she got quiet.

With one hand braced on the console and the other on the arm rest, she raised herself up. Stretching her neck, she looked out of the windshield. "Where's the mall?"

"About a quarter of a mile down the road."

"Look at all those cars. Are they all waiting to get into the mall?"

"Oh yes they are."

"All those people. This is going to be so much fun."

Resting his arm over the steering wheel, he refused to remark.

After about twenty minutes, they reached the parking lot. Following a line of cars in front of him, Franklin drove around in circles behind the slow moving vehicles, and it seemed as though he would never find a parking place. Whenever he found one, someone else took it before he could get to it. Maybe he shouldn't complain. "Princess, I don't think we'll be able to find a parking place."

She didn't respond.

He glanced over toward her. She had lifted her hands upward. Paranoid, he listened for the subject of her prayer.

"Lord, we need favor on a parking space."

At once, a gray Suburban pulled out of a space in front of him. He hit the brakes. A horn sounded behind him. After he had slipped into the parking spot, he shut down the truck. He stared out the windshield. Astonished that he had parked one row back near the mall's main entrance, he asked, "Maggie how did you do that?"

"Do what?"

"The parking space. Look where we're parked. You told God what you needed. Not only did He answer you, he gave us one of the best spots in the lot. Look, there's the mall's entrance. Right in front of us."

Grinning, she waggled her eyebrows. "You can't doubt it was Jesus, now can you?"

"What makes you think that?"

"Because you just admitted He gave us this parking space. I just heard you."

"You're correct, but I was caught up in the moment."

An askance expression appeared on her face. "What moment?"

Struggling for an answer, he opened his mouth, but nothing came out.

"I'm waiting for your explanation."

"It was a mere coincidence. I don't have any other explanation." Except that his pride got in the way.

Rubbing her hands together, she grinned and nodded. "Oh yes there is another one. I believe that I receive whatever I ask Him. And I have the favor of God because Jesus loves me."

"How do you know Jesus loves you?"

She leaned back against the door. "Jesus died for all of us when we were His enemies. It's in the bible. When we get back home, would you like me to read it to you?"

"No. You don't have to read it to me."

"Okay Grampy. Can we go shopping now?"

She just dropped the subject like a hot potato, and he refused to complain. He knew when he had it good.

Playing with Maggie's hat, he pulled it over her eyes. "Come on, let's go shopping and have some fun."

She straightened it out. "I'm ready."

"But wait in the truck until I come around and get you."

"Okay."

When he opened the door for her, she had a huge smile across her face. "Grampy, God told me that He's going to use me to help someone today. Praise the Lord, I can't wait." She hopped out of the truck. "I love it when the Lord uses me."

Franklin shrugged it off as her over-active imagination had gone into full throttle.

CHAPTER 13

While at the Mall. . .

THEY FORCED THEIR WAY through the packed food court and meandered down a busy corridor. He got a headache from the racket in the mall. The loud voices amalgamated with secular Christmas carols were almost unbearable to tolerate. He wished he were in the quietness of his home.

Most of the stores had placed happy holiday sandwich-signs near their front entrances. Though at times he had irritated his brother-in-law with political correctness, Franklin despised it. It was Merry Christmas, not merry holiday.

"Grampy, doesn't anybody around here say Merry Christmas?"

"It doesn't look like it, does it?"

"No, it doesn't." Skipping next to him, she pointed at a sign on a store front window. "Look at that sign. It says 50 percent off and nothing about Christmas. Why don't the people like Christmas in New Hampshire? Everybody loves Christmas in Oklahoma."

Extending his arm, Franklin turned sideways. "Look all around you. Why do you think all these people are here?"

"Because they're Christmas shopping."

"That's right. It's not the people. It's our oppressive government waging an assault on free speech. It's a desperate attempt to silence the people by intimidating them through political correctness. And if they were to eliminate the second article of the Bill of Rights, tyranny would follow for sure."

Nose crinkled, she looked up at him. "You sound like Daddy. He taught me all about the U. S. Constitution and political correctness. Daddy said that our forefathers gave us the second article to keep us from tyranny, like the tyranny had in England. It's also so we can protect ourselves."

"Your Daddy is an excellent teacher."

"But Grampy, I didn't know that you had a political side to you. I can't wait to tell Mom and Dad."

"I try not to be, but there are idiots that force people like me into it."

"My daddy is very political, and he's angry at the media too. He calls them fake news like President Trump. Oh yes, and like Hannity and Lou Dobbs does too."

He busted out laughing. "You really understand what's going on, don't you little munchkin? You watch the news too?"

"Uh huh. With my father, I have no choice, since all he ever watches is the news. That's all he ever watches." "

You're a funny girl." Franklin stopped and looked around the mall. "By the way, where are we going?"

"I don't know. I'm following you."

"I don't know either," he cracked up. "We're two idiots talking politics, and walking aimlessly around the mall, and neither of us know where were going."

Hunched over with a hand on her stomach, Maggie giggled.

"I got an idea. There's a bench over there. Let's sit down and figure out what you would like to buy. After we figure that out, we'll know where to go."

"That's a great idea."

As she plopped down on the bench, she placed her small red patent-leather purse down by her side. With her fingers curled under the edge of the bench, she kicked her legs in and out.

"Now tell me, what would you like to buy for your parents?"

Before she could answer him, Franklin spotted Pastor Mark standing in the midst of the crowd, rubbing his chin. A young woman talking with another woman bumped into him.

"Well, I want to buy Daddy a "MercyMe" CD and my mom . . ."

Mark snapped his fingers, and hurried into the woman's clothing store across from the bench.

Franklin jumped up. "Okay, there's a Christian book store up the other way."

"But, but, I haven't told you what I want to get my mom."

"Come on, give me your hand. You can tell me on our way to the store."

Hopping off the bench, she pointed. "But I want to get my mom a sweater, and there's a ladies store in front of us that has 50 percent off."

"No. We're not staying here."

Maggie flinched. "You scared me! Why are you so angry?"

"I'm sorry. I'm not angry. We need to get out of here. Besides, there's a better clothing store up on the other end near the Christian bookstore. Give me your hand, and let's get out of here, now."

As he started down the mall, he felt her dragging him.

"Wait my purse."

He twisted around. His eyes darted toward the bench. A very tall elderly woman started to sit down on Maggie's purse. Quick, go get it."

"Excuse me ma'am, my purse is in your way." Maggie snatched it from under her.

The woman stood up straight. "Ooh, I almost sat on it."

"Yes, but I got it before it could hurt you."

"What a sweet little girl."

"Thank you, ma'am."

Maggie took Franklin's hand.

Franklin hoofed it as fast as he could. He headed for the mall's corridors junction.

Maggie ran beside him. "Grampy, please slow down. I can't keep up."

"Hold on for a few more minuets. We're almost there."

"But people are bumping into me!"

"I see the junction." He halted.

Maggie flung forward and stumbled over her feet. "You almost made me fall. What kind of Grandfather are you?"

"A clever one!" Proud he had an answer, he waggle one eyebrow at a time, but he forgot where the store was. He scanned down two different corridors.

"I don't think it's clever to almost trip your own granddaughter."

Franklin dropped his head.

"Well Grampy, do you think it's clever to make me almost fall?"

Embarrassed by how he had reacted when he saw Mark, he squatted in front of her. He placed his hand on her shoulder. "I'm so very sorry. You're correct. I was being thoughtless of you. Please forgive me."

"I forgive you."

"Look, you're mittens are falling out of your pocket." He shoved them in for her and straightened out her wolf hat. "There, you look beautiful. Just like a little lady wolf."

"Who were you running from?"

Franklin's heart sunk. Rendered speechless, his mouth opened and closed like a fish in distress, gasping for oxygenated water. His brain scrambled for an excuse. "Um, what made you think that?"

"Jesus told me. He said, 'Who is he running from?'"

"That's a question, not a said."

"Silly, sometimes He talks to me with a question."

He stood up. How did she know that? "I'm trying to get my bearings. I forgot where the store was. There's nothing more and nothing less."

Puffing up her cheeks, Maggie stared at him through squinted eyes.

"What's the matter? Don't you believe me?"

"The one thing that God can't do is lie."

He swayed his restless gaze. Only a rat would have lied to his granddaughter, but his big pride kept him from admitting it. "Why would you think I'm lying to you?"

"I'm sorry. I don't think you're lying to me, but . . ."

Turning his guilt on her graduated him to a despicable human being. He felt too awkward to admit his shenanigans, but somehow he planned to address it at another time. "Come on, I think it's this way next to Macy's." He reached for her hand.

"Please promise me you'll slow down. I have little legs, especially compared to yours?"

"I promise. I'll slow down for your little legs."

While meandering through the crowds, Maggie tugged on his hand. "Grampy, how do you know "MercyMe?"

"They were one of Nana's favorite groups. She had their CD's."

"Really? Do you still have them?"

"Yes, but I don't know where they are at the moment."

"Can you look for me?"

"Yes, when I have the time. Yes, here's the book store." He pointed at the other side of the corridor. "Look over there. That's the clothing store that I told you about."

"That is better. They have sixty percent off there. Thank you for bringing me here."

"You're very welcome. Your nana use to shop there."

"Really? That makes it even better to shop there."

The two turned into the Christian bookstore.

"I remember this store. Nana use to take me here." Pointing, she wiggled. The CD's are over there, by the front window."

"Lead the way."

"Can I let go of your hand, please?"

"Only if you promise to stay close to me."

"I promise." She skipped over to the CD's, and plopped her purse on top of the display stand.

Franklin stepped aside and rested against a wall. He crossed one foot over the other. While she pawed through them, he scanned the busied Christian store. It was like a stockyard for Jesus freaks. Chatter amongst customers and store clerks sounded from the aisles near him.

Since he stood in the midst of Christian paraphernalia, it hit him. Mark's presence had driven him into the store for holy rollers. Franklin found that quite funny.

A pleasant looking woman, with thick eyeglasses, approached Franklin. "Sir, can I help you with anything?"

"No thank you."

"My name is Tonya. If you need anything, just let me know."

"Thank you Ma'am. I appreciate it."

A scruffy and scrawny younger man hurried passed Franklin toward the CD display table. At once, Franklin fixed his eyes on the bum. The scoundrel had matted brown hair, an unzipped tattered kaki-green jacket, and a frayed black t-shirt.

The vagabond slowed his pace as he jerked his head from side to side, and over his shoulders. He neared Maggie, putting Franklin on high alert.

Franklin moved in and readied himself for a confrontation.

The man snatched her purse. Franklin seized his wrist. Maggie lurched backward.

Clenching the man's T-shirt, Franklin threw the vagabond against a nearby wall. He rammed his shoulder against the crook to pin him in, but the bum fought harder.

Screams and hollers boomed throughout the store. Books flew off a nearby bookcase. The more the low-life scuffled, the more forceful Franklin bulldozed his shoulder into the vagabond.

He clutched the crook's wrist. Through gritted teeth, Franklin demanded, "Let go of my granddaughter's purse before I break off your hand."

He dropped it. "Take your filthy hands off me!"

"I called mall security," a woman's voice shouted from behind them.

"I'm making a citizen's arrest, and I'm holding you until security gets here." Franklin snarled, "You're going to jail, you parasite."

"Jail! Please Mister don't call the cops. I only took it because I'm starving. I haven't eaten in three days."

Franklin snapped his head over his shoulder. As expected, the incident had drawn attention to him. It almost seemed like everyone in the store stared slack-jawed, or with hands over their hearts or mouths. But where was Maggie?

Panicked, he twisted around and eased his grip on the thief. "Maggie, where are you?"

"I'm over here, behind you Grampy."

The purse snatcher delivered him a fierce blow to Franklin's shin, forcing him to loosen his grip. Watery-eyed, Franklin sucked in his breath and expelled it through his gritted teeth.

A white haired, tall, and brawny man plunged in and thrust his body against the vagabond's. "Leave!"

The vagabond's face twisted into a grimace, and his body twitched. Within seconds, the man's head drooped.

That spooked Franklin. He pushed against the man's shoulder, holding it firm, but the vagrant stopped resisting, and the white haired man disappeared. Franklin snapped his head from side to side. "Where did he go?"

The bum grumbled, "I'm starving. My stomach hurts."

A muscled bound security guard stepped in and separated Franklin and the crook, as he hollered, "What's going on here?"

"He snatched my granddaughter's purse." Franklin declared, catching his breath.

A shorter and huskier guard held his hand out toward the bum, and he commanded, "Don't move."

At the same time, Franklin complained, "He snatched my granddaughter's purse; it's on the floor," as he pointed downward, he continued, "near my foot, and he kicked me in the shin."

The muscular guard picked up Maggie's purse. "Would you like us to call a medic?"

"No, I'll be fine."

Maggie ran over to Franklin.

He swept her up in his arms. "Are you alright?"

"Is this your granddaughter?" The taller security guard asked.

"Yes, she is."

"Would you mind waiting here for a moment, and I'll be right with you."

"Sure, no problem," Franklin complied.

"Grampy, why do we have to wait here?"

"They needed us out of the way. Are you alright?"

From the corner of his eye, Franklin spotted both security guards talking to the vagabond.

"Yes I am. I prayed for God's help. That angel appeared and helped you. And then I told Satan to leave that bad man. Then the angel told the devil to leave. And then the man made funny faces. Then he went limp. I took authority over the devil, and the angel helped me. Did you see that? I've always known what to do, but it was the first time that I have ever seen that work. Wasn't that. . ."

Angel and the devil? She was brainwashed.

". . .especially when the angel said leave right after I said leave."

"By the way, where is the man with white hair?" Standing in place, Franklin looked around the store. "Maggie, did you see him leave."

"Nope. He appeared and disappeared."

"What do you mean, he appeared and disappeared?"

"He appeared, and then," she threw her hands up, "poof, he vanished."

"Nobody goes poof and vanishes."

"He did. He went poof. I told you, God sent an angel to help you."

That confirmed it. She did have an overactive imagination. "An angel?"

"Grampy, yes, an angel."

Scouring the store, he saw the elderly store clerk with the thick glasses, standing a few feet behind him.

"Ma'am, did you happen to see that man who had helped me with that crook. Did you see if he had left the store or not? He was about a foot taller than me, and much younger than me with white hair."

A puzzle expression appeared across her face. "I'm sorry, but I didn't see a man with white hair, but I do see a lot of people."

"But that man helped me detain that crook. Didn't you see him?"

"I'm sorry, I didn't see anybody." She backed up a few steps and walked away toward the register.

Scratching his head, Franklin figured that she might have preferred not to get involved.

Before he had a chance to ask someone else, the muscled-bound guard approached Franklin. "I'm Lieutenant Maxwell. Would you like us to call the police?"

Franklin spotted the other guard escorting the crook out of the store. "Yes. I want to press charges."

"We need to take a report of. . ."

"No," Maggie interrupted.

"Maggie, you shouldn't interrupt. That's not polite."

She pursed her lips and crinkled her forehead. "But he's hungry."

"I do apologize for my granddaughter. She's eight."

"Grampy, so what does that have to do with anything? That man is hungry and he needs something to eat. Remember God told me that He was going to use me today?"

If there were a whole for Franklin to crawl into, he would. "I'm sorry for her interruptions. She has a big heart."

Lieutenant Maxwell responded, "No worries. Let's take this out in the mall. It shouldn't be long."

Franklin and Maggie followed Maxwell into the mall, away from the store front, and into a hallway with public restrooms.

Maxwell reached into his front shirt pocket and slid out a pen and a small notepad. I need your name and your granddaughter's name."

"Dr. Franklyn."

"You're first name, please?"

"Hold on a minute. Where did the other guard take the thief?"

"Sir, we're taking the man's picture before we escort him out of the mall."

Franklin snapped, "What do you mean you're escorting him out of the mall? I told you I wanted the bum arrested."

"I'm sorry, but we only have the authority to kick the man out of the mall. We can't make any type of arrests unless we witness a crime committed."

"What? He snatched my granddaughter's purse! That's not a crime?"

"Well, technically nobody witnessed it. Tonya—I mean, the store's owner reported a fight not a purse snatching. The only reason why I'm not throwing you out is because the owner believed the other man started the fight. Frankly, you don't look the type to cause trouble."

Hotter than a burning house, Franklin fired out, "What! Technically, nobody witnessed it! You considered throwing me out? What kind of bureaucratic nonsense is this? This is unbelievable!" He pressed his lips together. "I don't believe this. What about the man with the white hair? He witnessed it, and my granddaughter is a witness too!"

Wearing a deadpan expression, Maxwell asked, "What man with the white hair?"

Throwing his hands up in the air, Franklin refused to consider himself as delusional as the rest of the idiots around him. "Why did you offer to call the police in the first place?"

"We can call the police for you if you would prefer that, but we can't make an arrest."

Franklin found himself dealing with idiotsville, incorporated.

Maggie tugged on Franklin's jacket sleeve, "Grampy."

"Maggie, what's the problem?"

"You can't have him arrested," she pleaded.

Holding back his temper, Franklin quizzed, "Do you understand this man tried to steal your purse?"

"Yes, but he did it because he was hungry."

"Maggie, if we don't have him arrested, he'll do this again to somebody else."

"I understand, but God said no."

Inside, he could feel the pressure building up. "Lieutenant, throw him out of the mall!" he surrendered.

"Phew," she slid her hand across her forehead, "Thank you. I thought telling you what God said would help you understand."

Maxwell added, "I'll guarantee you that he will attempt to rob someone else."

"Lieutenant Maxwell," Maggie removed a ten dollar bill out of her purse, "we need to be obedient to the Lord. The poor man tried to take my purse because he said he was starving. He hasn't eaten in three whole days. Before you throw him out, would you please tell him I forgive him," she handed Maxwell the money, "and would you please feed him? He's really hungry, and it's really cold out there."

The guard looked at Franklin, but Franklin refused to engage in such lunacy. He shrugged, "It's her money."

"Okay. Sure I'll get him something to eat."

"And please, don't forget to tell him I forgive him."

She sounded like Katie and Kitty. Through much observation, Franklin concluded for some reason forgiving low-lives and idiots was paramount within their Christian rituals.

Maxwell scratched his head. "Yes, I'll tell him."

With Franklin's nerves tighter than a winch cranked to capacity, he took in a deep breath through his nose and let it out of his mouth. After giving the information Maxwell needed for his report, Franklin and Maggie resumed shopping.

"Princess, would you like to go back to the Christian store?"

"No Way!"

"Why not? I thought you wanted to get your father a "MercyMe" CD."

"That store was expensive. I was about to tell you that I wanted to leave when that man tried to steal my purse. I'd rather go to a place like Target or Wal-Mart. They're much cheaper."

"Would you like to go to Walmart?"

Her face lit up. "Yes, where is it? I can buy a lot more stuff there. Like Daddy says, 'you can get more bang for the buck at a big box store.'"

Franklin busted out laughing. "Okay, give me your hand, and let's go see what bang you get for your buck."

Walmart must have been the busiest store in the state of New Hampshire. For two hours, the massive heard of people had pushed, shoved, nudged, banged shopping carts into Franklin's heels, and stepped on his feet.

In the pet aisle, a woman caught Franklin with a handicap cart and shoved him down the crowed aisle. He held onto the cart and ran backwards. "Lady, stop!"

"Why won't it stop?"

"Just let go of the handles."

She halted. He flung back on his rear. The frail woman apologized several times.

Out of breath, he brushed himself off. "Lady, don't worry about it. I'm fine."

"Would you mind reaching that box of cat food first?"

"No ma'am."

"Thank you, sonny."

That made his day. Even though he had graying temples, she called him sonny.

Holding a dog's squeaky toy in each of her hands, laughing, she paced back and forth.

"Maggie, what are you laughing at?"

"You looked so funny—your eyeballs . . ."

But Franklin found no humor in the calamities that he suffered throughout the store. "It's not funny."

"Oh yes it is!"

That aggravated him further. "Maggie, it's time to go."

Within seconds, Maggie's laughter waned. "But Grampy, I don't know if Harry would like the squeaky ball or the squeaky bone."

"Get him the bone." He marched off pushing the cart with Maggie chasing him.

The lines at the cash registers flowed into the aisles behind them. Franklin stopped between two registers to observe the situation. It seemed every single person's cart overflowed with items.

He threw a hand up. "Look at this! Look at all the registers they have closed. Unbelievable! It'll take another hour to check out."

Since his cart had five items and a few Christmas cards, he looked around for a quick checkout, but they were packed too. "That's ludicrous. What kind of idiots close registers during a Christmas rush?"

A petite and dark haired female clerk approached him. "Come with me. I'm opening up register twelve."

"Praise the Lord. God had mercy on you." Maggie declared.

With one hand on the front of the cart, the clerk led the way.

He glanced at Maggie. "What do you mean mercy?"

"When you were griping, I prayed for God to forgive you and have mercy on you, so He could give you favor. And voila, the lady came and took us ahead of the others."

"I wasn't gripping!"

"Oh yes you were."

"I was stating a fact."

"Okay." She skipped along side the shopping cart.

The clerk rushed around the counter, and five other customers pushed their carts behind Franklin.

It hit him. "By the way, cashiers do this all the time." He handed her the cards.

She placed them on the conveyor and proceeded to help him with the rest of the stuff. "Then why didn't she grab someone else on either side of her register rather than coming four registers down from hers to get us?"

Her rationale made sense like Katie's rationale had at times, but he believed he had done nothing that required forgiveness. But since he knew it was best not to argue with a Christian's rational, he dropped the subject. "Maggie, I appreciate you helping me."

"You're welcome. I like to help."

He took the bag from the cashier, and left the cart with the other carts. "Let's get out of here. Wait a minute. Where's the mall's front entrance?"

"Why do we have to go back in the mall," she pointed, "when outside is right there?"

"Remember, you prayed for favor, and God gave us a parking space near the mall's main entrance? We have to go back there."

"Oh yes, I forgot," she giggled.

"Why are you giggling?"

"You just admitted that it was God, again."

"No. It's just that—forget about it. Let's get out of here."

"Okay, Grampy."

When they had reached the food court, it was packed beyond his imagination.

"Unbelievable. Don't let go of my hand."

"I'm starving. Can we get something to eat?"

He glanced at his watch. "It's a quarter to one, so am I. Let's get out of here first."

"Can't we eat here and then go?"

The crowds surrounded him like a swarm of bees protecting their hive. "No princess, not here. Its way too crowded. We'll get something on the way home. Besides, there's no place to sit."

"But I don't need to sit. I just need to eat."

"No buts, we're out of here."

"Okay, I would like you to know that God agrees with you."

He held open the door to exit the mall. "What do you mean?"

"Jesus also said 'Not here.' I can't wait to see what Jesus has in stored for us next. How 'bout you?"

Oh no! God if you're real, please no more holy spook stuff.

CHAPTER 14

On the Way to Chili's

FRANKLIN COMPARED THE TRAFFIC in the parking lot to rush hour in a metropolis. Wearing his patience, he swore that he would never shop at a mall again. Online shopping was the best thing that happened to society.

"Grampy, I'm so hungry."

"I know Princess. We're almost to the exit." He pulled onto the roadway. "Finally, we're out of there. What would you like to eat?"

"I want chili rellenos and enchiladas with refried beans and flour tortillas. Oh yes, guacamole too."

That sounded fantastic, but Franklin would have added street tacos to that menu. "But that's Mexican food. Princess, you're hat is in your eyes, push it back."

"Okay, but don't you like Mexican?"

"Yes. I love Mexican food, but not in New England. "

"So what does that mean?"

"We have excellent Italian food, but the best Mexican food around here is Taco Bell."

She crinkled her nose. "Ew, that's fake Mexican."

"You don't like Taco Bell? I thought all kids did."

"It's okay. But we don't eat fast food. It's not good for you. But why doesn't New Hampshire have real Mexican food?"

"We have some Mexican restaurants here, but they're not authentic." Franklin maneuvered into the left turning lane. "It's just a different culture."

"What do you mean?"

"Different parts of the country have different cultures, different accents, and different food favorites. New Hampshire has great seafood and Italian food."

"And good pizza."

The left arrow turned green. The line of cars ahead of him moved ahead like a bunch of snails. Just as he reached the light, it turned red. *That figures.* "Bingo, I got an idea. Do you like Chili's? At least it's Tex-Mex."

"I love Chili's, and I love Tex-Mex. That's the type of food we have in Okla." She fell silent.

Franklin glanced at her. She froze with her mouth hung open.

"I get it now," she proclaimed. Oklahoma specializes in Tex-Mex. New Hampshire specializes in Italian food."

"Yes, exactly. But Chili's is about twenty minutes from here. And with all this traffic, it could take a little longer than usual. It's in Tilton."

"I don't care. I want a steak fajita quesadilla."

"Are you sure you can wait?" The light turned green, and he turned onto the interstate.

"Yes, I can wait. If you take me there, you'd make me a very happy granddaughter."

Watching traffic, he merged into the first lane and moved over into the middle lane. "Okay, young lady, Chili's it is."

"Can I get salsa and chips and guacamole too?"

"Absolutely, anything you want."

"Yes!"

Traveling down the highway, she hummed and wiggled like she created her own musical composition.

Maggie blurted, "Claudia is like you. Her favorite color is red."

"Who's Claudia?"

"She's my best friend?"

"Okay. That's good to know. But what makes you think my favorite color is red?"

A smart car passed him, reentered in front of him, and hit the brakes, forcing Franklin to press his brakes. *What an idiot! Why did you pass me?*

"Hmm, how did I figure that out? Let's see. You got a red truck, and you're wearing a red sweater. You have a red jacket in the back seat. You have a lot of red stuff in your house. Grampy, your whole world is red."

"Okay, okay, you smarty pants. That was you're Nana's favorite color too."

"Grampy, how did you and Nana meet?"

Though difficult for him to discuss it, she asked a perfectly normal question. "I met her in kindergarten."

"Kindergarten? You met her way back then?"

"Yes, it was a long-long time ago," he chuckled.

"How many rooms did you have in your school house?"

"What do you mean?" He glanced at her.

With an elbow rested on the door rest and the other on the console, she wore a huge grin. "Well, you said it was a long-long time ago. That leads me to believe you went to a school house like back in the old west days. Did you get to ride horses to school?"

"You're really on a roll today, little mischief."

Taking his eyes off the road, he reached over and tapped her freckled nose.

"Uh-oh!"

"Uh-oh, what?" He turned his head back. "Brake lights!" The rear of a white Suburban got closer by the second. He hit his brakes. "What happened?" His heart galloped.

Both the north and south lanes traffic stopped.

While gripping the steering wheel, his hands trembled. "Maggie, are you okay?"

Wide-eyed, Maggie pointed. "Look! There's a whole herd of deer running down that hill from that rest area."

He dropped his head against the headrest, and closed his eyes. "Something must have spooked them."

When deer crossed the highway, they leaped into the woods off the side of the road. The traffic started moving, real slow.

Down the road, he spotted a Subaru Legacy that resembled Sue Hamilton's vehicle. He rested his arm on the steering wheel and pointed out the windshield. "Look over there in the right lane. Just ahead of us. Is that Sue Hamilton's car?"

"I don't know. I've never seen her car. Which one are you talking about?"

"It's the red one. It's just ahead of that blue minivan."

Maggie lifted herself and peered out the windshield. "I see it."

"That sure looks like her car. Wow, it looks like it bottomed out. The left rear wheel is wobbling."

"I see them!" Maggie gasped, "It is them."

"It is them? It looks as though she has a shock problem."

"What's that?"

He moved ahead of the blue van and pulled up next to the Subaru.

She tapped on the passenger window. "Grampy, there's Lucas. He's sitting in the backseat behind Mrs. Hamilton." She waved."

The more Franklin watched her right rear tire shimmy, the more it concerned him.

"Grampy, you're driving faster than they are."

"I have no choice. I have to go with the flow of traffic." If he could have pulled her over and put Sue and the kids into his truck, he would have.

Maggie exclaimed, "Lucas sees me. He's waving back. But you passed them too fast."

"I told you that I have to move with the flow of traffic."

"I can't see them anymore." She sat back.

"Well, princess, maybe you can see them tomorrow."

"Grampy, did you forget? We're going to church tomorrow."

Though he hadn't, he had hoped she had. "Maybe you can see them after church."

"Aren't you going to feed me after church?"

He figured it out. Her stomach was her first priority in life. "Let not your little heart fear. I plan to feed you."

"Oh good, you worried me. But Grampy, when did you meet Uncle Johnny."

"What are you talking about?"

"You told me how you met Nana. Uncle Johnny is her brother. I was wondering when and how did you meet him."

It amazed him how she could resume a conversation right in the middle of another. "I met him the same time I met Nana. It was the first day of school when we were in kindergarten."

"You grew up with both of them? That's so cool."

"Yes it was. The next exit is Chili's."

He caught a glimpse of Maggie texting. "Who are you texting?"

"My mom. I'm telling her your favorite color is red, but my favorite color is blue."

"Don't tell her we went Christmas shopping."

"I already did."

"Why did you do a thing like that?"

"Why not?"

"Well . . ."

"There it is!" Maggie shrieked, pointing, "The Chili's sign."

Franklin turned off the exit. Though the light was green at the end of the ramp, he slowed and looked both directions before moving through that intersection.

She held her wristwatch up in front of his face. "It's twelve minutes after twelve. How did you do that when we left at quarter to one?"

"Maggie put that down. I need to see." He turned into the parking lot.

"But how did you get here before we left?"

"You must have forgotten to change the time an hour ahead."

"Opps, you're right." She giggled, "I thought that was strange."

He imitated the twilight zone song. "Maybe we time traveled."

She chirped, "That would be fun."

"I can't believe this. Again, there's no where to park. I thought people were eating at the mall. Where are all these people coming from?" He complained.

"Don't worry, I'll help you." She closed her eyes and prayed, "Lord favor, we need to eat."

A few seconds later, a car pulled out in front of him across from the front entrance.

She stretched her neck, pulling her body forward, and moving her head back and forth as he pulled into the space. "You did it! I was worried about how little the space was. You have a big truck."

"How do you do that?"

"Do what?" she removed her seatbelt.

"You pray, and I get a parking space. You pray, and there's a church across the street. You pray, and a strange man with white hair jumps in and helps me."

She dangled a crooked smile. "I didn't pray the church into existence."

"I know that, but you pray and things happen."

"Because I believe that I receive what I pray for, and my prayers are answered. And I have the favor of God. According to Proverbs 12:2, a good man, and a good little girl like me, obtains favor of the Lord. "

It all seemed plausible, but he had his suspicions. Nevertheless, since it benefitted him, he decided to go with the flow. "Come on, and let's get in there. I'm sure we got a long wait ahead of us."

She waggled her finger at him. "There you go again. I already prayed for favor for a table on our way here."

"Good. It's been working, so keep that favor thing going. But you wait in the truck until I come around and get you. There's too much traffic around here."

"Yes Grampy. I know the drill."

When he took her hand, a small car parked in a handicap spot pulled out and stopped the line of traffic. They dashed across the aisle.

Just then, Franklin spotted Mark's Chevy LUV. "You got to be kidding me."

"What's wrong?"

He led her to the LUV.

"Aren't we going inside? I'm starving."

"In a minute, I have to see something."

Standing in front of Mark's pickup, Franklin groaned, "No, no, no, no, no."

"Grampy. What's wrong?"

"That's my neighbor's truck. He's inside Chili's."

"Praise the Lord. It's a divine appointment. We can have lunch with him. Let's go in and find him." She yanked on his hand, but he wouldn't budge.

"I don't want to find him."

"Why not?"

Franklin exhaled. "Okay, I might as well face the music. It was going to happen sooner or later, so today is the sooner."

"What music?"

"Forget about it. Maybe we should go somewhere else."

"Please Grampy. I really want to eat here. You got me hungry for their food."

He gulped. "Okay."

CHAPTER 15

The Luncheon

WHEN FRANKLIN GRABBED THE handle of the front entrance, his hand trembled. He had no doubt in his mind that his worst fear would manifest. Somehow, he would meet up with Pastor Mark.

Several people blocked the way into the foyer. "Princess, we can't even get into the place. We should go."

A man stepped aside. "Oh excuse me. I'm sorry."

The man, and three other people, shuffled around, making room for Franklin and Maggie to come in.

Maggie hopped into the foyer. "See, the favor of God is working."

"Thank you." He maneuvered around others until he found the end of the line at the hostess station. The short line did not represent the traffic in the parking lot.

Maggie wiggled his hand. "Look. There are only a few people in front of us. That's favor."

"They're waiting to give their names," Franklin stretched is hand outward, "and all these people are waiting to be seated."

"Grampy, please, just watch God work."

Not seeing Mark, would work for him. "Okay, princess."

A much older couple stood first in line, speaking with a tall blond woman. A petite brunette walked in from the dinning room. She gathered some menus and led a large group away. That helped thin out the crowded foyer.

"Maggie, I think coming here was a mistake. It'll be at least an hour before we get a table, and you need something to eat."

She rolled her eyes. "Grampy, please don't worry. I'm fine."

"You haven't eaten since early this morning. Maybe we should have stopped at Taco Bell. There's a McDonald's nearby. Would you like to go there instead?"

She contorted her face. "Ew! I told you that I don't eat fast food, and neither do my parents. All those places use hydrogenated oils. It's plastic. God didn't create your body to process plastic."

"Okay, I get it."

"Besides, I told you I have the favor of God. I promise you. We won't have to wait long."

"Okay."

"Look, we're almost up to the lady. Do you see your neighbor, yet?"

"No." He twisted around. Only a young couple was in line behind him. He felt someone tap him on his shoulder. Startled, he spun around.

"Howdy neighbor!"

Mark! Franklin flinched.

"By gosh, I never expected to see you here. How are ya?"

"Fine."

Maggie wiggled Franklin's hand, "Is that your neighbor you didn't want to find?"

Franklin felt his face tighten and his blood rush to his head. A strange noise sounded out of his mouth, "Ooooooo."

Mark's smile grew wide. "It's mighty good to see you neighbor."

With Franklin's brain stuck between gears, he gaped at Mark while Maggie's voice sounded through his ears.

"So he is your neighbor? I saw him standing in front of us, and you didn't see him there. Isn't that hilarious? I told you it was a divine appointment."

Mark slid his eyes downward. "And who is this pretty young lady?"

She offered him her hand. "I'm his granddaughter. My name is Margaret Katherine Harris, but you can call me Maggie."

Mark leaned over and shook her hand. "Hi Maggie. I'm Pastor Mark. It's nice to meet you."

"And it's nice to meet you too."

"So tell me Maggie, how did you know I was here?"

"It was when we were standing in front of your truck, and my grandfather was chanting . . ."

Franklin raised his voice over hers. "I saw your truck parked outside."

Mark stood straight. "Oh, I see."

Placing her purse under her arm, Maggie asked, "Pastor Mark, are you the neighbor who's having church tomorrow?"

"Yes, and I'd love to have you both come visit us."

Oh boy!

"Oh we're going. I was really surprised when I saw your sign, and my grandfather was even more surprise than I was. He didn't want to drive 20 miles to church. I prayed and God showed me your church sign. You should have seen Grampy's face."

"I bet it was priceless."

"Excuse me, can I help you?" The blond hostess interrupted, speaking in a strong New Hampshire accent.

If she had a table for Mark, then Franklin would believe Maggie's favor thing.

"We would like a table for three please, and the name is Maggie."

"Three? Why three?" Franklin eyes blurred.

She pointed toward Mark and she contended with Franklin. "Isn't he your neighbor?"

Franklin froze like a Kakapo in the face of a predator.

Mark scratched the side of his chin. "Yes I am. That's so neighborly of you." Mark looked at Franklin. "I'd love to join you, but we should ask your grandfather first."

With a stoic nod, he indicated his faux approval.

"Grampy does that mean yes?"

He blamed Kitty for passing down the big and asserted mouth gene to his innocent and precious little princess. "Yes, Pastor Mark can join us."

"Yes!" Holding onto the edge of the podium, Maggie stood on her tippy-toes. "Ma'am, do we have a long wait? I'm really hungry."

The sweet faced blond looked downward as she rubbed the seating chart with a shammy cloth. "No. It'll only be a moment."

Maggie pointed behind her. "But, but what about all the people ahead of us?"

"That's a banquet." She tapped a blue marker against the chart.

"What's a banquet?"

The woman replied, "It's when you have a big group coming in to celebrate something. This one is a Christmas paaty."

"Paaty?" Maggie looked over her shoulder at Franklin.

By the puzzlement edge in her face, Franklin had an idea she didn't understand the woman's accent. "Party."

"Since it's only three of you, I can seat you in a few minutes."

That's the favor of God. She looked over her shoulder toward Franklin. "See Grampy, it worked."

Why is this happening to me?

"Yes that's favor." The pastor concurred.

"Pastor Mark, my grandfather and I had favor all day today."

Franklin mumbled, "Oh brother."

Maggie continued, "And because of God's favor we found your church, and the best parking spaces. And now, the lady has a table for us. And, meeting you is a divine appointment, even though my grandfather didn't want to find . . ."

Franklin stepped ahead and bumped her.

She stumbled forward. "Ow!"

Astonished that he almost tripped her, he grabbed her hand, and he held it until she caught her balance. "I'm so sorry." Franklin placed his hand on her back, and leaned his face near hers. "Princess, are you okay? I'm so very sorry."

"It was just an accident. No Worries. I'm okay."

That verified it. Franklin was a rat. "Are you sure?"

The petite brunette emerged with menus in her hand. Addressing Mark, she asked, "Would you like a kids menu?" Her New Hampshire accent was thick.

Maggie interceded, "No thank you. I don't need a menu. I already know what I want."

"Well then, follow me."

The cute and dainty girl had a bounce in her step. She held the menus against her chest, and asked Maggie, "You eat he'ah much?"

She snapped her head toward Franklin.

"She wants to know if you eat here a lot."

She mouthed, "Oh," and replied to the girl, "Not here, but I eat at the Chili's in Broken Arrow, Oklahoma."

"Do you live in Oklahoma?"

"Yes ma'am."

The hostess stopped at an empty booth. "How'd ya like N'hampsha?"

As Maggie slid into the booth, she replied, "I don't know. I never ate that before, but I like your fajitas."

Franklin and Mark cracked-up.

The hostess froze like a statue.

In stitches, Franklin spotted Maggie pouting. He removed his jacket and scooted in the booth next to her.

The hostess left the menus on the table and walked off.

Sitting across from Franklin, Mark rubbed his lips.

"Princess." Franklin placed his arm around her shoulders. "We're not laughing at you. I would never laugh at you. We're laughing at the situation."

With her bottom lip protruding, she asked, "What situation?"

"The girl has a heavy New England accent. When she asked you how you like N'hampsha, she was asking you how do you like New Hampshire."

The pout fell off her face. "I get it. I thought she was asking me about some strange food."

"That's because her accent confused you." He tapped her nose. "Take off your jacket, and put it next to you on the seat."

"Okay, but my mom is from New Hampshire, and she doesn't talk like her."

Franklin helped her pull her arm out of the sleeves of her jacket. "Well, some people speak differently. Before you moved to Oklahoma, you had a bit of a New Hampshire accent too."

"What happened to mine?"

"You moved to Oklahoma, and now you sound more like you're a native from the southwest rather than New Hampshire."

She giggled, "I get it now. I told her I never ate it."

"Yes, and you thoroughly befuddled her." With his arm around her shoulders, he squeezed Maggie.

Mark's hands were folded on top of the menu in front of him. "Maggie, may I add, I'm from out west and sometimes I too have trouble understanding their accents."

Sitting across from Mark, didn't seem as bad as Franklin had thought it would be. But he feared that his boorish and ungrateful behavior would be revealed to his beautiful princess.

Maggie's eyes grew big. "What do you do when you don't understand them?"

"Well," Pastor Mark removed his nit hat, "I simply ask them to repeat themselves. That's all I can do."

"You do? Do they get upset with you?"

"Nah, not at all. They understand, and sometimes they do the same to me. You should never be concerned about being truthful."

"That's what my father says, but some people don't like to hear the truth."

"You're right. But like Jesus, we speak the truth in love."

As soft spoken as Mark was, he never deserved the tongue lashing he had given him. Ready to face the embarrassment, Franklin attempted to apologize. "Mark, I—um—the other day . . ."

Mark raised a dismissive hand. "Hey, I was glad to give you a hand."

"But . . ."

"And I'm glad we're having a meal together." Mark seemed to reassure Franklin.

"Thank you."

That easy? Mark forgave him that easy?

"You're very welcome," Mark replied.

Though he couldn't understand it, he sat back in the booth.

Opening the menu, Mark kept it on the table. "So tell me, what've you two been up to today?"

Franklin answered, "We stopped to get something to eat."

"Grampy, you forgot to tell him we went Christmas shopping."

Oh boy, here we go again.

"You went Christmas shopping? I bet that was fun, especially with your grampy."

Maggie's face lit up like a hundred watt bulb. "It was a lot of fun. Today was the first time in my life I got to go shopping alone with my grandfather. We went to the Maple Edge Mall."

"By golly, I just left that mall. I bought a few gifts for my wife, and I got to witness to a stranger."

"Did that stranger get saved?"

Why the God stuff?

"He sure did."

Maggie slapped her hands together. "Praise the Lord!"

"Hello, I'm Tom, and I'm going to be your server. Can I get you a Strawberry Margarita, Loaded Potato Skins, or. . ."

As the well-built young man delivered the procedural recommendations, Franklin gave his undivided attention due him. That is, until he felt a poke on his side. Maggie beckoned him to lean closer to her.

"When can we order?" She whispered.

"We need to wait until he's finished."

After the waiter had completed his robotic spill, Franklin waited for her to order, but she didn't say a word. "You can order now."

She beckoned him again. As he leaned toward her, she edged closer to him and cuffed her hands over his ear. "Aren't you going to order for me?"

"But you just asked me if you could order."

Taking her hands away from his ear, she bit her lower lip and slammed her eyes shut, letting out a breath. "No I didn't. I asked when we could order. You're supposed to order for me."

"What?"

"My mom says a real gentleman orders for the lady. Daddy orders for us all the time. Remember, I told you what I wanted."

At the time she told him her order, he had no idea she had expected him to follow Emily Post's rules of etiquette by ordering for her. If he had known, he might have paid more attention to her meal order.

"If you haven't decided, I can come back."

Tom appeared antsy. But since the restaurant was packed, Franklin understood. He raised one finger. "Could you hold on for a second more, please?"

She put her elbow on the table and rolled her eyes. "Please just tell him. I'm starving."

Pressured by a rushed server and Maggie's expected gentleman protocol for him, Franklin blurted without thinking. "She would like a fajita steak with the chips and the avocado."

Straightaway, the man's head cocked forward and his eyes popped. "I'm sorry, but I don't think we have that on the menu."

Maggie expelled a deep breath. "No. You said it wrong. It's a steak fajita quesadilla, and chips and salsa with guacamole."

His Kitty turned his princess into a primadonna.

Okay, your Royal Highness. Trying not to laugh, Franklin cleared his throat. "My granddaughter would like the steak fajita quesadilla. But first, bring us an order of chips and salsa with a side of guacamole."

As the server wrote it, he repeated it. While Franklin was listening, he felt a tug on his sweater. Again, she spoke under her breath. "Can I have a Shirley Temple?"

"Absolutely."

When he lifted his head to order the drink, he caught Tom rolling his eyes. Franklin shot him a fiery scowl. "What's that all about?"

The young man flinched.

Franklin glared at the waiter as he waited for an answer. Out of the corner of his eye, he noticed Mark swaying his head between them like a medium speed oscillating fan.

Mark clapped. "By golly, that quesadilla sounds mighty good to me! I'll take one of those."

Still angered by the server's derogatory eye roll, Franklin snarled, "I'll do the same, and you can bring my granddaughter a Shirley Temple, but I'll have lemonade."

Mark raked his fingers through his clean-cut and light-brown hair. "I'll make it easy, ditto that lemonade."

That was the first time Franklin had seen him without a hat. Since the first time he saw Mark, he either wore that stocking hat or cowboy hat.

The server rushed off like an Olympic power racer with his long dark pony-tail flopping around on the back of his shoulders.

Mark asked, "So Maggie, tell me, where did you learn about the favor of God?"

"My mother and father are going to Bible College, and they let me read their books. But I have to wait until they get done with them. My parents taught me that we have the favor of God, but we have to declare it with your mouth. I get miracles when I declare it."

"That's amazing. How old are you?" Mark asked.

Though amazed by Maggie's willingness and ability to read college level books, Franklin found it difficult to process it. She had to have been a prodigy child, and that made him proud.

"I'm eight." She replied.

Mark looked at Franklin. "So is she your daughter's or your son's child?"

"She's my daughter's child."

"Your granddaughter is a blessed child."

In order to prevent any religious conversations, Franklin avoided the blessed thing. He propped his elbows on the table and rubbed his hands together. "So, Maggie, you read your mother's and your father's textbooks?"

"Uh-huh."

"And you understand the information?"

"I've been reading books since I was three. Don't you remember? When my mom and Nana read me the bible, I learned how to read."

He recalled, since Maggie was an infant, Katie and Kitty had read the bible to her. Soon after her third birthday, Katie had told Franklin that Maggie had started reading along with her. Though surprised by it, Franklin had found it remarkable, and believed he had a prodigy grand-daughter. "Yes, now I do."

Mark inquired, "Maggie, are your parents visiting too?"

"No, my parents are in Arizona right now"

Franklin inserted, "My daughter and her husband are there on business."

"And I get to stay with Grampy for five days."

Franklin hung his head. That prompted a bitter reminder that his family would soon be moving to Thailand. He decided that he would rather worry about it when he had to deal with it.

Mark unrolled the green napkin and removed the tableware. "I use to love to stay with my grandparents, especially when they took me on cattle drives." He placed the napkin on his lap and arranged the knife and fork off to the side. "I loved it because we brought the chuck wagon with us, and we camped out under the beautiful Wyoming stars. When I gazed at them, I knew only God could make something that majestic."

Unless Franklin had lost his mind all together, he recalled that Mark had told him he was from Montana. "Wyoming?" His vehicles had Montana Plates as well. "I thought you said you were from Montana?"

"I was born and raised in Sundance, Wyoming. But before my wife and I moved here, we pastored a church in Libby for the past ten years."

"Pastor Mark, where's Libby?"

"Well Maggie, it's a small community in the Northwest area of Montana, and it's not too far from Idaho."

"Is that far away from here?"

"It sure is little lady. It's more than twenty-five hundred miles away."

"Wow, that's a long way."

Mark scratched his stubble-beard. "I was thinking. We've been living across the street from you for a few months. And now we're having lunch together, and I don't know your name."

"Yes, your right. We never did discuss it, did we?" Franklin chortled a bit.

Maggie slapped her hand on the table. "I don't believe it! Why do you think you have to discuss your name? Just tell him what it is."

Cracking a half smile, Mark remarked, "She's a wild one."

"Oh she is, but you don't know the short of it."

"Grampy, are you going to tell him your name is Frank or not?"

"Well actually, my name is Frank. But most people know me as Franklin."

"So Frank is short for Franklin."

"No."

Mark squinted. "So your given name is Franklin."

"No. It's B. Francis Franklyn."

Mark's eyes slid back and forth. "Oh, then most people know you by your last name."

"No, my last name is spelled F-r-a-n-k-l-y-n. I'm talking about Franklin with an i."

Maggie sounded out, "Jesus help us."

Franklin looked at her.

With her head drooped, she had her palms pushed against the sides of her checks. "Grampy I don't believe you."

Franklin felt a bit insulted. "That wasn't nice."

"I'm very sorry Grampy, but Pastor Mark only wanted to know what your name was." she stretched her forefinger over her thumb, "Instead of giving him little tiny answers to a whole lot of questions, please just tell him your name."

"Maggie, that was rude. I'm trying to answer the man's questions."

Her jaw dropped as she sucked in a sharp breath.

Franklin continued his conversation with Mark. "My legal name is Dr. B. Francis Franklyn. My high school coach called me Franklin Franklyn during roll call on the first day of school. As a joke, I answered to it. Since my buddies thought it was hilarious, I kept the name, and it stuck throughout my life. Ever since," Maggie tapped him on the hand, distracting him, "and, um, I've been known as Franklin. That is, by my colleagues and friendly acquaintances."

Maggie placed her hand on Franklin's arm. He placed his hand over hers.

Franklin glanced over to acknowledge her.

Mark asked, "So you're a doctor?"

Franklin looked back at him. "No, I'm an English professor."

"Okay, but how would you like me to address you? Professor Franklyn? Dr. Franklyn?"

"No, neither. Just call me Frank. That's what my real friends call me." His mouth had erupted and his brain had malfunctioned.

It hit him like an aftershock after a large earthquake. Franklin had just called a Jesus freak pastor friend. At once, Franklin's mind scrambled for an excuse out of his idiocy, but it was too late.

Mark had intercepted those words like a quarterback near the goal line with one step in for the touchdown. "Well Frank, it's nice to meet you friend."

"Grampy, why do you have a B for a first name? What kind of parents did you have?"

"Oh silly, my name isn't a B. it's the initial for my first name."

With her eyebrows furrowed, Maggie asked, "Then what does the initial B stand for?"

"Benjamin."

"Benjamin Franklyn?" Maggie hollered. She added, "I remember . . ."

A man in the booth behind Mark looked over his shoulder.

Franklin snapped, "What are you looking at?"

The man jolted back and Mark glanced behind him.

"Frank, nobody needs to guess what's on your mind," Mark commented.

"Unless you gotta ask him his name," Maggie injected.

Franklin nudged her shoulder.

Mark chuckled, "You got a point there, little lady."

"Grampy, I'm starving. How much longer do you think it'll be?"

While looking around, Franklin remarked, "I know. He hasn't been by since he took our order, but it's really busy in here. If he doesn't come by in a few moments, I'll ask somebody to find him."

"Okay, but my stomach is starving."

Mark played with the table knife. "By the way, is there a Mrs. Franklyn?"

Such a harrowing question for Franklin, but it was a normal one. He looked away for a second. "There was. Katie died two years ago in an auto accident."

Mark's smile dropped into a stoic look. "I'm so sorry."

"Thank you."

If Mark had only known that he was about to dine with a murderer, he would run out of this restaurant.

Maggie twisted around and searched through her purse. "Here it is." She held up a picture of Katie with Maggie on her lap. "Pastor Mark, this is my Nana, but she's in our future, and not in our past."

Stunned by learning she kept Katie's picture in her purse, Franklin's eyes welled up.

As Mark gazed at the picture, his eyes widened. He looked at Franklin. "Maggie's almost a spitting image of your wife."

Franklin sucked in his breath, forcing his tears back. His lips trembled.

"I'm sorry it took so long." Tom interrupted, placing a tray of food and drinks down on its stand. "We're short two people, and it's been hectic." He served Maggie her Shirley Temple first. "Little missy, I gave you two extra cherries."

She pulled a cherry off the plastic toothpick. "Thank you Tom. I'm so starving."

As he gave each of them a small appetizer plate, he added, "Good, I have a surprise for the little missy. I brought you our famous queso skillet. It's on the house since you've been so patient."

Maggie declared, "Now, that's the favor of God!"

No, that's the fear of losing a tip.

"And missy, you aught to dip your chip in the queso first, then in the guac, and then the salsa. Try it, it's my favorite way of eating it."

Her eyes sparkled as she took the chip and dipped it in the condiments. She bit into it. "Mmmm," she flashed him a thumbs up. "I'm so starving. I really appreciate you bringing this out for me. Thank you much."

"You're welcome." He added, "Gentlemen, I'm sorry, but it's going to be a few more minuets before I can bring out your food."

Franklin responded, "I do appreciate you bringing out the dip."

"Sure. If you need anything else, let me know." With the tray in one hand and stand in the other, Tom hurried off.

But before they finished their appetizers, Tom returned with their food.

The three of them spent another half hour together, engaging in casual conversations about the food, the area, hunting and fishing, and such.

But at Franklin's surprise, throughout the entire meal, never once Mark attempted to preach to him or pry into his business. By the time they had gone their separate ways, he had grown fond of the Jesus freak. Nevertheless, that didn't make him any less anxious about attending church the next day.

CHAPTER 16

A Quick Stop for Gift Wrap

On their way home from Chili's, it seemed as though the sun had fallen out of the sky. Franklin merged into the line of the northbound traffic, on the highway. Blinded by headlights behind him, glaring into his review mirror, he flipped the mirror's tab to night mode.

"Grampy, why is it so dark? It's only three-forty-two on the truck's clock."

"The sun is setting and the dark clouds are overshadowing the sunset."

Maggie leaned forward and looked up through the windshield, swaying her head back and forth.

A truck's headlights approaching him from the left lane reflected in his side mirror. At the same time, he felt a blast of cold air.

"Where in the world is that coming from?" He glanced over at Maggie. "Why are you hanging your head out the window? Pull it back in before something hits it and chops it off."

She drew it back in, pushed it against the seat, and held her hand against her throat. "That's a horrible visual!"

"People have lost limbs that way." From the driver's side, he closed her window. "It's freezing out there! Do you want to catch your death?"

"I've told you that don't catch death. Death has no power over me!"

It dawned on him. He figured out what she meant by that. He recalled something Katie had told him. If he would believe what he confessed with his mouth, it would come to pass. But he believed that it would only work if one used their common sense. "Not if you hang your head out the window for some bypassing truck to take cut it off."

"Ew, Grampy, please stop saying that. I don't like the visual. It's scary."

"Maggie, if you confess you'll never drown. But if you jump into the deep end of a pool when you don't know how to swim, what's going to happen to you?"

"I'll drown."

"That's right. What were you thinking when you stuck your head out the window with traffic racing past you?"

"I'm sorry. I was trying to see the clouds."

"Do you see the sun, the stars, or the moon?"

"No," she answered.

"That's because of the overcast."

"Oh. That makes sense. If I don't see anything in the sky besides black, it's cloudy."

"Yes, but it can happen when the sky is polluted with light like in a city."

"Oh, oh, I learned about light pollution in school. My teacher said that man destroys the environment, and light pollution keeps us from viewing the stars. But that was just before my parents put me into the home school co-op.

About a half a mile from his exit, a slow-moving dump truck slowed his speed from sixty-five to forty. Even though it annoyed him, he refused to pass the truck and miss his exit.

Maggie started tapping her fingers on the console. "I had fun with Pastor Mark. He's really a nice pastor. I can't wait to see him in church tomorrow."

I can.

"Grampy, what are we going to do this afternoon?"

Since he had woken early and his day had been hectic, he was ready to go home, put his feet up on his ottoman, and relax for the rest of the day.

He yawned. "What would you like to do?"

"Wrap gifts, and have another one of Annabelle's gingerbread cookies with a cup of your hot chocolate."

"I like that idea! But I don't believe I have any wrapping paper at home. Or do I? Well, instead of taking a chance, we'll stop at Walgreens before we go home."

"Can we get bows and ribbon too?"

"Absolutely."

"Can I pick out the Christmas wrapping and stuff?"

"Absolutely."

When he landed near his off ramp, he accelerated into the exit. He turned onto the main road through town, and turned into the strip mall. But at that time of the day, the parking lot was packed. All the stores were open with the exception of Dina's Donut House.

At his surprise, a mini-van pulled out of a spot in front of him near the Walgreens entrance. He glanced at Maggie. "Well, did you pray?"

"Not this time. But I told you I have the favor of God." She grinned like Garfield.

It reminded Franklin of the night of her Christmas play when she had grinned at the audience. Though a sweet memory, it also reminded him of Katie's death.

If he had known such a joyous evening would have evolved into the most horrific and traumatic life changing event of his life, he would have held Katie tight in his arms. And he would have never gone to the play that night.

When he pulled into the space, Franklin let the engine idle as he gazed out the windshield.

"Grampy," Maggie called out, "Are you okay?"

Forcing back the tears, he wished he had died with Katie to end his endless nightmare.

A tapping on his side window startled him. "It's Bob!" He let down the window.

Bob's face appeared small with the fur-lined hood over his head. "Hello my friend. I never expected to see your ugly face with such a pretty little lady."

"She's much safer with me than in the range of your long-French ugly beak."

"You got me!" Bob laughed out loud.

Franklin released his seatbelt. "What are you doing here?"

"I come to pick up Annabelle's prescription."

"Is Annabelle sick?"

"She has a," Bob tapped his forehead, "a sinus infection. But she'll be okay."

With Bob's forearm leaning on the edge of the truck's windowsill, he put his face near the open window, and waved to Maggie.

She waved back vigorously. "Hello Mr. Bob."

"Hello little missy! Did you have fun today with your grampy?"

"Uh-huh, I had lots of fun. And we're going to wrap gifts, and we're going to eat another one of Miss Annabelle's cookies with hot chocolate."

"Ooh, that sounds good. But I never get cookies and hot chocolate for supper."

With her top teeth on her lower lip, Maggie declared, "Oh no, they're not for supper. That's just an appetizer. Right Grampy?"

That comment amazed Franklin. They had just got done eating a huge meal at Chili's. "How much can you eat?"

"I told you that I believe I have a fast metabolism. I can eat lots more than the average little girl."

Both men cracked up.

Reaching for his keys, Franklin shut down the truck. "By the way, I saw your tenant, Mrs. Hamilton."

"Yes, Sue Hamilton."

"I saw her on the highway earlier. Her legacy bottomed out when she hit a rut. . ."

"Yes, yes."

" . . .and her left rare wheel shimmied. It appears that her shocks may be worn."

"Yes, you're correct my friend. She has a lot of problems with that car." Bob tilted his head and narrowed his eyes. "I like to tell you what I planned. Maybe you can help, yes?"

"Yes maybe. But first I need to know what your plan is."

"We talk inside where it's warm, yes?"

Franklin heard Maggie pop the passenger door open. "Maggie wait until I come around to get you."

"Okay, I'm sorry."

When he helped her out, she put her hat on, and tugged it straight. Franklin took her hand, and she skipped along his side until they went through the automatic doors. Bob followed them in.

Inside, Franklin took one of the last two shopping carts. Scooting the cart out of the way of the door, Franklin readied himself to hear what Bob had in mind. "This place is a madhouse!"

"They have a big sale today." Bob tossed his hood off his head. "I go get Annabelle's prescription, and then we can talk. Where will you be?"

That was not what nosey Franklin wanted to hear. Nevertheless, he understood that Bob's wife of sixty years was his life. She always came first.

"We'll be in the gift wrapping aisle."

"Okay, I see you in a few minutes, yes?"

"Yes, my good friend."

Maggie slipped off her mittens and her hat, and she tossed them on the shopping cart's child seat. "Can I push the basket?"

Franklin looked around him. "What basket?"

"The one you're holding, silly," she chuckled.

"You mean the buggy?"

"You're the funniest Grampy, ever! Why do you call it a buggy? That's what baby's ride in."

"I'm glad you're amused. But as we agreed, I'll push while you pick out the gift wrap."

She wiggled her forefinger. "Unh-unh! Our original agreement did not include pushing the basket. Our plan was that I get to pick out the gift wrap."

"Well, that's the new plan. Grab hold of the side of the buggy, and let's get going."

Walgreens had allocated two aisles for Christmas decorations, which included prepackaged food gifts and gadgets, such as head lamps and manicure sets.

"Grampy, look how crowded it is. Isn't this exciting?"

"No."

"But Grampy, it's the hustle and bustle of Christmas."

"Then start the hustle and bustle through those rolls of Christmas paper."

Franklin stayed near Maggie and scooted the basket close to the shelves, so others could get by him, as he awaited her decision.

She hovered over a box of Christmas paper. Pulling out rolls of paper one at a time. She examined each one before she shoved the roll back into its spot.

Franklin spotted assorted bows packed in bags piled high on the top shelf, along with packages of ribbon tucked into two small shelves below the top shelf.

A woman with green hair, with two small children riding in the basket, entered into the crowed aisle.

"Maggie, can't you find anything you like?"

"Yes, I found two, but I can't make up my mind which one I want, and I need to make sure there's nothing better."

The longer Franklin stood in that crowed area, the warmer he got. "Buy them both."

"I can? Yes!"

She dropped them into the basket. With her hands down by her sides, Maggie started scanning the aisle.

"Maggie, what are you looking for?"

"I can't find the bows and ribbon."

"They're over your head." Franklin reached up and grabbed packages of bows and ribbon. "Let's get out of here."

"But Mr. Bob is supposed to meet us here, and we need to get name tags."

While Franklin searched for the name tags, sweat beaded on his forehead. But every time he wiped it off with his handkerchief, his forehead became sweatier.

He threw his hands up. "This is ridiculous! This entire side of the aisle is allocated for gift wrapping, but I can't see the name tags."

Standing near the end of the shopping cart, Maggie requested, "If you move over some, I can look on the bottom shelf near you."

As he scooted the cart, she squeezed through the narrow space. "I can't see any name tags yet. Can you scoot over a little more?"

"Maybe they have the name tags across from us." But on the other side of the aisle were assorted Christmas stockings, garland, and boxes of Christmas lights.

A man passing Franklin commented, "I've search all the Christmas aisles. They don't have them. I called my wife. She believes Rite Aid might have the tags."

"Thank you. I appreciate the information."

"No problem."

"I heard him," Maggie yelled. She shimmied out, and she threw her arms over the end of the basket. "Grampy it's hot in here." She unzipped her jacket.

"I know. Let's get out of here."

"But we need to wait for Mr. Bob."

"We'll find him. I need air, and I need it now."

With Maggie by his side, Franklin shoved his way out of the aisle. He rushed to the front entrance. As he stood near the doors, cold air flowed as the automatic doors opened and closed. The air felt good against his face. He unzipped his jacket, and opened it wide as he breathed in the fresh crisp air. "Oh man, that feels so good."

"It does. It feels so very good," Maggie concurred.

He glanced over. Maggie held her jacket wide open as well.

Just then, a teen clerk pushed a line of shopping carts through the front entrance. When the young man shoved them into the cart area, Franklin hurried over to him. "Can you please tell me where you keep your name tags?"

The man described where they were, while moving his hands according to the direction he gave Franklin. "They're at the end of aisle seven, past the motor oil, and on the top right side, across from the office supplies."

"What? The name tags are in auto parts?"

"No. Auto parts are on aisle eleven. Would you like me to show you?"

"I don't care about auto parts," Franklin snapped, "Why aren't the name tags with the gift wrapping supplies?"

"I don't know. You'll have to ask management."

"Management?"

"Would you like me to call her for you?"

Franklin barked, "No!"

The teen winced.

"If she's the idiot responsible for organizing this store and training you, I have nothing to say to her." Franklin stomped off murmuring about the idiots with Maggie sprinting along his side.

When he turned into the aisle, he spotted Bob on the other end passing by.

Pointing and out of breath, Maggie blurted, "There's Mr. Bob."

Bob halted and raised a greeting hand.

"Wait there. That's where we need to be," Franklin called out.

"Grampy, why are we the only ones in this aisle? All the other aisles were busy."

"Nobody expects the name tags with the motor oil."

"My good friend, you don't look very happy, no?"

Wounded up tighter than a traffic jam after the Fourth of July fireworks, Franklin vented his disgust with the store. "Bob, you won't believe this!" He placed his hands on his hips. "Name tags are down here with the motor oil. But everything you need to wrap Christmas gifts is down aisle four and auto parts are on aisle eleven."

The corners of Bob's mouth turned up. "Maybe they ran out of room, yes."

"You would find it amusing." Tight lipped, Franklin tilted his head off to the side.

"Tell me, how does it benefit you to get so upset over something so little?"

Franklin stared motionless. His sharp-witted friend whacked him with an eye-opener.

"Why get sick inside over where the store puts the name tags? How does that make sense?"

Franklin dropped his head. He closed his eyes. He lifted his head. "You're right, my friend. I let too much bother me. I feel so foolish."

"Foolish? Why? We've all done it. One day I asked my self, self why get sick over something stupid? Then I laughed at the ridiculous matter. I use to have high blood pressure. No more. I learned to laugh. Now the doctor tells me that I have blood pressure like a man that runs in the marathon."

Maggie snapped her fingers. "Grampy, Jesus said that a merry heart is good like medicine."

Bob raised his forefinger upward. "A-ha! Maggie this is true. It's in Proverbs 17."

Though Bob was a faithful Catholic, Franklin had never heard him refer to scripture before then.

"Frank remember, it's the little things that build up and make you bitter, and it's not good for your health."

Franklin nodded.

Bob pointed his hand toward Maggie, "You want to stay healthy for this little one, yes?"

Franklin glanced at Maggie. She stared at him with her hands on her hips. By the look in her eyes, he knew she was waiting for an answer.

"Of course I do."

Maggie beamed. "Praise the Lord!" She leaped with her feet tucked under her. "My prayers have been answered."

"What prayers?" Franklin asked.

"Ever since Nana went home to be with Jesus, I've been praying everyday that you'll be at my wedding. And my little girl can know you like I do. Because I know she'll love you almost as much as I love you."

Franklin's eyes flooded with tears. It hadn't dawned on him that since she had lost her Nana, she was afraid of loosing him too.

Out of the corner of his eye, he spotted Bob wipe tears from his eyes. "Tell me Maggie, why would she almost love him as much as you do?"

"Nobody can ever love Grampy like I do."

"Princess," Franklin said as he squatted and opened his arms. She ran into them. He held her close, rubbing her back. "I promise you, I will do whatever it takes to keep myself healthy, so I can be at your wedding and be there for your little girl."

"Thank you, Grampy. I thank you Jesus, too."

He kissed her on the head. "I love you." He noticed Bob with his back toward them removing his handkerchief from his back pocket.

"I love you too Grampy."

A foghorn type of nose blow sounded.

Maggie jerked backward. "What was that?"

"Mr. Bob blowing his nose." Franklin chuckled.

"That was Mr. Bob?" She cracked up. As she held her stomach, she tottered around the aisle.

Bob turned around with a grin on his face as he rubbed his nose with the handkerchief.

Franklin declared, "You sounded like a tugboat in distress."

Chortling, Bob shrugged his shoulders.

He noticed Bob's swollen and bloodshot eyes. Maggie must have touched Bob's huge and warm heart too.

"By the way, Bob. What do you have on your mind for your tenant?"

"You know Tony Bianchi?"

Maggie stopped laughing and moved closer to Franklin.

"Yes, he opened Bianchi Chrysler dealership. But now his grandson runs the place." Franklin replied.

"Yes, that would be Mitchell Bianchi. He added Subaru to the dealership. Tony told me Mitchell has a used Subaru on his lot. He believes it's in good shape, but he doesn't know what Mitchell's asking price is. And he was sure I can get a good deal for it.

Sue, she tries very hard, but she doesn't make much money, and now she has two children to support," Bob hung his head and swayed it, and added, "Those poor little ones. They're too young to suffer so much. But if the vehicle is good and I can get a good deal, Uncle Taki is going to chip in with me. Then we buy it for her."

It seemed like the right thing to do. The woman was in need for a car. "So Bob, would you would like me to chip in something too?"

Bob swayed his head. "No. Do you remember my granddaughter, Alice?"

Since Bob had twenty-three grandchildren and eight great-grand children, Franklin made an intelligent guess. "Isn't she the Marine biologist?"

"Yes, Alice and her husband both study Manatees in Florida. She's expecting her first baby any day, and I'm taking my wife to Florida next week. Annabelle, she wants to be there for when the baby comes."

"Okay, so what does that have to do with me?"

"You know a lot about cars. It wasn't to long ago when you and Johnny use to restore old trucks and cars together. I would like you to check out the car for me, and see if it's reliable. If you can, I would like you to help make the deal for me. And you can call me. Taki can't go. He has Christmas parties and a wedding to cater next week."

"Cater? When did he start catering his doughnuts?"

"Last year. The people want doughnut cakes." Bob shrugged, "Don't ask me why. It's the new generation." He raised his hands up. "If they like it, let them have it. It's good for Taki. He makes good money doing doughnut cakes."

"Grampy, remember the wedding I told you about. The one where I had lobster for an appetizer."

"Yes."

"They had a doughnut cake and a cupcake cake, and they were real good."

Bob noted, "See, there you go!"

"Yes, I see what you mean. But I won't be able to get to the dealership until Thursday or Friday. I have Maggie, and Kitty's returning from her trip on Wednesday."

"I understand. You and Maggie need to visit together. Thursday, Friday either is fine."

"But the car may be gone by then?"

"No. Tony said Mitchell will keep it in the back lot for us. Can you check it out for me?"

"Absolutely."

A huge smile popped on his face. "Thank you. I knew I could depend on you."

"Praise the Lord! Grampy, do you realize Jesus gave us two divine appointments today?"

Bob's brows bumped together and his head cocked and tilted. "What did she say about appointments?"

Oh boy. Before Franklin could intercede, he heard Maggie's voice blast in his ears.

"Mr. Bob, Jesus set this appointment up so Grampy can help you and Mrs. Hamilton, and earlier. . ."

Franklin darted wide-opened eyes at her as he pressed his lips together.

She flinched.

Bob slid his eyes back and forth. "Okay. I better get Annabelle's medicine home before she worries. She's making Cog au vin for supper."

"What's that?" Maggie asked.

"It's a chicken cooked in red wine. It's my favorite. Your Grampy makes good Cog au vin. But sorry my friend, my Annabelle makes the best."

Just then, an elderly man with a walker came into the aisle. After a brief few seconds, a woman appeared and hollered, "Dad, you're in the wrong aisle. It's the next one over."

"Bob I'll talk to you next week. You have a good trip."

"Thank you, my friend." Passing by Maggie, he rubbed her head. "You be good."

"I will."

Franklin placed his hand on Maggie's shoulder. "Come on, princess. Let's get out of here."

As Franklin turned the cart half way around, Maggie grabbed it. "But we have to get the name tags."

"I forgot. Let's get them and get out of here."

When Franklin reached for the tags, Maggie asked, "Why didn't you let me tell Mr. Bob about our two divine appointments today?"

He tossed the package of name tags into the cart. "I understand you have a lot of faith. You also have an excellent understanding of the bible. But you don't shove your knowledge down others throats. It's like feeding a baby. You don't shove steak down a baby's throat if he doesn't have any teeth."

"Wow, you talk like Daddy does. When you get saved, you're going to have a lot of wisdom."

He had enough talk about him becoming a Jesus freak. "What makes you think I'm going to get saved?"

Skipping along, she simply answered, "Because I prayed for you," and she proceeded to play imaginary hop-scotch as they headed for the check-out.

Though her nonchalant confidence alarmed him, Franklin was an intelligent human being, and incapable of being fooled by the tricks of the hypocritical Jesus freaks. Not that his daughter or Maggie were hypocritical. He understood they were brainwashed. But he couldn't be brainwashed. He was too smart for that.

CHAPTER 17

Johnny Attends Mark's Church

THE NEXT MORNING, FRANKLIN opened his front door. A line of cars were turning onto Mark's property. He pushed open the storm door. A rush of cold air smacked him in the face. A whoosh of wind slammed the door against his shoulder. He held the door open. The numerous cars parking on Mark's plowed hay lot nerved him.

Franklin zipped his jacket all the way up to his throat and tossed his hood over his head. He stepped out onto the porch, and he closed the storm door behind him. With his hands in his jacket pockets, he couldn't understand why he had never seen all that activity around Mark's place before that day.

Maggie stepped out onto the porch. "Grampy, I'm ready." Wearing a red French beret in a cutesy tilt, she raised her arms, holding her blue bible case. "Do you like my outfit?" She swayed back and forth, showing off her red woolen dress coat.

"Who's this pretty little lady?"

She giggled, "You know it's me."

"By gosh this beautiful little princess is you!"

"Thank you. Mom and I bought this outfit just in case we went somewhere special, like church." She leaned over and pulled up her coat exposing the black lace along the hem of her dress. "I really like the lace. My mom helped me pick out the dress, and the red tights were my idea."

Looking downward, she rested her foot on the small square heel of her black boot. "And, I picked out the boots. Mom liked them too. She said they have a lot of tread on them like a tire."

"That's what you want so you don't slip when you walk on snow and ice."

"Yes, my mom looks for safety in items as well as pretty."

Another gust of wind came swirling through. She grabbed the top of her hat. "So you like my new outfit?"

"That's a pretty outfit, but you make it beautiful."

A sparkling smile popped across her face. "Thank you. And you look very handsome too."

"Well thank you princess."

She walked over to the porch banister with short quick steps. "Look at all the people going to church. This is going to be so much fun!"

She called church fun? Hunting was fun, but he dreaded church, especially that day. "Give me your hand before the wind blows you over there."

"You're funny." Her eyes widened. "Opps," she shoved a hand in her front pocket and pulled out the wolf mittens. "I forgot to put these on. My mom wants me to wear the red gloves with this outfit. But I left them inside, because I like these better. Can I wear them instead?"

If it were up to him, he would allow her to wear the gloves of her choosing, but he couldn't go against his daughter's instructions. "I don't mind whichever pair you wear, but we have to honor your mother by doing what she had told you to do. Run inside and get them, and I'll wait here for you."

"Okay Grampy. You're right. Can you hold my purse and my bible?"

She came out wearing red-ski gloves. "I'll take my stuff back now."

"Here's your purse. But I'll hold your bible. so you can hold my hand."

"That's a good idea. You get to touch the Word of God, and that's a good thing. The Word of God is alive."

"Paper was alive when it was in tree form." He took hold of her hand. "Ready?"

Wide-eyed and wide-grinned, she nodded.

At his surprise, she didn't address his comment. "Good, let's get at it."

As they stepped onto the road, he could feel his heart race. Franklin hadn't been in Mark's house since Rita Steinberg's funeral. In spite of the Steinbergs had led Katie to the holly roller religion, he loved the kind-hearted and selfless couple. He missed them more than he had imagined he would.

Maggie wiggled his hand. "Why are you so quiet?"

"I was thinking about the people who use to live in Mark's house."

She swung his hand. "I kind of remember them. They were very, very old with lots of wrinkles, and gray hair. She gave me cookies, and she wore a blue apron with little red roses on it. He laughed a lot. What were their names?"

"Rita and Joe Steinberg."

"Grampy, do you miss them?"

"More than you can imagine. Whenever one of us got a cold or the flu, Rita made us a big pot of her scrumptious Matzah balls in her delicious hot chicken broth. She called it her Jewish medicine."

"What's a Matzah ball?"

"They're a big Jewish dumpling made from a meal called Matzah."

"I like dumplings, but what does a Matzah ball taste like?"

"Stand back!" A silver mini-van rushed by and continued down the road. "What kind of idiot is that?"

"Grampy remember? Don't let the little things make you angry."

"You're right, princess." *But the man is still an idiot.*

As they drew closer to Mark's place, images of Rita waving to him flashed in his mind.

That autumn day when he had approached his driveway, he had spotted Rita standing on her white porch. Before turning into his driveway, he stopped, and let down his truck's window.

With her blue glove over her tiny hand, she waved as she shouted, "Frank, don't ever forget what I told you. God is not a religion. He's a person, and don't ever forget that Jesus loves you!" A few hours later, they had gotten the news that she had passed away in her recliner."

"Grampy."

"Yes."

"Are you still thinking about those people?"

"Yes, I was thinking about the day Rita had passed away."

"Did she know Jesus?"

Franklin could never figure out why Christians had to ask a question like that. They must have trained Maggie good. He believed in God and he figured anyone who believed in God would know He existed. "Both of them were Christians. They taught Nana about God, and that's why Nana became a Christian."

Maggie hopped onto Mark's property. "Really. Then that's why almost all of us are Christians now. But soon it'll be all of us."

Though he had enough of her delusional faith stuff, he shrugged it off. He had no doubt that the Jesus freaks couldn't brainwash him, like they had done to his innocent wife and daughter.

"Grampy look," she pointed, "Pastor Mark's house is beautiful."

"Yes it is."

"I like that light yellow. There's a house in Tulsa that has a dark yellow, and it's ugly."

"I imagine. Is it the blinding type of yellow, like being blinded by the sun?

"Exactly."

While studying the new features on the house, he spotted a sign nailed to the front porch column. It read, "Church in the guest house" with an arrow pointing toward the left of the house.

Several people were walking along the new cobblestone pathway in front of them.

"Are we going to that house?" She pointed toward the two bedroom guest home.

"Yes, that's where it is." About seven years prior, Franklin had helped them remodel the guest house. Though it looked different on the outside, it couldn't change the fact that the home belonged to Rita and Joe.

"It's so cute. It looks like a miniature of the big house."

"Yes it does." He did like the modern facelift their son had given the house before he had placed it on the market.

Maggie swayed his hand. "I'm so excited." While climbing up the three front steps, Maggie added, "Thank you for taking me today. I love you."

"You're very welcome. I love you too, princess."

When he reached for the door handle, the door opened. Taken by surprise, Franklin stepped back. "Johnny, what are you doing here?"

Franklin couldn't think of any worse scenario than being seen in church by Johnny.

Wearing a mischievous grin, Johnny replied, "I attend church here. What brings you to church today?"

"How long have you been coming here?" Franklin snarled.

"Okay, Frank. You don't have to answer my question." He looked down at Maggie. "I have a feeling I know who brought you here. I've been coming here for about two months, now."

From inside, Mary waved.

"Aunt Mary," Maggie ran into her arms. "I can't believe you're here."

Infuriated, Franklin edged toward Johnny. "Why didn't you tell me there was a church here?"

Johnny chortled, "You live across the street from it. Why don't you look out your window?"

Someone tapped Franklin on the shoulder. He jerked his head around.

A round faced man with bright red cheeks stood behind him. The man asked, "Would you mind going in? It's cold out here for our baby."

Franklin twisted around and noticed a woman holding a toddler in her arms. "I'm sorry, Ma'am." He stepped inside, and he allowed the young couple to pass by him.

Franklin spotted Mary leaning over Maggie whispering in her ear. He suspected Johnny had plotted a scheme to get him in church.

Maggie held onto Mary's hand. "Grampy, isn't it too cool that Aunt Mary and Uncle Johnny come here? I'm so happy. Aren't you?"

He gritted his teeth. "Yes, I'm as thrilled as a mouse finding cheese in a trap."

"But Grampy that doesn't sound like you're happy to see them, and that's not nice."

Glaring at Johnny, Franklin gave Mary a half hug. "Like always, it's a pleasure to see you Mary"

Hugging him back, she replied, "It's nice to see you too."

Johnny's smile fell off his face. "What about me?"

After catching Mary whisper in Maggie's ear, he had no doubt that Johnny had used Maggie and Mary to get him into church. He gritted his teeth, "I'll talk to you later."

"What?" Johnny asked, "What's the matter with you?"

Franklin took Maggie by the hand. "Let's go find a seat."

Resisting his lead, she asked, "Can we sit with Aunt Mary and Uncle Johnny, please?"

Johnny clapped his hands. "That's a fantastic idea!"

He snarled at Johnny.

She dropped her hand out of his, and placed her hands on her hips. "Grampy please. They're our family."

"But they're probably sitting in the front row, and I. . ."

"You're correct." Johnny placed his hand on Maggie's shoulder. "Can you see our coats hanging over the chairs?"

"No. There are too many people in the way."

Johnny lifted her up. "How about now? They're in the front row just like your Grampy said. Do you see the empty seats next to ours?"

"I can see them. You can put me down now."

Franklin moved close to Johnny and sneered, "Thank you for the front row seating, brother-in-law."

"You're very welcome. Anything for family."

Maggie tugged Franklin's hand. "Come on Grampy."

Aggravated, Franklin followed Maggie.

He felt strange in that great room without the Steinbergs there. The entire space had changed. The familiar warmness of the Steinberg's furniture and décor were gone as though it had never existed. The color theme they had replicated from the shades of the blue and white in Israel's flag had been replaced with neutral beiges and neat rows of tan church chairs.

But the basic shades made a great backdrop for the Christmas tree adorned with large-red-glass ornaments, silver bows, and ice-blue garland with numerous glittering white lights.

It thrilled Franklin to see the original woodstove kept the great room cozy as it did when the Steinbergs owned the place. It was a wonderful and familiar sight.

When they reached the front row, it irked Franklin even more that their seats were in front of the preacher's wooden podium.

Since he did not have enough room for his legs, Franklin kept his feet tucked under his chair. Fuming over his seat, he crossed his arms across his chest. Though there were no people on the row, every seat had either bibles or coats left on the seats. It seemed he always ended up with the bad deal.

CHAPTER 18

The Church Service

MAGGIE SWUNG HER FEET and played with her fingers, whereas he sulked about his situation. Just then, the four members of the worship team sauntered over to their instruments, which consisted of a keyboard, a set of drums, and two electric guitars.

To avoid eye contact, he lowered his head, pretending to read the church bulletin.

"Grampy, are you going to take off your jacket?"

"I forgot." He slipped it off, twisted around, and hung it on the back of his chair.

Maggie poked him in his side. "Look! Somebody's waving at you."

"What? Who's waving?" Franklin twisted back around.

"That guy. Right there. He's holding a black guitar."

He muttered, "Craig Mason?"

Seeing Craig delighted Franklin. His former student, from that past fall semester, was the brightest student he had in a long time. Excited about seeing Mr. Mason, Franklin raised his hand and waived back. But it dawned on him that Craig saw him in church. Embarrassed by it, Franklin's smile melted."

Franklin felt someone sit down on the other side of him.

"Howdy neighbor!"

Startled, Franklin blurted, "Pastor Mark! I didn't expect to see you here."

"Really? Every so often, I come by to preach."

Maggie cracked-up, "Grampy he's the pastor. He has to be here."

A woman sitting close to Mark busted out laughing. Franklin surmised she must have been the preacher's wife.

Franklin stumbled over his words. "I didn't mean that—I meant—you surprised me!"

Mark leaned forward. "Sometimes I do that to people, especially when they find out I'm a pastor."

Franklin chuckled, "That I believe."

Pastor Mark leaned closer to Franklin. "Speaking from experience, brother?"

"Absolutely, I'm quite familiar with your heart-stopping stentorian introductions."

Wiggling his finger, Mark bantered, "Now, now, now, it's obvious you had never attended the Emily Post Institute of Etiquette."

"I didn't need to. I found my good conduct list in a box of Cracker Jacks!"

Maggie shook Franklin's arm. "I don't get it. What's so funny?"

Franklin touched her nose. "I'm sorry, it's grown up jokes."

"Frank, I'm embarrassed, I forgot to introduce you to my wife, Grace."

The long-legged woman looked different up close. Though he had imagined she looked more like Popeye's girlfriend, Olive Oil, she was much prettier than she had appeared from a distance. Her sandy-blonde and shoulder-length hair complimented her button nose.

"It's good to finally meet you, Frank. Mark told me a lot about you."

He leaned to reach around Pastor Mark to shake her hand. "Was it good or bad?"

She placed her finger under her short chin. "Let me see."

He had no doubt that the lady was a prankster. "It was all bad, wasn't it?"

"No, just kidding." She shook his hand.

While strumming his guitar, Craig's gentle voice sounded through the microphone. "A brother I admire and have the utmost respect for is visiting with us today."

Franklin didn't know Craig had a brother. He knew he had two sisters.

"He's a man with a prestigious reputation, and it was an honor to have studied under him."

Uh-oh, No! Don't!

"Everyone, let's give a big welcome of applause to the distinguished Professor Franklyn."

Everything went blur. Franklin's ears deafened. He couldn't feel his heart beat. He placed his hand over his chest. *Hooray! I'm dead.*

Maggie patted him on the leg. "Grampy, stand up so everyone can see you."

"By golly, that's quite a welcome. Stand up brother." Pastor Mark's voice reverberated through Franklin's ears.

Oh No! I'm still alive. Franklin glanced at Craig.

Clapping and wearing a bright and sunny smile, Craig animated a gestured for Franklin to stand. "Professor, please stand up so everyone can see you."

With his body stiff like a piece of petrified wood, Franklin stood.

Maggie's face was compared to a mother who had been filled with pride over her child. "Come on Grampy, turn around so everyone can see your face."

I can't ditch the kid. He turned around and nodded with a counterfeit smile as he mouthed, "Thank you." *I think I'm going to faint.*

Craig leaned into the microphone, "Professor, I would like to thank you. You have inspired me to change my major from psychology to English. Thank you sir. It was an honor to be in your class. And to see you in my church is a miracle."

The applause resounded.

Miracle? Why did he say that?

Franklin nodded as he mouthed, "sure." The room started spinning. He felt faint. It was as though, the floor got closer to him. He sat down. Nauseated, the thought of barfing up his breakfast added to his anxiety.

The clapping stopped and the music sounded. Craig shouted, "Let's stand up and worship our Lord for all His goodness and grace!" As he strummed the guitar, he added, "He's worthy of our praise!" His straight golden hair bounced on his shoulders.

Franklin felt his knees buckling under him when he stood for Maggie's sake. His legs wobbled.

He attempted to devise an escape plan, but he couldn't think straight with all the noise blaring in his ears.

Mortified by the crowd, he spotted Johnny, with a few other men, placing folding chairs in the middle aisle along the rows. *I'm surrounded by Jesus freaks.*

He saw Mary, standing next to Maggie. How could she have gotten into the row without him seeing her?

After the crowd had repeated lyrics to several Christian Christmas songs, the music stopped, and Mark strolled to the podium. The church remained standing until he signaled for them to sit. After his salutation, a few comical one-liners, and several announcements, the pastor opened his black-leather bible.

"I would like you to turn with me to Luke 2:13-14."

While he turned the pages of his bible, Mark spoke a bit on God's love.

Maggie slid one side of her bible onto Franklin's lap. Under her breath, she said, "You can share with me."

Oh, Brother! He whispered, "Thank you."

"Is everybody in Luke?" Mark glanced around the church. "Let's place our eyes on the Word."

> And suddenly there was with the angel a multitude of the heavenly host praising God and saying: Glory to God in the highest, And on earth peace, goodwill toward men."

With his bible opened in one hand, Mark moseyed away from the pulpit.

"A multitude, it was a multitude of the heavenly host shouting. There was so much excitement in Heaven that the Angels voices rumbled on the earth. Do you understand what I am saying church?" He raised his palm upward as he emphasized, "The rumbling and thundering of voices from the Heavenly Hosts were so powerful, it was heard on earth."

Several voices sounded behind Franklin, shouting Hallelujahs.

While pacing with his bible draped over his hand, he continued, "Their voices blasted down from Heaven because Christ was on the earth to consummate God's great plan of redemption. Prophecies of His birth were fulfilled. Jesus became man to redeem us from the law of sin and death. Church, now that's something to shout about!"

A rumbling of applause and more shouts of Hallelujahs as well as praise the Lord boomed throughout the room, piercing Franklin's ears. He winced.

"Before we move on, let's do a word study on peace. It's not the English passive version. . ."

Franklin snapped his head toward Maggie. It hit him. She had gotten the word study concept from church.

". . .like in the sixties." Mark flashed the peace sign with a stupid grin on his face. Laughter erupted throughout.

"This word peace in the Greek is translated as nothing missing nothing broken, whole, wholeness, complete, putting everything back into order, and victory over the enemy."

Fascinated that the word study meant translating words from its original Greek text, it interested Franklin to learn more. He stretched his arm over the back of Maggie's chair.

"Sometimes violence may be involved to put things back in order like destroying an enemy through war. Who's the enemy?"

Several people shouted out "Satan," as a few shouted, "the devil."

"Yes folks, your right. Satan is the enemy. He came to steal, kill, and destroy. But God created the earth for man. Turn with me to Genesis 1:26.

> Let us make man in our image, after our likeness: and let them have dominion over the fish of the sea, and over the fowl of the air, and over the cattle, and over all the earth, and over every creeping thing that creeps upon the earth.

"When Adam gave his dominion over to the devil, sin, sickness, and disease came onto the earth . . ."

The preacher got Franklin thinking. If God had given man dominion, then God expected man take the dominion over the earth, period. If stupid Adam didn't turn the dominion over to the devil, there wouldn't be any tragedies, sicknesses, or pains. Franklin found it amusing that Pastor Mark got him to think like a Christian.

". . .in His image. Therefore, He created earth and everything in it for man. God did not make man for the earth. Contrary to popular opinion, earth is not our mother."

"He's got a point there," Franklin muttered.

"God put all the resources on earth for man. God created the garden with everything man needed before he put man into the garden. When the Lord created Adam, he blessed man. In the Hebrew, the word blessed means to empower."

He liked Mark's technique of teaching rather than preaching.

"God empowered man and gave man dominion over the earth. But Adam committed treason."

Treason?

"Back in the garden, Adam gave dominion over to Satan. Then sin entered when man fell. And Satan thought he ruined God's plan and he destroyed man. I imagine he had a party with all his demon folks. But the devil is a stupid devil. He has an IQ of three.

Along with the rest of the church, Franklin cracked-up.

With his eyebrows lifted and a broad smile across his face, Mark declared, "But God is smarter. In fact, about ten years ago, I had a revelation. God is smarter than me."

This guy made church fun.

"God had a plan. And His plan was Jesus! Folks, let's jump over to chapter three and, ahh, verse fifteen.

> And I will put enmity between thee and the woman, and be-
> tween thy seed and her seed; it shall bruise thy head, and thou
> shall bruise his heel.

This is the first promise of the Savior. And in this verse, Jesus was the seed that bruised Satan's head and heel. Now, that's something to shout about!"

When Franklin had gone to church with Katie, on rare occasions, her pastor bored him.

"Paul said in Romans 16:20. Folks, you don't have to turn to it. I'm reading it from the New Living translation.

> The God of peace will soon crush Satan under your feet. May
> the grace of our Lord Jesus be with you."

There's that word peace. "Interesting, peace will crush," he mouthed.

"Folks, God is a God of peace, but Jesus had to die. I'd like to read Hebrews 2:14–15 from the New Living Translation as well. We'll put it up on the screen.

> Because God's children are human beings—made of flesh and
> blood—the Son also became flesh and blood. For only as a hu-
> man being could He die, and only by dying could He break the
> power of the devil, which had the power of death."

Pastor moved closer to the front row. "Jesus had to die. Folks that's violence. Jesus disarmed, defeated, and put Satan to open shame at Calvary. When God rolled that stone away, the veil tore. God and man were reconciled.

That's the peace the Angels were shouting about! Through Christ Jesus, the dominion is ours. The devil has no more authority here unless we give it to him. And when Jesus comes back, the devil is finished. Jesus is coming! That's something to shout about!" Mark's feet took off dancing, hoping, and kicking as he shouted, "Glory to God! He's coming! Hallelujah!"

Since Jesus destroyed Satan's power over death, then who killed Katie? Franklin did. He couldn't even blame the devil for that. Franklin has no one to blame but himself. He killed his wife when he stopped for milk.

The church exploded into a frenetic worship, sending some dancing into the aisles and others running around the room.

But Franklin didn't feel so joyous. If everything Mark had just said were true, it proved he had escorted Katie to her death. He didn't believe this stuff. But at the same time, Mark's rational made sense. Franklin was confused more than ever before.

When the church quieted, Mark resumed. "The heavenly host shouted, 'peace and goodwill.' Through a virgin birth, Jesus landed on the earth. God of Shalom landed! Because He so loved us.

It was God's love that destroyed the power of sin and death. God is love! Folks, everywhere love is in the bible, you can change it to God!"

Maggie leaned her head on Franklin's arm, averting his attention. She was too precious. He admired her cuteness.

Mark bellowed, "The entire plan was conceived from love. God's greatest gift of love to all mankind was Jesus. The Father sowed His Son for our sins and we're His harvest."

I get it. Like farming.

"It's like farming," Mark declared.

After hearing that, Franklin commended himself for being brilliant.

"The Father loves us as much as He loves Jesus." Mark stopped and looked around. "You're staring at me like a bunch of cows looking at a new gate. What is this preacher talking about?"

But that rational made sense to Franklin. If God had given His son for man's sins, He did it because He loved man.

"Turn with me to John 17:23

> . . . I in them, and You in Me; that they may be made perfect in
> one, and that the world may know that You have sent Me, and
> have loved them as you have loved Me."

Mark lifted his bible and put his finger on the page. Look, the word here is loved. Now, who did the Father love? 'THEM! And That's us folks!

He was speaking about us. It's in red. Jesus said it, and I'm preaching it. Now don't shout me down when I'm preaching good!"

Maggie poked Franklin. With her finger pressing against the bible verse, she whispered, "Did you see it?"

"Yes," he whispered back.

". . . but Pastor, Jesus was praying for His disciples. Okay, let's back up and read the twentieth verse.

> I do not pray for these alone, but also for those who will believe
> in Me through their word.

Whose word? The disciples! They preached the Word, and His disciple John recorded it."

It made sense to Franklin.

"Now, repeat after me, the Father loves me as much as He loves Jesus."

Franklin slammed his mouth tight and sucked his lips inward. Even though he enjoyed Mark's style of preaching and found it interesting and sensible, he refused to participate in the Jesus freak antics. That trap he refused to stumble into. They weren't going to highjack him. He was way too intelligence for that.

". . .to Romans," flipping the pages, Mark added, "Um, the fifth chapter and the eighth verse."

> "But God commendeth his love toward us, in that, while we
> were yet sinners, Christ died for us . . ."

"Huh, that's why Maggie said He died for His enemies," Franklin muttered.

" . . .God gave us the best seed He had, and that was Jesus. Now, that's unconditional love folks. Jesus paid the price. All you have to do is receive it. When we repent and turn our lives over to Jesus, we take hold of His love."

Closing his bible, Mark walked back behind the pulpit. "On that first Christmas morning, Love was manifested. Heaven opened, and there was a shout that was heard on the earth.

I would like to add, if you haven't given your life to Jesus there's no better time than now. His love is tugging on your heart right now."

Craig's little band softly played, "Hark the Herald Angels Sing."

It pained him to hear that song in church, again.

Maggie poked his side. "Remember I danced to that song."

"Yes, I remember." He fought back his tears.

When Mark invited people to come up to receive Jesus into their hearts, five people marched up.

Maggie bent over, and placed her hands over her face.

Johnny and Mary, along with Pastor Mark, prayed for those at the altar.

In the same way that wondrous peace he had experienced that night of Maggie's play, inundated him. A chill flooded through him, causing an involuntary shudder through his body. The power of it welled up his eyes. He felt like a gentle tugged on his heart. He closed his eyes.

Submerged in the intangible presence of love, an unspeakable joy rose up within him. It convinced him to follow its lead. But how could he allow Johnny pray for him? It may influence Johnny to become brag-gadocious. If that would happen, he most likely would have never heard the end of it.

"Ouch!" The voice of a male child hollered.

Franklin jolted up and opened his eyes.

Maggie sat up.

"I'm sorry mister. I didn't see your foot."

"If you slow down, you wouldn't trip over people," Franklin remarked.

The boy scampered off.

He spotted Maggie gazing off.

The music stopped playing.

Franklin wondered where her mind had wandered to. "What's wrong with you? You look upset."

She expelled a huge breath. She turned her head toward Franklin. "Grampy, you're not ready to hear about it."

Taken back by her comment, Franklin responded, "Oh really! I'm not ready for what?"

A clean-cut man in his early thirties appeared in front of him. "Pro-fessor Franklin."

"Yes."

The man looked at Maggie, and back over to Franklin. "Neither of you recognize me, do you?"

Standing in front of Franklin, in living proof was a Jesus freak who had lost his mind. "Why, are we supposed to?"

With her head tilted and her face contorted, Maggie stared at the man. "I don't know who you are either."

The man hung his head and smacked his lips. "I'm sorry. I do look different." He raked his hand through his clean-cut brown hair. "I had a haircut and I've washed up, thanks to Pastor Mark."

"Grampy his voice sounds familiar. Does it sound familiar to you?"

"Sir, I'm the man who tried to steal your granddaughter's purse yesterday."

"What!" Franklin stood and snarled. He raised a tight fist. He growled under his breath. "I aught to . . ."

Maggie grabbed his arm. "Grampy don't!"

"I got saved yesterday because your granddaughter forgave me, and bought me lunch."

"What?" Franklin snapped his head downward to Maggie.

"Grampy, when you wanted to put him in jail, I told you God said no." She raised her hands. "Hallelujah to Jesus!"

Franklin held the fist position.

"Please, I would like to apologize, and I would like to explain."

Maggie nodded her head vigorously. She sat on the edge of her chair. She tugged on the hem of her skirt straightening it out. "I'm okay. I'm ready to hear your explanation."

Franklin threw his arms upward. "I'm not."

She tugged on Franklin's sweater. "Please sit down Grampy. Everyone should have a second chance. Jesus gave us all a second chance.

"Oh, this better be good, or I'm going to belt you in the mouth." He sat forward in his seat.

"May I sit down next to you?"

"Just explain," Franklin growled.

The man handed Maggie some coins. "First I want to thank you, um . . ."

"My name is Margaret Katherine Harris, but you can call me Maggie."

"Maggie! I'm Jesse Wilcox. This is your change. Please put your hand out." He hunched over and dropped several coins in her hand. "After the guard had bought me lunch, I had seventy-three cents leftover. Maggie you saved my life. If it weren't for your act of love, I would have never had run into Pastor. I want to thank you."

She shook her head. "No I didn't save your life. I just obeyed Jesus. But what happened next?"

"Well after the guard bought me a hot meatball sub, he wanted to throw me out in the cold to eat it. I pleaded with him to let me eat it inside. I hadn't eaten in three days, and I wanted to eat it while it was hot. I pleaded with him all the way to the Mall's exit. Pastor Mark overheard us, and he interceded for me. He promised he would send me on my way after I had eaten. At my surprise, the guard agreed."

"That's the favor of God," Maggie declared.

Jesse smiled at her. "Whatever it was, I sure am thankful I met Pastor Mark. He sat with me when I ate my sub. By the time I had finished my sandwich, I gave my life to Jesus.

Pastor Mark took me to the strip mall across the street for a haircut, and he bought me some new clothes. Afterwards, he took me to the weekly motel just a few miles south of Tilton, and he paid a weeks rent for me. I'm so grateful to him.

This morning, he picked me up for church. That's when he gave me this bible." He lifted it up. "But Maggie, it was your warm gesture of love that prepared my heart to hear the salvation message."

"Praise the Lord!" Maggie shouted, "Grampy, I told you that God was going to use me for someone when we went to the mall. Remember?" She extended her arm. "And here's the confirmation standing right in front of you."

Oh boy. "Yes I remember."

"Now we've had two divine appointments with Mr. Wilcox: here and on the mall. It's not just coincidence, Grampy. It's evidence. Do you understand it now?"

"Yes, I get it

But Jesse's story had a fishy smell to it. Even though he had cleaned up and claimed he had given his life to Jesus, Franklin did not trust him. "How did you end up homeless? Are you a drug addict?"

"No sir! I'm a scientist."

"What type, sanitation scientist?"

"No sir. I'm a pharmaceutical scientist. I developed HIV medications."

Franklin casted a skeptical eye as he questioned, "So, how does a scientist like you end up on the streets without a home or money?"

Jesse's head drooped. "Well sir, more than four years ago, when my wife and daughter were walking across the street to our neighbor's," he looked away and let out a deep breath. Tears flooded his eyes. "I'm sorry. This is difficult for me." He shut his eyes. Tears flowed through his closed eyelids. "I—um—a drunk driver plowed them down and killed them, instantly."

Franklin sat back and gazed downward. It felt like a dagger had punctured his heart. He took in a deep breath to keep his composure in tact as he listened to Jesse.

"The man, who killed them," Jesse choked-up, "illegal-immigrant—my Betsy—my little girl, she was only three. I couldn't face my life without my wife—my sweet Ashley, and without Betsy." Tears dropped off his eye lids. "I thought about committing suicide, but I didn't have the nerve to do it."

With tears flowing down her cheeks, Maggie rubbed her eyes. "I'm sorry. I'm glad you didn't kill yourself."

"Thank you. So am I. Jesus loves me unconditionally." Jesse reached for a Kleenex box off of Pastor's podium, and offered Maggie a Kleenex. "Are you okay?"

She sniffled, "Yes. Your story is very sad."

"I'm sorry. Would you rather I stopped telling it."

"No. Please continue. Since we're friends now, I would like to hear the rest of your story. " Maggie grabbed a few Kleenex out of the box,

In some ways, Franklin wished he had never asked him. Heartbroken, empathy filled his heart for the criminal. He rather had not known anything. At least Jesse wasn't a murderer like him.

Jesse blew his nose. "At the time, we were living in Costa Mesa, California, where we grew up together." His eyes glistened. "I met Ashley in the second grade."

Katie's face flashed in Franklin's mind. Her beautiful hair glimmered in the sun and flowed in the breeze. He leaned in to kiss her soft and full lips. Blood gushed from her mouth. He squeezed his eyes shut to clear the phantom from his head.

Maggie wiped the tears off her face. "But, how did you get out here?"

"Well, after the funeral, I was so depressed that I packed a bag, locked up my house, and started walking wherever my feet took me. I slept on the beach and in parks. Until one day, I found myself in El Segundo. That's one of the towns where the Los Angeles airport is.

When I heard a jet fly overhead, I looked up. I realized that I needed to get as far away from California as I could. I checked into a hotel. The next morning, I took the first non-stop flight out of the airport. It was a direct flight to Hartford, Connecticut.

At first, I stayed at hotels. A few months later, I started walking, again. I kept walking until I had lost everything, my home, my money, everything. And I was still walking when I saw Maggie's purse lying on top of the CD's through the store window. I'm so . . ."

"Pastor Mark, this is my brother-in-law Frank." Johnny interrupted.

Mark flinched. "Frank is your brother-in-law? By golly, that's amazing. You're both related."

"He's my wife's twin brother," Franklin responded.

Johnny's smile dropped. "You know Pastor Mark?"

Without hesitation, Franklin ceased the moment. "After all, we do live across the street from each other."

"In other words, you got to know the pastor without knowing he had a church across the street from you," Johnny riposted.

Mark clapped. "By golly, I see you got to meet Jesse too."

"Pastor Mark, do you remember the little girl I had told you about? The little girl who had bought me lunch yesterday."

"Yes I do."

Jesse stretched his hand out. "Maggie is that little girl."

Johnny's eyes swayed back and forth.

Maggie added, "Pastor Mark, I have never had so many divine appointments in my life. And they all started when I came to visit Grampy. God is definitely working on something."

Mark slid his eyes upward for a split second. "Now that's interesting. God is working on something."

With a slack-mouth, Johnny gazed off.

Their divine appointment's concept may have had some validity to it, but nevertheless it spooked Franklin.

Franklin slipped on his jacket. "Pastor Mark, I really enjoyed the service. And Jesse, it was real nice getting to know you too," Due to the familiarity of Jesse's suffering, Franklin couldn't look into Jesse's eyes. "I have to feed Maggie. I've planned a surprise for her." He zipped up his jacket.

"Surprise! What kind of surprise? Grampy, I love surprises."

"I know. I'll tell you later because it's a surprise."

As he passed by Johnny, he whispered, "Don't look so dumbfounded."

"I'm not dumbfounded. God is amazing."

Franklin took hold of Maggie's hand. He led Maggie out with Jesse's story on his mind.

CHAPTER 19

Christmas Town Theme Park

WHILE CROSSING THE STREET, Maggie jiggled Franklin's hand. "Are you going to tell me my surprise?"

"I'll tell you when we're in the house. Shoot, I forgot to ask Jesse if he saw the man with the white hair."

"Oh well Grampy, it's called a missed opportunity. His story reminded me of Nana. It made me cry."

"I know. It made me cry too."

"Grampy, I feel too sad to think about that story anymore today."

"I agree. Let's not talk about it anymore."

When he opened the front door for her, she hopped over the threshold into the living room. She yanked off her hat. "Grampy, please tell me my surprise."

"Let me take of my jacket and settle in, and I'll tell you. Hand me your coat."

From the kitchen, Harry came running in. "Hello Harry," Maggie squatted.

Wagging his entire rear-end, Harry licked her chin. She hugged him, and rubbed her face on his furry neck. "I love you."

He wiggled out of her arms and ran over to Franklin. "You need to go out fella?" Harry curled himself around Franklin's legs. "Come on boy."

Maggie followed behind them. "After you let Harry out, can you tell me my surprise?"

"Yes I will, but sit down at the table and wait for a moment."

He opened the door. A blast of wind pushed against it. Harry ran out onto the deck. Franklin closed the door and sat at the table next to Maggie.

She drummed her fingers on the table top. "Well, can you tell me now."

"Tell you what?"

"Grampy please, tell me my surprise."

Teasingly, he answered, "Oh you would like to know what your surprise is!"

"Yes. Please just tell me, I can't wait any longer."

"Oh, Okay," he sat down at the table. "About ten miles north from here is a theme park called Christmas Town, and every night they have a lighted Christmas train event, until the twenty-third."

"Yes, Grampy. I would love to go." She batted her eyes.

He sounded out a hearty burst of laughter. "I thought you would."

"Can we hurry up and eat, so we can leave?"

"Hold on for a minute so I can finish explaining. There's a nice Danish style diner there where we can get a bite to eat. They have meals like beef stew and turkey dinners."

Biting her lower lip, she stared at him like a lion scoping its prey.

"But if you'd rather eat now, I can make peanut butter and jelly sandwiches before we go."

She stretched her palm out. "No. I wanna go to the diner."

"But yesterday you were worried about me feeding you. Are you sure you can wait?"

"You just made my mouth drool for beef stew. How can I eat a peanut butter sandwich, now? It really wouldn't be very satisfying eating a little sandwich while thinking about beef stew."

He loved her preciousness.

"Well then, if you're sure, go up stairs and change into your jeans."

"Okay," she leaped up. The chair skidded behind her. She ran off shouting, "I'll be down in a minute."

He chortled, "That's a girl who loves her food."

On their way out, Maggie took the last gingerbread cookie from off of Annabelle's platter. Franklin raised an eyebrow.

Maggie stopped in her tracks with the cookie near her mouth. "Well, it's an appetizer."

"An appetizer?"

"Uh-huh, I'm a growing little girl."

"A growing little girl? I see. Grab a napkin and let's get going."

Half way up the route to Christmas town, Franklin hadn't seen anyone else on the road. It seemed strange. Maybe he should have called ahead to make sure the park was still opened.

"Grampy, are we almost there? I'm starving."

"Why? You just finished your appetizer a few minutes ago."

"It didn't work. It made me hungrier."

Before Franklin could respond, he noticed in his side mirror a black Hummer following him too close. He glanced in his rearview mirror. "Get off my bumper you idiot!"

Raising herself upward, she twisted around. "I don't think he can hear you, and you shouldn't judge him."

"Judge him?" He pointed over the steering wheel. "Look. There's nobody else on the road," He glanced at her, "and he can legally pass me. But instead of passing me, he's riding on my rear-end."

"I know, but you don't know if he's an idiot."

"Moose!" Franklin slowed to a stop. The vehicle behind him squealed.

Up ahead about fifty yards, a mature bull moose stopped in the middle of the road. The majestic animal's antlers spread were at least six feet. The enormous animal stood like a crowned monarch of the forest. But his cold stare and laid back ears concerned Franklin. "Great! That idiot squealing his breaks spooked him."

"Is he going to charge us?"

"It might." Franklin looked over his shoulder. The male driver threw his hands up. "The moose thinks his space is threatened, and that moron behind me is angry."

Franklin waved at the man to back up, but he didn't move. "Doesn't that idiot see the moose?" He looked out the windshield. "Terrific, the animal is urinating."

With his eyes on the animal, he reached for his forty-four magnum pistol in his shoulder holster.

Maggie let down the passenger window, stuck her head out, and pointed at the twelve-hundred pound animal. She shouted, "In the name of Jesus, moose go back into the woods, now!"

That instant, the majestic creature took off into the woods.

Franklin gazed through the windshield. His little eight-year-old granddaughter ordered the moose, and it obeyed her. That unexplainable had no explanation. "That's impossible! Why would that moose obey you?"

"When God said He made us in His image, He made us speaking creatures. For an example, God said let there be light, and there was light.

When God breathed into our nostrils, He gave us His Spirit. Our words are powerful like His. That means were speaking creatures."

Though Franklin listened, his mind stayed on that animal running off.

"Your words can be used against you or for you. In Mark 11:22-23. Jesus said if you believe what you say, you can have what you say. That's why . . ."

If he hadn't witnessed the animal run off, he wouldn't have believed it.

The man behind them honked his horn, squealed around them, and took off. But Franklin didn't flinch or blink an eye. He just stared out the windshield.

"Grampy, are you in there?"

He heard her, but he didn't want to respond. He was too busy mulling over all those so called favors and divine appointments. It just didn't seem plausible that they might not have been just coincidences. No matter how many angles he looked at it from, he had no explanations for the various phenomena. Maybe there was something legitimate about that God stuff.

"Hello Grampy, are you okay?"

"Yes, I am. I'm starving. Let's get going."

"Good. Because I'm starving too."

Since all this Christian stuff caused him a huge headache, he no longer had interest talking about the moose incident. But Maggie kept chattering in his ear about it. He preferred she'd stay quiet. But she had never seen a moose in the wild before that day. He couldn't fault her for that.

The amount of cars in Christmas Town's parking lot amazed Franklin. "Where did all these cars come from? We had no traffic coming up here."

Maggie raised her hands. "Lord, we need favor. Yes Lord, show us the spot You've chosen for us."

He found that prayer odd. She hadn't prayed for parking that way before, but did she? "What did you mean by God to show us His chosen spot?"

"I don't know. I felt in my spirit to pray that way."

He turned down the front aisle in anticipation of finding a place to park in near the entrance. But there were no parking spaces. He drove around in the second aisle and then the third one back. Just then, a vehicle pulled out of a parking space.

"It's the favor of God." Maggie declared as he turned into the space.

Franklin gave a sigh of relief. He almost got taken in by that Christian hocus-pocus stuff. That obedient Moose must have seen a Cow in the woods. That had to have been what happened.

When he shut off the truck, he noticed a familiar vehicle in front of him. "Wait a minute. Is that Mrs. Hamilton's car?"

Maggie clapped her hands. "Another divine appointment! That's why God chose this parking space." She removed her seatbelt and sat up closer to the windshield. "That's her car." She looked over at him. "Wow Grampy. God has a lot of divine appointments for you. He's working on something. I wonder what this one's about. How about you?"

He preferred not knowing, but he had no doubt she'd point it out for him. "Wait until I come around and get you."

"I know the drill."

As he approached Mrs. Hamilton's Subaru, he noticed a puddle of oil under the front end. He beckoned Maggie to come to him.

She opened the passenger door, and she shouted, "But you told me to wait."

"Just come around the front of the truck."

With one hand on the hood, he leaned a knee on the ground, and he dipped his finger in the oil. After smelling it, he rubbed it between his fingers.

Maggie squatted next to him. "Why are you rubbing that black stuff between your fingers?"

"I'm examining the oil. There's a lot of grit in this oil. That's why it's black. Whoa. There's water in the oil."

"What does that mean?"

"It looks like she may have a blown head gasket." He braced his hand against the bumper and looked under the vehicle. "Wow, the insides of the tires are almost bald."

Maggie shadowed him, as he walked around the car.

He examined the right rear tire, and then he kicked it. "That's soft."

"Is her car broken?"

He placed a hand on a hip. "It has some serious issues." He pushed a knee down on the rear bumper and let it go. The car bounced three times. "The shocks are shot."

"Will she be okay?"

"I hope so, but the kids must be with her. That's not good."

In a panic tone, Maggie raised her forefinger toward the sky. "Lord, You need to show us how we can help them!"

"Princess, I would like to help her, but I don't even know where she is. If we see her, I'll talk to her."

"Okay Grampy, I'll pray that we'll see them."

Though he wasn't a praying man, he believed Mrs. Hamilton needed someone to help her. Maggie's prayers couldn't hurt, but maybe by chance they could help. "You do that. But right now, we need to eat."

"Me too, but give me a minute to pray first." She raised her hands, looked heavenward, and prayed, "Lord lead us to Mrs. Hamilton and her grandchildren, in Jesus' name, amen.

"That's all?"

"God heard me and answered me. We'll see her before the day is out."

Why should Franklin complain? The prayer was short, but to the point. "Good, give me your hand."

Only a few people stood in line at the gift shop entrance.

Pointing at the building, Maggie exclaimed, "I remember that place!"

"How can you? You were only three when Nana and I took you here."

"Because I'm not a man, I'm a little girl with an excellent memory."

"What does that mean?"

"My mom said that men are born with special devices in their brains to help them forget things."

This is going to be good. "What do you mean a special device?"

"She called it a selective memory device. With this device, a man can choose which memory he wants to keep and which one he wants to throw away. Daddy was born with that selective memory device in his head. We're you born with one?"

Franklin chortled, "No, your mother is still quite the character."

"Grampy look, a handicap ramp. May I run up it?"

"No. You have two good legs that work. That's for people who are in wheelchairs."

"But my mom let's me when there's nobody using it."

"She's not here. I am. Now watch where you're going. It's slick out here."

"Okay." She put her feet together and hopped onto the first step of the porch.

"Is that being careful?"

"Opps. I'm sorry. I forgot."

Two elaborate wreaths hung on the front entrance doors. After waiting in line a few moments, automatic sleigh bells rang as they stepped into the shop.

A cheery gray haired man stood behind the counter. "Can I help you sir?"

As he pulled his wallet out of his back pocket, Franklin responded, "Yes, I need one adult and one child ticket."

Maggie scooted in front of him and pointed at a jar on the counter, filled with foot-long peppermint candy canes. "Grampy look at those humongous candy-canes! May I have two?"

"Two? But there's only one of you."

"Yes, but I got a feeling I need to buy two. It's the Holy Spirit."

It amazed him how much she talked like Katie that night, but he wouldn't interfere with that kind of thing ever again. "You can have two."

"Thank you. You're the best Grampy of all time."

He took two out of the jar. "I'd like to add these candy canes, and two tickets for the four-thirty train ride, as well."

The cashier wore a huge grin. "You got blessed. You got the last two tickets for the four-thirty train, and that's the only train for the night.

"That's strange. Why only one ride?" Franklin put his debit card back into his wallet.

"The park is rented for a wedding tonight. We posted it in the paper. If you didn't read it, it's not my fault."

"Praise the Lord!" Maggie blurted, "That is the favor of God!"

Franklin explained, "My granddaughter likes to pray a lot."

"There's nothing wrong with that," the cashier declared.

Maggie's face lit up. "You're a Christian too?"

"Yes I am." The fellow handed Franklin the tickets and his receipt.

"My grampy will be a Christian soon."

"You don't say," the man glanced down at Maggie, "That's a good thing."

With her finger tips pressing down on the edge of the counter, her smile glowed. "It is."

Franklin refused to allow that to bother him. He handed her the bag of candy. "Thank you, sir. Have a good day."

"You too, my good man."

"Grampy, now do you believe me that I have favor?"

"It seems reasonable. What time is it?" He glanced at his watch. "We better hurry. We have less than two hours to eat and to catch the sleigh ride to the train station."

"Don't worry, Grampy. That's lots of time."

"Not if the place is packed. We might have to wait a while before we're seated."

"That's what you said about Chili's, but we got a table within minutes. And may I add, we also got to have lunch with Pastor Mark." With her hand in his, she ran along side of him. "Lord we need favor for a table—wait a minute?" Maggie halted.

A woman almost tripped over her, "Excuse me, little girl." She hurried by.

"Why did you stop like that? You almost tripped that woman."

"I'm sorry. I didn't mean to. I wasn't thinking. But where's the diner?"

"You need to think. This place is crowded. It's down the breezeway."

"What's better, the beef stew or the turkey dinner?"

"They're both good, but I thought you wanted stew."

They turned down the breezeway.

"I know, but I've been thinking about the turkey dinner too." She pushed her hat off her eyes. "If I don't know what to order, how will you know what to order for me?"

"Oh yes, I forgot, my little princess. I'm getting the beef stew. They pour it over a flaky pie crust. And for desert, I'm having a piece of their warm and luscious caramel-pecan pumpkin bread pudding with a scoop of their creamy-homemade French vanilla ice cream."

Wide-eyed, she stared at him. "Mmmm Grampy, ditto that for me"

"Absolutely."

Christmas carolers dressed in Currier and Ives type of costumes sang in the corner of the diner's foyer.

Franklin took her hand. "This place is crowed. Don't let go of my hand."

"Okay, but why do you look so worried?"

"Princess, I'm not worried. It's just crowded. I don't want you to miss the train ride."

"Oh my goodness, haven't you figured it out? Remember, I have the favor of God? I promise you, we'll have a table in a few minutes."

When he gave his name to the hostess, there were about ten or more names ahead of his. He doubted it. "Okay, we'll see."

But in less than ten minutes, the little device lit up and vibrated. There had to have been a mistake.

"Look! The thingy lit up. It's the favor of God."

They approached the hostess station.

"Franklin?" A young hostess, dressed in an elf costume, asked.

"That's me, but what about all these other people ahead of me?"

"Those are bigger parties. We just had a deuce open."

While they followed the hostess through the dinning room, Maggie asked, "Grampy, what's a deuce?"

"A booth that seats only two people."

"Hallelujah, hallelujah! It's the favor of God."

When Franklin and Maggie slid into the booth, the hostess laid the menus on the table. "Your waitress will be right with you."

The red booth's table cloth had little Christmas tree prints through-out it.

A small framed girl with most of her blond hair tucked under a Santa's hat approached their table. "Merry Christmas! I'm Jamie, and I'm going to be your server today."

"You got the whitest teeth I've ever seen in my entire life," Maggie commented.

The cute teen blushed, and she giggled, "Thank you."

Franklin looked around the packed dining room. "Are you ready to take our order or do you need to come back?"

"If you're ready to order, I can take it now."

"Thank you. We'll each have your stew and the pumpkin bread pud-ding with ice cream for desert. And you can start us with two cups of hot butterscotch apple cider."

"With or without whip cream?"

Since he had no clue, he looked at Maggie. She nodded yes.

"One with and one without."

"Thank you." The girl took the menus as she left.

Maggie flashed Franklin a thumbs up. "You did a great job this time."

He chuckled, "I'm glad I got your approval."

Maggie slid out of the booth, stood on her tippy-toes, and scanned around the dinning room.

"What are you doing?"

"I'm looking for Mrs. Hamilton."

"There's a lady with a tray of food trying to pass you."

"Opps, I'm sorry ma'am." She plopped back down on the seat.

"Why were you looking for Mrs. Hamilton?"

She folded her hands in front of her. "God told me that we're going to see them before this day is out. Remember, and Grampy, you have to help her. She has Lucas and Mackenzie with her. They need you."

He would help her if he could, but he didn't have a lot of options on a Sunday afternoon, especially in the rural areas of New Hampshire. "Maggie, Thursday after you leave, Mr. Bob and Uncle Taki are buying her a newer car, and I'm going to help them. But if we do run into her, you are not to say a word about it. It's a surprise."

"Okay, but what if they break down on the way home."

"She should be fine tonight. She has only about ten miles to go. Where her house is, it's a bit closer to here than my place."

Maggie rested her face on the palm of her hand. She seemed bummed out.

"I promise, if we see her, I'll check her fluids and have a talk with her. I never leave the house without being prepared for an emergency. I can fill up her fluids before she heads out. Okay?"

"Thank you, I feel much better about this now. When we see them, you can help them. You're really a smart Grampy."

"Wow, I'm a smart grandfather. Now you know what kind of grand-father I am."

"You're funny," she giggled.

"Boy it smells good in here," he raised his head and sniffed the air, "It's making me hungrier."

Opening her mouth wide like a hippopotamus, she drew in a deep breath. "Did you say we're going on a sleigh ride?"

"Yes I did. You just realized it?"

"Yes," she leaned forward, "I've never been on one before. This is going to be so much fun."

Jamie appeared with the two mugs of cider. "I have your hot cider." When she sat it down in front of Maggie, Jamie warned, "Now be careful. It's very hot."

"Okay. Thank you." She touched the whipped cream. "Grampy look, there's cinnamon on top of the whipped cream."

He grabbed her finger, "She just told you it's hot."

"I know. I'm touching the cold stuff."

Jamie laughed, "Your meals should be out in a few moments."

"Thank you," Franklin responded, cuffing his hands around the warm mug.

After the two had finished their meals, Franklin waited for Maggie while she was in the restroom. They were near the exit that led into the theme park. He watched countless people coming in and going out of the diner.

A couple with eight children came through the door. "Wow, they got a litter," he muttered.

Straight way, a tall and muscled bound man appeared in front of Franklin. Wearing a brown derby hat, he had whitish sideburns down to his chin. His round-wire rimmed spectacles sat on the tip of his plump nose. He peered over them, and pointed his finger at Franklin. "Help her."

Stunned, Franklin winced. "Help who?"

As the strange man walked out the door, he disappeared.

"What? Help her? Who? Oh no." Franklin hollered, "Maggie!"

"Grampy! I'm right here!"

He spun around.

She was walking down the short hall from the ladies' room, tugging on the waist of her jeans.

He ran to her. He squatted and grabbed her shoulders. "Are you okay? Did anything happen to you? Did any man touch you? Did a man approach you?"

"No. I'm fine." Whispering, she informed him, "Girls take longer."

He grabbed her and held her tight.

"Are you okay, Grampy?"

He took her hand. "I don't want you to let go of my hand for one second."

Her brows knocked together. "Why? What happened?"

"I saw a strange man, and it concerned me." He opened the door for her.

"You shouldn't get so nervous when you see people that are different than you."

"You're correct, princess."

Franklin stepped off the wooden sidewalk with Maggie. Across the dirt road, two black draft horses, harnessed to a buckboard wagon, were parked at the sleigh-ride stop. He spotted the man with the derby hat. "There he is."

"Who?"

Without hesitation, he dashed across the road with Maggie. Rushing in front of the sled, he barked, "Hey you! What did you mean?"

The baby-faced young man jolted. The horses shifted their weight. The silver bells tied to their harnesses jingled. One of the horses looked over his shoulder.

Franklin halted. Maggie stumbled. He helped her regain her footing. "You're not him?"

The young man held his hand over his heart. "Sir, you startled me."

"I'm so very sorry. I thought you were somebody else. I'm so embarrassed. I'm so sorry for spooking the horses."

The young man responded, "You sure got their blood flowing, but they'll be fine. Glad I'm not the one you're looking for."

Whenever Franklin lost his foot, he'd most certainly find it inserted in his mouth. "This is so embarrassing."

"It's not important. My heart only missed one beat," the driver chortled.

Several people lined up along the other side of the wagon. The young driver glanced over toward them. He asked Franklin, "By the way, are you taking the four-thirty train?"

"Yes we are. I guess we better get in line. But thank you for being so understanding."

"No worries. You were here first, get in front of the line."

"Praise the Lord!" Maggie sounded out. "Mister, thank you."

"Sure. No problem little one."

Franklin lifted Maggie and set her up on the wagon. She chose the first seat behind the driver. Every seat filled up within moments.

On the way to the theme park's train station, the sleigh ride took a detour through a snow covered hay lot. Watching Maggie's long hair blowing in the wind like Katie's use to, reminded him of the longing in his heart for his wife. With his eyes welling, he pushed back on the pain. Nothing would ruin his short time he had with Maggie, especially when Kitty would most likely take her to Thailand.

Maggie tugged on Franklin's jacket. "This is so much fun." Shivering, she pulled strands of hair out of her mouth, and then she wrapped her arms around herself. "I love the sounds of the sleigh bells. It's like I'm in a Christmas movie."

Putting his arm around her shoulders, he held her closer to him. "It's freezing out here. Does that feel better?"

"Yes it does, thank you. The horses look like they're marching in a parade, don't they?"

"They do."

She pointed upward. "Look how big the moon is behind that cloud."

Recalling Pappy's full moon theory, he let out a hearty laugh. "It is big for this time of the year."

Two brass bells reverberated through the darkened sky "Carol of the Bells" tune as the sleigh pulled in front of the train station. A black, red, and green nineteenth century steam engine with golden smoke stacks, awaited on the tracks. A green and black coal car hooked behind the engine. Behind the coal car, was a red passenger car. The green diner car would only be used for a dinner train ride. The entire open-sided platform arrayed in white lights. Nothing had changed since he had been there with Katie several years before.

Maggie squealed like a baby pig. "This is so exciting!"

If only Katie were with them. "Princess, it sure is."

On board the train, the conductor punched Franklin's and Maggie's golden tickets, and he instructed them to lower the trays in front of them like on an airplane, but they were wooden like the seats.

"Grampy, can I keep my ticket forever?"

"Absolutely."

She ransacked through her purse and lifted a golden pen in the shape of a bullet, which caught Franklin's eye.

"Where did you get a pen like that?"

"Daddy. He got it from the National Rifle Association." She leaned over hers and wrote something on the back of her ticket. "May I have your ticket too?"

Curious of what she was writing, he handed her his ticket.

"Look Grampy."

She had written the same thing on each of them.

We shall never forget the wonderful day Grampy and Maggie took a train ride together in Christmas Town.

"Here, you keep yours and I'll keep mine forever.

"I'll treasure this forever," and that he did.

As the train rolled out, the whistle blew.

A young man and a young woman dressed in red shirts, green bow-ties, and black trousers passed out small bags of three large and warm chocolate chip cookies. Two others followed them offering hot chocolate.

While carolers and a man dressed in a Santa suit entertained the passengers, the train passed through a winter wonderland country side of oak, maple, and conifer trees adorned with numerous Christmas lights and decorations.

CHAPTER 20

The Rescue

AFTER THE HOUR AND half train ride, the temperature had dropped, significantly. While holding Franklin's hand and swinging her bag of cookies and candy canes, Maggie took an opportunity of the slippery conditions for playtime. She attempted to slide across the parking lot. He almost lost his footing.

"Opps, I'm sorry Grampy."

"I love you, but this is not a playground. This is dangerous. You don't play on ice."

Before he jumped in his truck, Franklin noticed Sue's vehicle was gone. It disappointed him. He had hopes that Maggie's prediction of seeing them before ends day would come to pass. As he warmed the truck, he wondered if Sue had made it home safe with the kids.

"Grampy, can we turn on the heat now?"

"Yes," he switched the heater and blower on high.

She placed her hands in front of the heater vent. "That feels so good."

"It does!"

"Grampy, thank you for the best day ever. I loved the Christmas lights the best. Weren't they beautiful?"

While driving down the dark-two-lane-country road, Maggie kept his tired bones awake with her chatter. The more she discussed Christmas Town's lighted displays, the more Franklin considered decorating the outside of his home for her. But before he could discuss it with her, he spotted flashing red lights down the road.

"Grampy, look! What is it?"

"It's probably an emergency vehicle, maybe a tow truck or something. Oh boy, that's Mrs. Hamilton's Subaru in the snow bank."

"Are they dead?" Maggie shouted.

"Dead!" He glanced at Maggie. With both hands crossed against her chest, her lower lip was drawn in between her teeth. "Maggie, you can relax. I'm positive they're not dead." He pulled on the side of the road behind them.

"Are you sure?"

Before he got out of the truck, he switched on his emergency flashers. "They're not dead. They're moving around in the vehicle." He grabbed a flare out of the glove box. "You wait here where it's warm and don't get out."

"Okay. Jesus help Grampy help Mrs. Hamilton."

After he lit the flare and placed it on the road, he noticed Mrs. Hamilton's driver's door open with her upper torso twisted outside of the vehicle. He ran to her, shouting, "Are you okay?"

"Professor Franklyn, I'm stuck." Sue shouted back.

Catching his breath, he placed his hand on the Subaru's top. "Is anybody injured?"

He checked through the vehicle. Lucas waved at him from the front seat, while McKenzie stood in the rear behind her brother. Though they were bundled up in heavy winter clothing, he surmised the temperature inside the vehicle was below freezing. "No one's injured, "Sue replied, "We're okay, but we're cold."

"What happened?"

As she explained, Franklin could see her breath. "The engine died when we crashed into the snow bank, and I can't start it," as she continued, Franklin noticed her hands trembling. "It was horrible. I must have skidded on ice. It spun out of control and we landed here. Oh my car. What am I going to do? How am I going to get to work?"

He reassured her, "It'll all work out, but let's get you and the kids out of this freezing weather and into my warm truck."

McKenzie started crying, "Professor Franklyn, are we going to die?"

"No. Nobody is going to die." He opened the rear door. "Come on, come to me." With the little girl in his arms, Franklin tucked her long soft-blonde hair under the hood. "Let's get you inside my truck where it's warm."

Lucas pushed on the passenger door. "Grandma, my door won't open."

Franklin interceded, "Lucas, please wait until your grandmother gets out. Then you can get out through the driver's door."

With her vehicle slanted and trapped in the snow bank, Mrs. Hamilton had difficulty getting out.

Since Mackenzie was in his arms, he had difficulty assisting the woman. "I have an idea. Let me put Mackenzie in my truck, and I'll be right back for you and Lucas."

"Thank you."

He put McKenzie in the backseat of his truck. "Maggie, climb over the seat, so Mrs. Hamilton can sit in the front seat."

As soon as he shut the back door, he hurried over and he took hold of Sue Hamilton's hand. "Mrs. Hamilton, your hand is freezing."

"We were at Christmas Town. I lost one of my gloves in the park." Even with his assistance, she struggled out of the Legacy. Lucas climbed out behind her.

"My car. What am I going to do?"

"Mrs. Hamilton, let's get you two in the truck, so you can warm up. Then we'll figure something out. Okay?"

She nodded.

Lucas fell as he rushed alongside his grandmother. Franklin helped him stand up. Mrs. Hamilton took his hand.

From the interior light shinning on all of their faces, Franklin noticed how bright red all their faces were. "Mrs. Hamilton, how long have you been in that snow bank?"

"Please call me Sue. We've been out here for about an hour."

As Franklin opened his mouth, Maggie's voice came out of it. "And you can call my grampy, Frank."

Franklin looked over his shoulder, and shot her a tight-lipped scowl.

"Grampy, I'm sorry for interrupting. But when you discuss your name, it's exhausting."

Since he was in the middle of a rescue, he ignored her comment.

"Sue, nobody else would stop for you?"

"Nobody else drove by."

Franklin had a flashback of that man who had told him "help her." He darted his eyes at Sue. *No, it's only my imagination.*

"In all my fifty-seven years on this earth, I've never been in this position."

Ever since Maggie had arrived, the holy spook stuff never ceased. He glanced at his watch. *Six forty.* The day hadn't ended, and he found Sue Hamilton. *It's a coincidence.*

". . . always had a dependable car. My wages are less here in New Hampshire than back home. I don't know what I'm going to do now."

"Sue, I'm going to check a few things in your vehicle, and I'll be right back. Can I have the keys?"

"They're in the ignition. But I told you, it doesn't start. I tried, but there's nothing."

"Let me take a look anyhow. I'm good with mechanics, maybe I can do something. Do you have your cell phone with you?"

"Yes, why?"

"Call a wrecker. I'll be back."

As he was about to close the door, she called out, "But I don't have towing on my insurance."

Franklin dropped his head. "First, let me see if I can get it started. Okay?"

"Thank you."

"If we need to tow it, Rifferton is only three miles back. I'll call Charlie's. They're a good company. I know Charlie personally. I'll try and work out something with him."

He marched down the crunchy snow covered edge of the road.

The front end of the Legacy was crushed against a pine tree. Though he couldn't look under the hood, with one foot on the ground and the other on the gas peddle, Franklin turned the key.

The engine went clack melded with that bonus grinding and metal carnage sound of a seized engine. He shoved the keys in his jacket pocket. He looked at the rear and front tires. The right front wheel was bent inward against the tree. He stood back. Due to the issues and damage of that vehicle, he figured the Subaru was totaled.

It broke his heart. He wanted to help her. But he couldn't figure out how. Then it dawned on him. If prayer worked for Maggie, it might work for him. With his hands on his hips as he observed the car, he mumbled, "God, it feels strange to talk to you, but I think I need to now. Just tell me how I can help her. The poor woman needs a car."

Just then, he heard a diesel engine behind him.

A newer white Dodge Ram stopped on the opposite side of the road. Franklin watched as the passenger window rolled down. A younger man, maybe in his early thirties, shouted out, "Are you folks okay?"

Franklin replied, "It's not a good situation, but I'm going to call a wrecker, and take the owner of the car home. Thank you for stopping, anyhow."

"My uncle owns a wrecking company. In fact, he's at my place right now. We're having an anniversary party for my grandparents. I ran out to pick up something at the store. I'm a mile from home and he's got his wrecker with him. I help him part-time. If you can wait a few moments, I'll give you a hand. I can tow it to my uncle's place back in Rifferton."

"Rifferton? By chance would your uncle be Charlie Weston?"

"Why yes. Do you know him?"

Franklin walked over to the man's truck. "Yes I do. I went to school with him. Tell him you saw Franklin Franklyn. He'll know who I am."

Charlie was a native of New Hampshire, but his parents had moved to York, Maine when he was a freshman in high school. After he had graduated, he moved back to his home town. His little brother, Eliot, had followed him the following year. Though he had met Eliot once, Franklin had never gotten a chance to know him.

"I sure will. By the way, I'm Tommy Weston. I moved up from Manchester two years ago."

Eliot had attended college in Manchester. Afterwards, he had made his home there.

Franklin shook his hand. "I'm Frank. It's good to meet you."

"It's good to meetcha, too."

"I appreciate you giving us a hand."

"Glad to help. I'll be back in a jiffy." As he slid the window up, he drove off.

"This is wonderful!" Franklin shouted. He spun around, placed his hands in his jean's pockets, and he whistled the Andy Griffith theme song until he got back to his truck. "I have some great news. Remember, Charlie was the man I told you about?"

"I remember," Sue replied.

"The man I was just talking to is Charlie's nephew. His name is Tommy. Well, I went to school with Charlie, and we've been friends for years. But I haven't spoken to him for the past two years. Charlie is at his nephew's place with his wrecker. Tommy is coming back to tow your car to Charlie's place back up the road a piece."

With her elbow propped on the console, she rubbed her forehead. "I can't afford this. I don't have towing with my insurance. Remember?"

"Don't worry. I'll work something out for you. Sue, I have to tell you that I think you're car has seen its last days."

"I have no car!" her head drooped. "Thank you. I do appreciate everything you're doing for us."

For some reason, she seemed to avoid eye contact with him as much as possible, and that confused him.

The wrecker's bright headlights shined into Franklin's truck. He jumped out.

Charlie's head hung out the window. "Franklin Franklyn, it is you! I had to come and see it for myself." Charlie stepped out of the wrecker. "Man it's good to see you."

Tommy came around from the other side of the wrecker.

"It's good to see you too," Franklin replied, as he shook his hand. Charlie reached over and gave Franklin a partial embrace, and both men slapped one another on the back.

Charlie asked, "How've you been?"

Franklin placed his hands on his hips. "I'm doing better, but it's been difficult for me without Katie."

"For a while there you kind of checked out of society."

"I sure did. But a few days ago, Kitty and Jake left Maggie with me. And now I'm back."

"You got Maggie? Is she still the rascal?"

"Yes and yes."

"I bet she is. Anyhow, is that the vehicle in the ditch up there?"

"Yes," Franklin turned half way around and pointed, "The engine seized, and her front end is crushed against that tree."

"Whose is it?"

Franklin rubbed his chin. "The woman's name is Sue Hamilton, and she's Bob Lapierre's tenant. She doesn't have towing, and she's raising her grandchildren. To top it off, the woman has no husband."

Charlie shook his head. "That stinks. Poor woman. She doesn't have much money, does she?"

"No, but I'll pay for the tow. Her car is totaled."

"Hey, don't worry about the money. If she'll sign the title over to me, I'll sell it out for parts. That'll pay for the tow. She can bring it to me when she can."

"That sounds like a great idea. I'll ask her."

"Okay, while you do that, Tommy and me will put it on the hook."

Franklin opened the driver's door of his pick up, and he rested his arm over the top of the door. "Sue, your car is most likely totaled. If you try to fix it, it'll cost more than what the car is worth."

"How much?"

"You'll have to drop a new engine it, and there's a lot more than that that needs fixing. It'd be cheaper to buy another vehicle than fix it."

"How much will it cost to tow it?"

"Charlie said if you sign over the title to him, he'll tow it for free. He can use it to sell parts."

She pressed her forehead. "But I don't have the title with me."

"That's fine. He'll wait until you have a chance to get it to him."

"I guess I have no other choice."

As her head drooped, Franklin felt bad for her. "Sue, every thing will work out."

She nodded and shrugged. "I better get out and talk to him."

"You don't have to. Stay in the truck where it's warm, and I'll take care of business."

"Thank you. You're so nice." Her eyes welled up.

He wished he could tell her about the other car Bob had planned for her, but Bob had him promise to not tell her.

After Charlie drove off with her legacy, Franklin noticed Sue's lips quivering. She screwed her eyes shut. Silent tears escaped through the corners of her eyes.

Within seconds, she hunched her shoulders and cried, "What am I going to do? I need my car. I can't work without it. I can't go to the store, and I need to buy food for supper." She swayed her head back and forth. "I can't now, and I promised them hamburgers for supper. I can't now."

Leaning forward in his seat, Luke reached around his grandmother's neck. "Grandma, don't cry. We don't need burgers tonight. We can eat whatever's in the house."

Sue placed her hand on his. "You're such a good boy," shedding tears, she raised her shoulder. She touched his hand with her face.

Maggie held the bag of cookies upward. "I got two more cookies in my bag."

"Hold on a minute!" Franklin interrupted. With a hand on the steering wheel, Franklin twisted around. He leaned against the driver's door. "Nobody's going to miss out on those burgers."

Sue, you and the kids have been through a lot tonight. You sat out in the cold, and your car went down the road on a hook. Everybody is hungry, including me. I planned to take Maggie to Wally's Burgers and Shakes for supper tonight. Sue, may I take you and the kids to supper with us?"

"Oh no Frank, Wally's is way to expense to feed all of us. I can't . . ."

Though Wally's was pricey, they grounded their own beef and formed the burgers by hand. They seasoned them with an outstanding special secret spice mix.

"Please don't worry about that. Please just say yes. The kids are hungry," Franklin placed his hand on his chest, "and I want a juicy half-a-pounder with bacon and cheddar cheese." He looked over his shoulder, "How about you kids? Would you like a burger and milk shakes from Wally's?"

Lucas popped a smile. "I'd like that very much, Professor Franklyn."

McKenzie smiled as she nodded vigorously.

Franklin glanced over at Sue. "Well, will you be my guest?"

"Yes, thank you."

"That settles it. I'm headed to Wally's."

"What about me!" Maggie blurted, "You never asked me if I wanted a burger and milk shake!"

He glanced over his shoulder. "Because I already know you're starving."

"You're right."

On the way to Wally's, the kids chitter-chattered in the back seat, but Sue stared out the passenger's window, and never said a word.

Franklin presumed she must have been too heartbroken to speak. He tried to cheer her up. "After we eat, I'll stop at the store so you can pick-up a few things."

As her head tilted off to the side, tears fell from her eyes. "I can't thank you enough. You're such a kindhearted man. I really appreciate everything you're doing for us."

Maggie hung the bag of cookies and candy canes over the seat. "Mrs. Hamilton, can I give my cookies and candy canes to Lucas and McKenzie?"

She responded, "That's so sweet. Yes you can. But Lucas and McKenzie you can't eat them until after supper."

Lucas poked his grandmother on the shoulder. "Grandma, look how big these candy canes are."

"Wow."

Maggie scooted up toward the front seat. "They're a foot long."

"I never seen any that big." With her head turned toward Franklin and her eyes cast down, Sue remarked, "Your granddaughter is such a sweet little girl."

Why couldn't she make eye contact? What happened to this woman? "Thank you, Sue."

On their way back home, Maggie strummed her fingers on the counsel. "Grampy, I have something very sad to tell you."

"What's that?"

"When I told Lucas and Mackenzie that Jesus had me buy the two candy canes for them, they asked me who Jesus was. They never even heard of Him. Isn't that sad?"

Franklin had thought everyone had heard of Jesus, at least in The States. Those poor children must have had a horrible experience with their mother. Did they even know why people celebrated Christmas?

That evening, Franklin had difficulty falling asleep. Did he have the strength to give Katie's Ford Explorer to Sue? But the poor woman needed it. But how could he watch someone else drive around town in his wife's car. That would only be a constant reminder of his crime and rotten life. But those poor children need a break. Exhausted from overthinking, he fell asleep.

CHAPTER 21

A Vehicle for Sue

MAGGIE SAT DOWN AT the kitchen table. "Grampy, what are we going to do today?"

Franklin placed a plate of scrambled eggs and toast in front of her. He sat down with his food.

"Those look good." She picked up the salt shaker. "So, what are we going to do?"

"Well, I've been thinking. Mrs. Hamilton needs a vehicle. I had bought Nana a new red Ford Explorer for Christmas three days before the accident, and it's been in Uncle Johnny's garage ever since."

She smacked the shaker down. "Can we give it to her, please?"

"I've been considering it."

With palms up, Maggie responded, "Consider no more. It's the right thing to do."

"It's not that easy. Eventually, I'll see Mrs. Hamilton drive Nana's car around town."

"Oh brother," she fell back in the chair, "I don't believe you! Did you ever give it to Nana?"

"Maggie, that question was out of line. You know we lost Nana before I could. Now eat your breakfast."

"But Grampy, it was never Nana's in the first place. Haven't you ever bought a present for someone and decide to give it to someone else? This is the same thing. Just because you bought it for Nana, it doesn't mean it was hers. It belongs to the person you give it to."

How could his eight-year-old granddaughter's rational make more sense than his own brain? He sat silent for a few moments.

Maggie placed her delicate hand on top of his. "Grampy, we're both sad we lost Nana, but Nana would tell you this is the right thing to do. She no longer needs it, but Mrs. Hamilton and her grandchildren need it."

He took hold of her finger tips. "What you just said makes sense. If it were the other way around, Nana would give it to Mrs. Hamilton. She had a giving heart."

"Exactly. So we give it to her?"

"Yes, but I need a few moments." He muttered, "How am I going to get to her?"

"Grampy, I would think the easiest way to get it to her is to drive it to her."

"It's more complicated than that. Let's eat before the food gets cold."

"Let's pray before we eat it." She shot him a Garfield grin.

Like an obedient soldier, he bowed his head and took her hand. When she said amen and he didn't, she flashed him a dirty look.

"Okay, amen."

"But Grampy, I don't understand. How can that be complicated?"

"Some things are too personal for me to discuss. Look. For my own reasons, I'd rather not take it over to her myself."

"Okay, but can't Uncle Johnny take it over for you?"

Franklin bit off a piece of toast. "I don't know, but that's a great idea. I'll have to call him."

"Please call him right now."

"I will, but not until I get done eating."

After he was done, he poured himself a cup of coffee.

She shoveled her eggs into her mouth, and scraped her fork across the plate, gathering the last bit of eggs. After she chomped down her toast, she pushed her plate aside. "I'm done!"

"I'm not. I'm enjoying my coffee."

"Hurry please."

"No. The coffee is hot. This is the deal. Since you have so much energy, let Harry out for a few minutes and give him some water. By then I should be done and I'll call Johnny."

"Okay, will do."

Franklin rinsed off their plates. "I'm going to my den to call Uncle Johnny."

"Yippy! I'm so excited for Mrs. Hamilton."

After he sat at his desk, he took his cell phone out of his pocked, and stared at it for a few moments. He rubbed a hand along his jeans. "Here I go." He pressed Johnny's name. "Hello Johnny, it's me."

"Frank? You're calling me?"

Franklin held back his temper. "Please don't be smart. I have something serious I need to talk to you about."

"What's wrong? Did something happen to Maggie?"

"No. Nothing happened. Can you come by?"

"Do you mean, come by your place?"

"Yes. Can you come by or not?" Franklin asked.

"I'm sorry, but I can't. I was just about to leave. I have a business meeting in Manchester today. Why? What's going on?"

"There's this woman who's raising her two grandchildren. The woman needs the Explorer."

Dead silence on the other end. Franklin couldn't even hear Johnny breathe. "Hello, hello, you there?"

"Yes."

"Then say something."

"I—ah—I'm sorry. You stunned me. You're willing to give Katie's car to another woman, who's total stranger?"

"What makes you think she's a stranger?"

"Hello, you've been a recluse for two years."

Franklin rubbed his forehead. "So you don't think I should help her?"

"No! I never said that, but what's the deal?"

"She's raising her two grandchildren and she doesn't have much money. She had a fifteen-year-old Subaru. The engine seized, and now she has nothing. She works as a cook at the hospital. She has a lot on her plate. I think the woman needs a break, especially her grandchildren. Besides, how can I leave the Explorer in your garage when I have the power to give it to her?" Franklin Explained.

"I agree. But how did you meet this woman."

"She's Bob's tenant."

"I see. I think it's commendable that you're willing to help her. If I didn't have to leave—wait a minute. I can drop it off to you. Then you . . ."

Help her! That's what the strange man from Christmas Town meant. Somehow, that man might have known he had the Ford Explorer, but he had never seen that man before. He titled back his black leather chair and rocked it.

"Hello Frank! Are you there?"

"Yes, I'm here. I was thinking about something. Hey, I really don't want it at my place. I don't think I could deal with that."

"So, how are you going to get it to her?"

"I just got an idea. Will Mary be home to unlock the garage door?"

"Yes, she's having a cookie exchange party today."

"Good, I'm going to see if Pastor Mark can pick it up and deliver it to the woman for me."

"Frank, that's a God idea."

"Whatever. Please let Mary know before you leave. If he can't help out, then we'll work on something tomorrow. I'll give Mary a call and let her know either way."

"Sounds good, but let me know how it goes too, please."

"I will."

When he left the den, Maggie was in the living room playing with Harry. "Maggie, bundle up. We're going over to Pastor Mark's place."

She leaped up. "Can Uncle Johnny help?"

Slipping on his jacket, he replied, "Not today, but I'm going to see if Pastor Mark is home. Maybe he can give us a hand."

"I'll pray."

"Put on your jacket while you're praying."

"Grampy, I'm sorry, but I need to pray first."

He rolled his eyes. "Okay, but hurry."

She looked heavenward and pointed her finger upward. "Father, Mrs. Hamilton needs Grampy's car. Work it out, in the name of Jesus, amen." She zipped her jacket. "Okay, I'm ready."

"Put your mittens on, too."

"I got them right here in my pocket," she pulled them out, "See."

"I see, but put them on."

On the porch, Franklin threw his hood over his head and took Maggie's hand. "Oh great, it looks quiet over there. I hope someone's home."

"Don't worry. You heard me pray. God will work it out."

As they walked across the street, Maggie babbled something about the consequences of worry, but he really didn't pay much attention.

Before Franklin could ring Mark's doorbell, Grace opened the door. She jolted, her eyes popped, and she tossed a bag of sandwich rolls into the air.

"Did we scare you?" Maggie giggled as she picked up the rolls for her.

Grace cracked-up. "Yes. It's called the element of surprise."

Without a doubt, Franklin got a good laughed out of that one. "Sorry about that. By the way, is Pastor home?"

"He's in the church. I was on my way to bring him some rolls so he can make sandwiches later. He's doing some work on one of the bedrooms. Come with me. I'm sure he'll be happy to see you both."

Sandwiches? It seemed odd that an average sized man like Pastor Mark could eat more than one sandwich, but it wasn't his business.

Grace shut the door behind her. "Are you having a good day?"

"I'm blessed and highly favored of the Lord!" Maggie declared.

"Praise the Lord." Grace took long strides as she swung the package of rolls along her side.

Franklin opened the church door for them. "It's nice and toasty in here."

"Yeah it is, isn't it? We love wood heat. It makes everything cozy," Grace hollered down the hall, "Honey, you have a couple of guests!"

"Hun, can you bring them back here, please?"

Grace dropped the rolls on the kitchen counter, and led the way. When they passed the first bedroom, Franklin noticed it had been converted to a small fellowship hall.

"Honey, Franklin and Maggie are here," Grace announced as they entered the second bedroom.

Standing on a wooden ladder with a hammer in hand, Mark looked over his shoulder.

Standing near the ladder, Jesse turned around. "Professor Franklyn . . ."

Maggie raised a dismissive hand. "No! Please call Grampy Frank."

Jesse stared with a gape-mouthed. "Grampy Frank?"

"Maggie, you interrupted him and you've confused him too. That was not nice," Franklin scolded.

"I'm sorry Mr. Jesse. I'm sorry Grampy. I really am sorry, but you take so long to tell people your name."

"Maggie, it isn't your place to tell people my name unless you're introducing me to someone."

She pouted, "I'm sorry," and then she perked up, "Mr. Jesse, I would like you to meet my Grampy. His name is Frank." Wide-eyed, she smiled at Franklin, "Did you mean like that?"

Jesse twisted around, and sputtered like attempting to hide his laughter.

Franklin pointed at her and opened his mouth. Then he closed it, and then opened it again as he started to speak. "Young lady, we'll discuss this later."

Mark chortled, "You have to admit. She did what you told her to do."

Though his pastor friend found humor in it, Franklin didn't. "I guess she did. By the way, what's your plan for this room?"

Mark laid down the hammer on top of the ladder. As he climbed down, he replied, "It'll be a guestroom, and Jesse will be our first guest."

He's going to put a thief in here? He's got a wife to protect?

Grace snapped her fingers. "That reminds me. I better get going. I have to go to the store. I'm going to a cookie exchange party this afternoon."

Before she left, Mark gave her a peck on the lips. "I love you."

"I love you too," she edged in for another kiss.

They reminded him of Katie and him. Neither of them had ever left the house before they had kissed each other. He loved kissing his wife, and he missed kissing her.

After Grace left, Mark asked, "So tell me, what brought you here today?"

Franklin placed his hands on his hips. "Well, I need a favor, but you're busy. Just forget about it. It can wait."

"I may be busy, but I'm never too busy to listen. You'll never know if I can give you a hand or not unless you tell me what you need."

"Well, if you have a moment." Franklin glanced over at Jesse. "Pastor, I'd like to talk to you alone. Would you mind? It won't take long?"

"No problem. Let's go into the sanctuary."

"Thank you."

Pastor addressed Jesse. "Would you mind hanging the curtain rod and the curtains? And I'll be back in a bit to do the other window."

"No worries, I'll get it done."

In the sanctuary, Franklin and Pastor stood near the back row seats. Maggie sat down sideways on one of the chairs.

After he glanced down the hall, Franklin placed his hands in his pockets. "Do you know where the wholesale Christmas tree farm is? The one up the road a piece?"

"Yes, it's about a mile or so from here. Grace and I went there to buy a Christmas tree. But when we saw several tractor trailers driving on and off the property, we assumed the trees were sold wholesale. Anyhow, why do you ask?"

"The man who owns the property is a good friend of mine. His name is Bob Lapierre. He has a tenant who lives in the manufactured home on the property, and his tenant needs a car. She's a woman in her fifties, and she's raising her two grandchildren. She's a cook at the hospital, she needs a car, and she has no husband."

Pastor nodded his head. "Oh I see. I don't know of anybody who has anything right off hand, but I can check around and see if I can find someone who's selling something." He smiled and raised his finger. "But I got an idea that might help that might help her until we can find something for her. Since Grace is a surgical nurse at the hospital, maybe she could ride into work with Grace."

That seemed odd to Franklin. Sue didn't attend Pastor Mark's church, and he was willing to help her find a car. The Pastor was a different type of Christian. That would have never happened in Katie's old church.

"I appreciate your offer, but I have a brand new Ford Explorer stored in Johnny's garage. Actually, the vehicle is two years old, but I bought it new, and it's been in his garage ever since, and I'd like to give it to her."

Mark's brows rose up. "Praise the Lord! You're willing to give her your best. Now that's a giving heart."

"Well, I'm only doing it because the woman needs a car, but I need a way to get it to her."

Maggie walked toward them.

"Why don't you just drive it to her?"

Again, Maggie interrupted, "That's what I suggested, but it's complicated."

Mark's smiley expression melted into a serious one. "Was it your wife's Explorer?"

Franklin tilted his head downward, and raised it again. "I bought it for her. It was her Christmas present. Three days after I had bought it, we had the accident."

Very solemn, Mark nodded, slowly. "I see. Would you like me to help you deliver it to the woman?"

"Yes. If you can, that is, I really would appreciate it."

"Of course I can. I'd be more than happy to help you out. When would you like me to do this?"

"The woman has no car. Can you give me a hand today?"

"Sure," Mark threw his hands up, "Oh man, I forgot, I can't today. I have two appointments, but I'm sure Jesse wouldn't mind giving you a hand," he glanced at his watch, "and I can take a few minutes to drop him off at Johnny's place."

"Jesse?" Franklin's heart sank. "I don't know about that."

"Frank, Jesse is a good man who has suffered a great deal of loss. But the moment I saw him, God told me to help him. I believe there's a special calling on his life. Besides, this might help you get to know him."

"Please Grampy," Maggie stood up, "God changes people. I trust Mr. Jesse because God didn't want him in jail. There was a reason for that. Remember, I told you about it? And meeting Mr. Jesse was a divine appointment from God. Please Grampy, Mrs. Hamilton needs the car. It's all part of God's plan."

Pastor Mark nodded his head. "I have to agree with her."

"Okay, I'll give him a chance. That is, if he doesn't mind helping out?"

Mark responded, "Good, I'll go talk to him. If you don't mind waiting here for a moment, and I'll be right back."

Franklin still had his doubts. "Sure, I'll wait."

A few moments later, Franklin spotted Jesse and Mark coming down the hallway. Jesse placed his thumbs in his jean pockets. "Professor Franklyn, I'll be more than happy to help you out."

Out of secret protest, he accepted Jesse's offer with a hand shake. "I do appreciate it. I'll give Pastor Mark the directions to Johnny's place."

Mark's eyes twinkled. "Oh, you don't have to. I've been to his place."

"You've been to Johnny's?" *Why didn't the pipsqueak say something to me?*

"Yes. I was just there this past Thursday. Their hospitality is impeccable. He invited us to his promotional party, and we followed him to the museum because we hadn't been there before. But I don't remember seeing you at the party," Mark gazed off. "Nope, I don't remember. Were you there?"

That made sense. Grace must have gone to Mary's party. Mark and Johnny must be tight. That didn't surprise Franklin a bit. The socialite pipsqueak knew everyone.

Maggie tugged on Franklin's jacket. "That was the night you and Mommy were at Uncle Johnny's."

Oh boy, here we go again.

"You were there when we were there?" Pastor Mark chuckled, "We crossed paths, and we didn't realize it?"

"Pastor Mark, that's a divine appointment," Maggie declared.

"By golly you're correct," Mark added, "But it's a part of God's great plan."

"Great plan. What great plan?" Franklin refused to become part of any holy spook plan.

Mark replied, "I'm not sure, but it's like a network of threads coming together to complete a section of a great tapestry. It will be interesting to watch it unfold."

Forget about it! It's not happening.

When he slipped his hands out of his pocket, he shook Mark's hand. "I really appreciate your help. But I have to go home and get the title, and then I'll give you the information where to bring the Explorer."

"Grampy! Didn't you hear what he said about the great tapestry?"

"Yes I did, but we need to get going."

Pastor Mark interceded, "Maggie, I think you need to give your grampy a chance to process it."

That was a great excuse for Franklin. "Pastor understands that I need a chance to process it."

Maggie grinned, "Okay."

Franklin glanced at the Pastor, "Can you bring Jesse over to my place so I can give him the paperwork on the Explorer?"

"After I finish up here, we'll be right over."

"Thank you. I'll see you in a bit." He took Maggie's hand and left.

At home in his den, Franklin swung the large framed photo of his vacation home in Fairbanks around to get to his safe. He hadn't opened it since he had put Katie's death certificate in it.

His hands trembled as he clicked the knob to each number of its combination. When he heard the last click, he inhaled a sharp breath as he gripped the safe's handle. He cranked it down. The metal door sprung open.

Katie's bible lied on top of everything. He wiggled his fingers, squeezed them against his palm, and formed a tight fist before he reached in.

Teary-eyed, he removed it out of the safe. He rubbed his thumb along the blood droplet stained on the center of her blue bible case. Uncontrollable tears streamed out of his eyes.

He plunked down on the leather straight chair by the safe, and laid the bible on the end of his desk. With his two hands over his face, he cried quietly. After several moments, he took hold of his composure. As he lifted himself out of the chair, he felt weak.

Wobbly-legged, he pawed through the documents in the safe. "Where's that title?"

He found the title under the small manila envelope with Katie's death certificate. He took a moment to force back the tears. "Why am I putting myself through this?" As he pulled out the title, he gazed at the death certificate's envelope. "I can't take this nightmare any longer." He slammed his eyes shut. "But Sue needs the SUV."

At once, he grabbed the safe's handle, slammed the door shut, and spun the combination dial to lock it.

With the title in hand, he hunched over the edge of his desk and laid down the title. As he picked up his Schaefer pen to sign it over to Sue, his hands shook.

He grabbed his right wrist. "Stop shaking. I have a mission to complete." Slanting the document, he hunched over and signed it off to Mrs. Hamilton.

The door bell rang. He dropped the pen, grabbed the title, and rushed to the den's door. As he hurried down the hall, he shouted, "Maggie, don't open that door until I get there!"

She hollered back, "I already did! It's Pastor Mark and Mr. Jesse!"

By the time he had gotten to her, she was between the front door and the storm door.

Franklin had Maggie move away from the door, as he invited them in.

Mark stepped into the small foyer next to Jesse. "I explained to Maggie that we didn't feel comfortable coming in without you in the room."

"I appreciate that."

"Grace and I never allowed our two boys to answer the door when we weren't around, and I'm firm on rules and policy."

It had never occurred to Franklin to ask him if he had kids. "You have two boys?"

"Yes we do. Our eldest son, Josiah, is a Navy Seal and Jeremiah is an army Green Beret." He started laughing, "These days, our boys answer the door for us."

Franklin chortled, "I bet they do."

"Pastor Mark," Maggie asked, "What are Green Berets and Navy Seals?"

Mark hunched over. "Do you know what Special Forces in the military are?"

"Uh-huh, my dad's friend is Delta Force."

"Navy Seals are Special Forces in the Navy and Green Berets are Special Forces in the Army."

Franklin shut the door. "And you young lady, I don't want you to ever answer the door when you're staying with me."

"That's my parents' rules too. But I thought since you knew they were coming, it'd be alright for me to answer the door. Besides, I saw them coming up the walkway."

"Maggie, I have no problem with you answering the door to Pastor Mark, but you need to stick with the rules your parents and I set down for you. It's because we're trying to protect you."

"I understand."

Franklin edged near Jesse, and handed him the title. "I signed the title over to her. The woman's name is Sue Hamilton. Since she has no vehicle, she should be home. My sister-in-law, Mary, she has the keys to the Explorer. She'll let you in the garage."

"Okay, does Mary know I'm coming?"

"Oh shoot, I forgot to call her. I'll call as soon as you leave, but how will you get back to Pastor Mark's place?"

Jesse's broad smile beamed. "Before we came over, we called Grace. She'll pick me up after she gets done at the grocery store."

Franklin crossed his arms over his chest. "But how will I know what happened?"

Pastor Mark responded, "I gave Jesse my personal cell phone. Here's the number. My business line is under it." Mark slid his finger to the bottom of the sticky note. "This one here is Grace's."

"This is perfect." Franklin put the sticky note in his shirt pocket. "Jesse, call me when you're done, okay. I would like to know how it went."

"Sure, when Grace picks me up, I'll call ya."

Nervous about the outcome, Franklin needed to do something to busy himself. "Hey, princess would you like to make that lobster stew with me tonight?"

"Can we?"

"We sure can, but we need to go to the store to pick up some things."

"Okay. This is going to be so much fun."

On their way into the garage, Franklin had his keys in his hand. "Maggie, would you like to decorate the outside of the house tomorrow morning?"

"Really? We can?"

"Yes we can."

She hugged him. "You're the best grandfather in the world."

While at the market, Jesse called Franklin, but he missed the call. "Maggie, Jesse called. We have to go to the front of the store to get service."

"Okay."

Since he was in the back of the store by the dairy department, he had to fight the crowds to get to the front. "Maggie, hold on to the buggy while I call my voicemail."

"Yes, Grampy."

"I pressed one. Get to it. I don't need to hear who, the date, and the time. I want my voicemail."

Jesse's message, "Done. Delivered."

He turned his phone, and gritted his teeth at it. "Are you kidding me? That's it? Done. Delivered."

"What's wrong, Grampy? He told you it's done."

"I would have liked to have gotten a little more detail."

"I get it. Maybe he doesn't like to talk to a voicemail. Mom doesn't."

At home, when they finished putting the groceries away, Franklin heard a soft knock. "Did you hear that? Is that the front door?"

Maggie stood by the dining table. "Yes, I heard it. Someone is knocking, listen."

Franklin laid his jacket down on the counter top. "I hear it. You don't open that door."

"I won't."

Just as Franklin opened the door, Jesse rang the doorbell. "Jesse, I appreciate what you did for me, but you could have been a little more detailed on the voicemail."

"I'm sorry. I thought you would rather hear it in person."

"Come on in. Have a seat."

Maggie sat on the rocking chair by the fireplace.

Jesse looked around the living room. "You sure have a beautiful home. It's real cozy in here."

Anxious to hear what happened, Franklin stood. "Thank you, but what happened? Was she happy?"

Jesse's broad smile appeared on his face. "Happy? Nah. It was more like she was dancing on cloud nine, and she just had a glimpse of heaven. But when Mrs. Hamilton noticed the name Dr. B. Francis Franklyn on the title, she asked me if you gave her the car."

"Oh boy, what did you tell her?"

"That I was only a delivery man. Which was true," Jesse replied.

"Thank you. I appreciate that, and I really do appreciate you giving me a hand."

"I was more than happy to do it. I'll never forget the look of joy on that woman's face. You should have seen the kids. Their faces were priceless. I have never seen two kids so happy in all my life.

The little girl jumped in on the passenger side, and she rubbed her face along the leather seat. When I assured the boy it really was their car, he started crying, he got into the back seat, and slid his hands all over the leather seats. I'll tell ya, this family was happy to get that Explorer. You're a big hearted man. I'm sure you made that family's Christmas."

Franklin choked up. He sat down on his chair, and folded his hands under his chin. He could feel something changing inside, but he couldn't put his finger on it. Looking skyward, he wondered about the validity of heaven. If Katie were looking down at him from heaven, she sure would be proud of his decision.

Because of feeling both humbled and elated, he wished he were alone so he could cry. "I never had an opportunity to do something like this before. Jesse, I have no words to describe how happy I am to hear all of this. I can't thank you enough for helping out."

"No problem. I was happy to do so. It blessed my heart to see that family's joy."

When Jesse left, Maggie waved from the rocking chair and said a simple "Good-bye."

Franklin found her quietness odd. "Princess, why were you so quiet? That's not like you."

"Because Jesus told me He was speaking to your heart."

Stumped, he couldn't reply. "Want to help me bring the decorations upstairs for tomorrow?"

"Yes, I'll help."

After Franklin and Maggie made the lobster stew together, they sat on the sectional with their bowls of stew as they watched an old classic movie. But he couldn't concentrate on the movie.

Jesus spoke to his heart? That's impossible. But maybe that change he felt inside of him—that seemed ridiculous. It had to have been her imagination because he had no explanation. Could Jesus have spoken to him?

CHAPTER 22

The Divine Design Manifesting

AFTER FRANKLIN AND MAGGIE had a quick breakfast, they hauled the lights and lawn decorations onto the front porch.

A wind gust blew off Franklin's hood. He threw it back over his head and pulled the strings. "All I need is my ladder. It's in the garage."

"I'll help you."

When he took hold of the ladder, he noticed Maggie standing by his truck with a vacant look in her eyes, wearing a silly grin. She appeared lost in a daydream. While he observed her, she slid her eyes upward and placed her hand on her chest.

Franklin whistled, and then he boomed, "Maggie!"

Without moving a muscle, she fixed her eyes on him. The longer she stared at him, the wider her grin grew.

"Hello, are you in there?"

"Jesus told me, 'Where's your diner?'"

He stressed, "A-ha! That was a question. And if I had a diner, I would know where it was, and so would God."

"But Grampy, sometimes when He tells me. . ."

"This time, I think you made a mistake. I guarantee you, I didn't misplace a diner."

"But. . ."

"No Buts."

She rolled her eyes. "Okay Grampy."

"If you think about it, it's not reasonable. If I had a diner, and I no longer desire one, I would know about it."

She swayed her head. "But Grampy, most of the time Jesus tells me something in a question form. He's not asking where your diner is. He's telling you that He has one for you."

If God had appeared before him and had handed him a diner, Franklin wouldn't accept it anyhow, not without Katie. "Princess, I will no longer participate in this discussion. Do you want to decorate?"

"Yes."

"Good, let's get started."

Several outlets were under the eves and around the bottom walls of the house. When Franklin built his house, He wired each outdoor outlet to one switch, so he could control everything from inside the garage.

By late morning, Franklin completed hanging the lights around the porch, first and second story windows. He started down the extension-ladder. "Maggie, how are you doing?"

"I got one more candy cane to stick in the ground, and I'm done with the walkway. Look!" Maggie pointed the solar candy cane outward. "Pastor Mark and Mr. Jesse are coming over."

Franklin stepped off the ladder. "Is Mark holding a shopping bag?"

Jesse raised his hand and waved.

"Howdy neighbor and Miss Maggie," Mark greeted.

Franklin briskly opened and shut his hands by his sides. "Nice jackets. Are they new?"

Jesse rubbed his hands together. "Thank you, Professor Franklyn. Grace bought it for me. She said she couldn't let me wear that old shabby jacket any longer." He raised a hand. "She got me these warm ski gloves too."

"That was neighborly of her. You do need something like that to keep you warm in this neck of the woods."

"Yeah, and it's warm."

Pastor Mark's new jacket seemed extra nice and expensive. Franklin sniffed inward. "You look more like a cowboy today than a pastor. I really like that shearling, sheepskin coat. I had one like that once, but mine was a darker tan, actually, more brown than yours."

"Thank you much. It's a gift from my parents. I got it yesterday."

Bundled up in Kitty's old green snowsuit, Maggie's nose and cheeks were quite rosy. "Pastor Mark, you're not supposed to open your Christmas present before Christmas."

"This is true missy, but my parents asked me to open it when they were on the phone with me yesterday."

She twirled the candy cane like a baton. "But why? It's supposed to be for Christmas."

"Well little one, my parents left for Haiti this morning. They're helping *Samaritan's Purse: Operation Christmas Child*, and they wanted me to open it before they left."

"I know them." Franklin had helped Katie when she had prepared her shoebox for underprivileged children, and he enjoyed doing it with her.

Maggie lit up. "I know them too. That's Franklyn Graham's organization. Me and my parents send them a shoebox filled with all kinds of stuff. We've been doing it ever since I've been alive."

Franklin responded, "And you've been around a long time."

"Grampy, I'm serious."

"Oh by the way, I got a little something for you." Mark handed the shopping bag to Franklin.

"What's in here?"

"It's a gift, but it wasn't my idea. It was God's. Remember when we had lunch together last Saturday, I told you that I too had gone to the mall?"

"Yes, that's how you found Jesse."

"That's right, and that's how I found that. God told me to buy it, but He didn't tell me who it was for, or why. This morning, I had a stirring in my spirit to give it to you. So think of it as a gift from God."

"Thank you." With one hand, Franklin held the bag up near his face. As he gazed at it, he rubbed his chin. "It's heavy."

Maggie rubbed her nose. "Well, aren't you going to open it?"

"Don't be so impatient. I'm trying to figure out what it is."

"I don't believe this." Maggie tapped the bag with the candy cane. "Grampy, if you look inside, you can see what it is."

A huge grin extended across Mark's face. "Brother, I think she's got a point."

Jesse cracked up.

"I'm glad you're all amused!"

"Grampy please, just open it." She stood on her tippy toes as she tried to look in the bag. "Hurry please. I want to see what it is."

"I will. Just calm down."

As he slid it out of the bag, Maggie blurted, "It's a picture. What's the picture of? I can't see it. You're holding it too high."

Flabbergasted, he analyzed the print of a log cabin diner in the mist of snow-covered conifers. Surrounded by a few other rustic town buildings gave the impression of a small wilderness village, during Alaska's gold rush days. Over the front entrance hung the business's name, Bear Bones Diner, in faded blue letters. A sled team of huskies lying on hay near the front of the building helped captivate the historical period. All against a clear night star filled sky with a light display of Aurora Borealis.

This must have been the diner Maggie imagined that God asked her about. But he had never known anyone with an intuitive ability like his little princess's. "Um, this is beautiful. Thank you."

He lowered the plaque so Maggie could see it.

She touched it with the tip of her finger. "Look! It's a diner. It says so right there." She slid her finger across the plaque. "Grampy, look at the post office. It says Fairbanks, Alaska. Where's that?"

"Fairbanks?"

"Yes, look its right here. Do you see the Fairbank's post office sign?"

"I see it. It's the second largest city in Alaska."

Recognition dawned on Maggie's face. "This must be the diner . . ." she stopped and pressed against her diaphragm. "Sorry Grampy, it's not."

When Franklin heard that, it nerved him. "It's not what?"

"It's not the diner God is giving you. It's just more confirmation."

Mark crinkled his forehead. "God's giving you a diner?"

"No! Absolutely not!" He caught himself barking at the pastor. "I'm so sorry. I didn't mean to jump like that. I'm really . . ."

In a gentle tone, Mark interrupted, "Hey, no worries. It's okay. But I'm curious, what's all this about a diner? If you don't mind, telling me that is."

"You see, Katie and I had planned on opening a diner before she died. But I have no more interest without her."

"Was Katie your wife?" Jesse inquired.

Of course he must have known. All Christians gossip. At least that was Franklin's experience. "You didn't know that I had lost my wife too?"

Squeezing his lips together, Jesse turned away for a moment. "No, I didn't. I did inquire about your wife, but Pastor Mark told me that 'If a man has a question about another man, he should ask that man.'"

Franklin shot his eyes toward Pastor.

Mark gave one nod. "My grandfather taught me that when I was a boy."

A moment of silence fell among them. Mark appeared deep in thought, and Jesse gazed out with his eyelids drooping. In awe, Franklin thought on how trustworthy Pastor Mark had proven himself.

A gusty wind howled through the eerie silence. And then, Maggie's voice sounded. "But Mr. Jesse, my nana and your family are in our future."

"Thank you, Maggie. That helps." Jesse lifted an eyebrow. "You know, my wife was a Christian before she passed. But at that time, I refused to bother with Christianity. You know, I'm sure glad I have Jesus now."

"I'm glad you found Him too. And when Grampy gets saved, he'll be happy that he has Jesus too."

Franklin squeezed his lips shut. All this stuff about him joining the holly rollers got on his nerves. But how could he stop her from talking about it without hurting her feelings?

With his winter boot, Mark kicked some snow off the walkway onto the lawn. "So, do you like to cook or was it your Mrs. who cooked?"

`Before Franklin could reply, Maggie did. "Grampy is the best cook ever. Last night, he taught me how to make Pappy's lobster stew." She rolled her eyes behind her head, "It was the best thing ever."

"Really, Dr. Franklyn? You can cook?" Jesse chortled, "Cooking is a science, but it's a science I have no clue about."

"Yes, I have a passion for it. I learned everything I know from my grandfather, who was a chef."

Pulling his stocking hat over his ear, Mark asked, "Did your wife have the same passion?"

"For the diner, yes. But she was a baker, and she loved baking. When we were in high school, she worked for my grandfather as a baker apprentice. In fact, the summer before the accident, Katie and I had decided to open one in Fairbanks for the summer months. Tourist season. That's where we have our vacation home. I mean—um, I own a vacation home."

"Interesting, the picture depicts Fairbanks." Mark's cell phone rang, "It's Grace. I have to get this."

"I've been to Fairbanks," Jesse commented, "If you had opened the place, you would have raked in the money. That town is hopping in the summer."

"Jesse, Grace is on her break, and she's on her way to pick you up."

"Praise the Lord! I have an interview at the hospital."

"That's great," Franklin declared. "You're life is really turning around. What position did you apply for?"

"Lab tech. It's a beginning." His entire face lit up. "I just remembered something. I told that lady you gave the car to how good Jesus is, and about all the great things he has done for me. I let her know it was God who had given her the Explorer, and that she needed to thank Him for it . . ."

Jesus freaks always gave God the credit instead of the person who had done the good deed. After all, the Ford Explorer didn't just fall out of heaven.

" . . .I'm not sure if she received it. But like Pastor taught me, God's word does not return to Him void." Jesse glanced over at Pastor Mark. "That's correct. Right?"

"That's right." Pastor confirmed.

"Well, I better get across the street before Grace comes. Professor Franklin, it was nice visiting with you."

Franklin shook his hand. "Jesse, please call me Frank."

"Thank you sir. I appreciate that. You have a great day."

"You too."

Jesse ambled across the street.

Once again, Maggie slid her finger across the plaque. "Look Grampy, there's a general store over here on the left side. It's even got little sale signs on the windows. This is so funny. Pickles three cents each? You can't buy just one pickle. You have to buy a whole jar. Isn't that funny?"

Franklin put the plaque back into the bag. "Princess, at one time, stores had huge wooden barrels of pickles. Customers bought a pickle out of the barrel. That's what the artist had depicted here when he painted it."

"That must have been a long time ago. Way before me."

When Franklin chuckled over his princess's remark, he caught a glimpse of Pastor Mark nodding his head with his finger pressing against his lip. He attempted to get into Mark's thoughts, "So, pastor, a lot has transpired these few days, hasn't it?"

"Yes it has. But I just had a thought. It seems like this picture is part of a divine design." He brightened. "Oh yes, I almost forgot. When I saw you two folks out here, I thought maybe you can use a hand."

That divine design sounded important, whatever it meant. Franklin had never heard that term used before. "Absolutely, I could use a hand. But I don't want to keep you from any plans you may have with your bride."

"No, we have no plans. Grace doesn't get off until six, and I'm taking her out for dinner tonight. You got me for the rest of the day."

The divine design thing kept gnawing at Franklin's heart. Added to all the holy spook stuff, it was time he had a conversation with Mark. "It's after noon and I'm hungry. Pastor, would you like to join us for grilled cheese sandwiches and hot tomato soup?"

"That sounds mighty good."

After getting Maggie up before the crack of dawn, along with working in the cold air, Franklin hoped she'd be tuckered out. He wagered that once she hit the warm air and got hot food in her tummy, she'd fall asleep. If she did, he'd have enough time alone with Pastor. "Then it's settled. Let's take a lunch break."

"But Grampy, I didn't have a chance to put the last candy cane in the ground."

Franklin rubbed her head. "Well, go ahead. Pastor Mark and I will wait here until you get it done."

CHAPTER 23

Franklin Seeks Answers

When Maggie finished with her tomato soup, she plopped down her Wolfuss mug and yawned. She rubbed her droopy eyes and yawned again. "Why do I feel so sleepy?"

Maybe Franklin will have some time alone with pastor after all. "Well, when you're in the cold air and come in where it's warm, you relax, especially when your belly is full. Would you like to take a nap?"

"Yes, but just a little one. Please wait for me before you finish decorating."

Franklin was proud of his success. "Of course we will. I'll wake you up in about an hour."

"Thank you." Maggie moseyed off.

Pastor Mark placed the empty tumbler down near his plate. "Boy that hit the spot. I really do appreciate you having me for lunch."

"Sure anytime, but I'm sorry. I forgot to ask you if you mind waiting for Maggie before we go back out."

"Not at all. This gives us an opportunity to fellowship. Besides, it's cozy in here."

Franklin paused to gather his thoughts. He rubbed under his chin as he eyeballed the pastor across the table.

Pastor Mark pushed up his blue tee-shirt's sleeves above his wrists. "Is there something on your mind?"

"Well, yes."

"I'm all ears."

"Well, that picture. I've been wondering, what did you mean by a divine design?"

"May I ask you this? What happened the night your wife passed away? That is, if you don't mind telling me."

That was a reality check that Franklin wasn't ready for. "Boy that's a zinger. What does that have to do with the picture?"

"Everything, as long as you're willing to tell me. It'll help me and you understand God's divine design for you."

Though Franklin hadn't known him long, he found Pastor Mark a different kind of Christian. He never heard preaching like his before, and he enjoyed it. In just a short time, he found the man trustworthy.

When Franklin opened his mouth, his heart poured out like a bucket of water. And at his surprise, he poured out without resistance. "It was my fault."

With his hands crossed behind his head. "I see, but how was it your fault?"

"I'm not a Christian, and I'm sure you've already figured that out by now."

"Yes, I have."

"It's not that I'm an atheist. I do believe God exists, but I base my belief system on . . ." Ever since Maggie had arrived, he no longer knew for sure what he believed. "So much has happened these past several days. I'm not sure if they're from God or not. I just can't explain it. I don't know anymore."

Mark lifted his shoulder in a half shrug. "Okay. God has been revealing Himself to you."

Could that have been possible? Franklin sat back. "Where do I start?"

"It'd be best if you start from the beginning."

"Well, we were at Katie's church down in Concord for Maggie's Christmas play. I had promised Maggie that I would attend the Christmas party after the play. She was only six at the time."

Recalling how adorable Maggie looked in her little angel costume dancing around on the stage, he paused.

"It's very obvious that she's very close to you," Mark remarked.

"Yes, we are very close. She'll always be my little princess."

"I bet she will. So, you were planning on going to Maggie's party after the play."

"Yes we were. Katie told me that she had a warning from God. She told me that it was a feeling inside her diaphragm. She insisted that we needed to skip the party, and go straight home, but I dismissed it. You have to understand that I had never heard of God using someone's stomach to speak to them."

With one hand over the back of his chair, Mark clicked his tongue. "It sounds as though she attempted to explain to you that the Lord's Spirit speaks to us through our spirit. It's more like a gut feeling."

"That sounds like what she had tried to explain to me, but I didn't understand it back then." Franklin combed his fingers through his hair. "But now, it seems clearer. Anyhow, when I saw how much it bothered her, I agreed to leave after the play. I promised I would go straight home." Franklin looked away. He forced back the tears. "But I didn't keep my promise."

While losing his composure, Franklin slid his eyes downward and squeezed his trembling lips together. "You see, after Christmas, Kitty and her husband, Jake, had planned to move to Tulsa for school. They were taking Maggie with them for two years. It was hard on both of us." His eyes welled up. "But since they were going to leave Maggie with us the following evening," he lowered his head and placed his hand against his throat as he choked back the tears, "I wanted to make something special for her, her favorite biscuits and gravy. But we had no whole milk in the house.

Katie pleaded with me not to stop, but I insisted." Tears flooded his eyes, "I told her it wouldn't kill her to wait a few minutes, while I ran into the store." With his lips pulled inward, he squeezed his eyes shut. His eyes popped opened. After sucking in air, Franklin blurted out, "But it did! It killed her."

From his tear-rimmed eyes, silent streams of salty droplets cascaded down his face, dripping into his mouth. Mucus secreted from his nose onto his upper lip. He took a few napkins, wiped his eyes and nose, but the tears kept flowing. He took in a few sharp breaths, but the tears kept flowing.

He formed one of the dampened napkins into a ball. White-knuckled, he squeezed it in his hand, as he continued, "She was killed because I stopped for milk."

Though he tried, Franklin couldn't stop pouring out his heart. "On the way into the store, I changed my mind. I started back to the car. But when a woman bumped into me, I turned around and went into the store." He groaned.

Pastor Mark placed his hand on Franklin's arm. "In the name of Jesus, Father help Frank feel Your love, and shower him with Your peace." Mark whispered, "Sweet Jesus," several times.

Trembling, he continued narrating his story. "After I came out of the store, it was freezing rain. At that point, I realized she must have had a premonition of the bad weather.

When I got back to the car, she asked me to wait for the weather to let up before we went home. But I wanted to take her straight home where she'd be safe and warm."

Pastor's half shut eyes glistened with tears. "Of course you did."

"I raced through the green light. That's when we were t-boned by the so called Christian drunk driver."

He slapped his hand down on the table. "I can't tell you how many times I have sat alone on this very table, drinking coffee, and telling myself, I lost her over a gallon of milk. Do you understand what I'm saying? She's dead, and it's my fault! Over a gallon of milk, I escorted my wife to her death." He bowed his head.

While Franklin mumbled, "It's my fault," over and over again, he felt pastor's hand on the back of his shoulder.

"Comfort Frank with your peace, Lord."

Franklin threw his fist heavenward. "The hypocritical Jesus freaks at Katie's church comforted me, alright." He snarled, "Their excuses why she died were preposterous. The best one was God sacrificed her to save others." He gnashed his teeth together. "But only the so called saintly holy rollers attended her funeral. That is, except for me, the heathen."

With his finger shoved against his chest, Franklin growled, "So tell me Pastor, God had me kill my wife to save me? God mangled her in a car wreck to save me? That's real comforting, isn't it?"

In a firm, but gentle tone, Mark responded, "God did not sacrifice your wife, and He did not have you kill her."

Franklin plopped against the back of the chair with his arms hanging off to the sides.

Pastor Mark proceeded, "Since God said, 'thou shall not kill,' and the word kill in the Hebrew means murder. So, why would He allow you to kill your wife when He commands you to not murder?"

"Huh! What are you asking?"

"Why would God have you murder your wife when thou shall not murder is the sixth commandment? Would God break His own commandments?"

Franklin placed his elbows on the arms of the chair. "Of course He wouldn't. But why would those Christians tell me that? Even the pastor preached it during the funeral."

Shrugging, Pastor answered, "I'm not sure where it comes from. Why would God sacrifice a human being to save others when Jesus is the once and for all final sacrifice for all sin? Now, that's according to Hebrews seven.

But God said that all things come together for the good to them who love God. That's why we see good things happen at Christian funerals, such as friends and family members getting saved. When most people attend funerals, they think about their own mortalities, and many of them get saved. It might be because of this, Christians think that God had sacrificed a loved one to save their other loved ones. But the scriptures say something different."

"Makes sense. But you can't deny that I dismissed her warnings, and that makes her death my fault."

"Let me show you something." Mark reached around and removed his jacket off the back of the chair. He pulled a small bible out of a pocket. "I never leave home without it." He thumbed through the pages. "Here we go. He leaned forward and turned the bible for Franklin to see. "Look here, in John 3:17.

> For God did not send His Son into the world to condemn the world, but to save the world through Him.

If God didn't condemn you, why do you condemn yourself?"

That question jabbed Franklin's heart like a dagger shoved into his chest. "Are you suggesting that I'm a self-condemning delusional nut? Look it, Pastor, my wife warned me," he raised two fingers, "twice: once to go straight home and the other to wait. If I had done either, she'd be alive today. No matter how you look at it, it's my fault."

"Did you know that if you stopped at the store, your wife would be killed in an auto accident?"

"Of course not."

"Did you do jail time because of her death?"

Leaning forward, Franklin placed his forearm on the table. "That's ridiculous!"

Pastor Mark closed his bible. "No it's not. God didn't condemn you and the police didn't condemn you. If it were your fault, you would have gone to jail. God condemns Satan. You're not delusional either.

Satan blinded you. That's why you dismissed her first warning. Then Satan came like an angel of light and convinced you to take her straight home so you can protect her. You were unaware of Satan's tactics. Satan came to steal, kill, and destroy. He killed your wife, and he's been trying to destroy you by accusing you. He's the accuser."

"Hold on, so are you saying that Satan led me to believe that I escorted Katie to her death?" Franklin questioned.

"Self-condemnation comes from Satan, not from God. Satan is the prince of lies. He's the inventor of lies. Satan tried to murder the both of you, but God thwarted his plan."

"I beg to differ with you. My wife is dead."

"Her body is, but she's not, and you're still here."

Franklin pounded his fist on the table. "But I don't want to be here without her! We were together since we were five. She's the only woman I've ever dated. I ever kissed. I miss her." Tears poured out of his eyes. "How can I live without my wife?"

"You can with Christ. God loves you! Frank, be thankful for the beautiful family that you still have. Maggie is a beautiful little girl, and she loves you. Start the healing process today. Your family needs you whole, so they can heal too."

Rubbing his tear soaked face, Franklin cried out, "How?"

"You need to repent and ask Jesus into your heart."

Franklin slid off the chair and fell to his knees. "Father, in the name of Jesus, I repent all my sins. I repent for denying you. I repent for hurting my family. I repent for keeping my family from being healed. Oh, God, I'm so sorry. Have mercy on me. Forgive me, and heal my family. Help me live without my Katie."

Rubbing the tops of his thighs, Franklin's tears fell off his chin. "I've known to do this ever since I was a boy. If I had done this sooner, Katie would still be alive."

"Frank, don't do this. It's the devil's trap. Let it go."

"You're right. I got to let it go. God help me." Just then, he felt a tap on his shoulder.

Pastor Mark offered him his hand. "Here let me help you up."

"Thank you." Franklin reached deep into his pocket for his handkerchief. He blew his nose. "Hey, praise the Lord, I feel like a veil has been lifted off my eyes. It's weird but it's real. Wait a minute! Did you hear me? I said praise the Lord."

"The Holy Ghost is living in you now. You'll be saying that a lot."

"All along, Maggie has been saying that I'm not saved, yet, and she would put an emphasis on yet. She knew this would happen."

Pastor Mark chuckled, "For a little girl, she's got a lot of faith."

"Oh yes, she does," *especially when it comes to parking spaces.* "And when she finds out I gave my life to Jesus, she's going to be one happy little girl. But it might disappoint her that she didn't lead me through the sinner's prayer."

"Frank, she tilled and watered the ground. All I did was pick the fruit that she produced. I guarantee you, she'll be thrilled."

While Maggie napped, Pastor discussed God and the goodness of His love with Franklin.

"Grampy, Grampy," Maggie's screams blared throughout the house.

Franklin darted his eyes at Mark. Both leaped out of their chairs.

Maggie ran into the kitchen. Trying to catch her breath, she exclaimed, "Grampy, God showed me the angels rejoicing over your salvation! I saw them. They were in heaven rejoicing over you. I saw them, I saw them. I did. You will get saved. You will, you will, you will. Hallelujah!" Lifting her arms in the air, she twirled around on her heel. "Hallelujah!"

By the look on Pastor Mark's face, he seemed as much in awe as Franklin was.

Franklin placed his hand on her shoulder, slowing her from spinning. He squatted down in front of her, and he took a hold of her hands. "Princess, you saw angels in heaven?"

"Yes, so many of them that I couldn't count them all."

"How did you see them in heaven?"

"In my dream."

Dumbstruck, Franklin looked at Pastor.

"One of the ways God speaks to us is through dreams," Pastor Mark explained.

"I remember! My pappy told me God gave him a dream about marrying my grandmother before he had met her."

"Really, Grampy?"

The more Franklin thought about it, the more he wished God would talk to him someday. But at the young age of eight, his little princess talked to God. Why hadn't God ever spoken to him?

"I got something to tell you."

How long will it take before Franklin begins hearing from God?

"Okay, but I saw the angels . . ."

"Shh, I know. I have news for you."

Hit with a revelation, Franklin bolted to his feet. "Pastor Mark, God has spoken to me all along. That night when I had thought about going back to the car, God was speaking to my heart. If it weren't for a woman bumping into me, I wouldn't have gone into the store. I get it. The devil used her."

"Exactly," Pastor confirmed.

"Furthermore, I couldn't have gotten saved today, if God hadn't been speaking to my heart . . ."

"Grampy." Maggie tugged on his shirt.

" . . .God used you and Maggie to . . ."

"Grampy, you got saved?"

"Yes, hold on a minute. God used you and Maggie to speak to me too. Correct?"

With a sudden thrust, Maggie slammed her body against his, and she flung her arms around his waist, almost knocking him off his feet.

To catch his balance, Franklin grabbed the top of a chair. "What's going on?"

When she looked up, her chin pressed against his stomach. "You got saved."

"Yes I did," Franklin cheerfully replied.

"I told you God was going to save you. Now my whole family is going to heaven. This is the best day of my life, ever."

What a fool Franklin had been wasting all those years. He could have missed that day if Kitty hadn't given him Maggie, but he gave his life to Christ too late for Katie to see it. Oh how he had caught her praying for him. A missed opportunity he could never have back. But everything that had happened helped him realize how much his family really needed him for their healing, also. "Princess, let's sit down."

Franklin lifted Maggie onto his lap. He wrapped his arms around her, and he gave her a big squeeze. "Thank you for all your prayers and for never loosing faith in God."

"You're welcome, but I can't breath. You're squeezing me too tight."

Both men had a chuckle over that.

"Well, it's not getting any earlier." Franklin slid Maggie off his lap. "Shall we all go out and finish the job."

"Yes!" she rushed off, but stop dead in her tracks. "I left my cell phone upstairs. I got to call Mom and Dad. I need to tell them you got saved. I'll be right back."

When she pivoted around, Franklin took a gentle hold on her arm. "This is something I would like to tell your mother, myself."

"Why?"

He let go of her arm. "Because this is something I would like to do myself. Please respect my wishes."

"Oh, okay, but can you call her right now and tell her?"

"No, I would like to tell her alone in person when she comes home tomorrow. She deserves that."

Her brows bumped together. "But why?"

"It's something I need to do. Please respect my wishes."

"But—oh okay. I'll respect your wishes."

Franklin reached for his jacket from over the back of the chair. "Well, is everybody ready to go back to work?"

Little more than two hours later, the trio had completed the job, including the life sized Nativity scene with the exception of the baby Jesus in the manger.

When Franklin reached down into a wooden box of straw, he came up with the statue of Jesus in hand. "Maggie, would you like to do the honors of putting Jesus to bed?"

"Can I?"

"Absolutely."

While clapping her hands, she shouted, "Praise the Lord!"

Her emerald eyes twinkled as he placed the wooden figure into her arms. With her eyes glued on the statue, she knelt down by the cradle, and she laid the baby on top of the hay. After she kissed it, she slipped the blanket over it.

Mark encouraged her. "Maggie, you did a great job."

"Yes you did, my little princess," Franklin added.

Still kneeling, Maggie prayed, "Thank you Lord for saving my Grampy. That was the best Christmas present ever."

"It was for me too." Franklin started humming, "Hark the Herald Angles Sing."

Maggie took Franklin's hand and Mark held hers as all three sung in chorus.

Then Mark glanced across the street. "Well, brother, I had a great time. I best be getting back to my place. I need to go get my bride. "

Franklin shook Mark's hand, "Thank you for everything."

Mark cuffed his other hand over Franklin's. "I enjoyed every bit of it. I love ya brother." He slid his hands on Maggie's shoulders. "Love you too."

"I love you too." Maggie turned around and gave him a hug.

Mark rubbed his hand on top of Maggie's hood, "Behave." With his hands in his jacket pockets, he strolled across the street.

"And many blessings to you," Maggie called out. Afterwards, Maggie crinkled her nose. "Grampy, I can smell it. I smell snow. It's coming. I think I've been here long enough, don't you?"

He took her by the hand. "I believe so because I can smell it too." He hunched over. Looking upward, he pointed his finger. "Look how cloudy the sky is."

Without warning, she let go of his hand, and she grabbed him around his neck. "Thank you for being my Grampy. I love you too much."

"Well princess, I love you more than you could ever imagine."

Quickly, his mind drifted to loosing her again. Why do Kitty and Jake think they have to go to Thailand? Though the thought tore at his heart, he refused to allow the inevitable ruin their last night together.

While they embraced, his Christmas lights glowed through the darkness of the stormy clouds. Sudden strong winds whooshed, hurling heavy wet snow at them.

"Grampy it's snowing. I told you I smelled it coming." She raised her face toward the sky.

"Yes you did, and I'm proud of you."

"I'm proud of you too for giving your life to Jesus."

After Maggie settled in for the night, Franklin added another log into the woodstove. What would life be like when his family moved away? He gazed into the fire. Deep in thought, he locked the iron door. The door bell rang. He jolted.

CHAPTER 24

Sue Stops by to Thank Franklin

FRANKLIN HURRIED TO THE front door. "Who is that? It's late? Go to bed."

When he peaked through the peep hole, he couldn't believe his eyes. "Mrs. Hamilton? What in the world?" He opened the door.

Shivering, she held a square Tupperware container near her chest. "Frank," her teeth chattered, "I'm sorry for coming by so late, but I wanted to wait until the kids were in bed."

"Sue, did you leave the kids alone in bed?"

"No. They're with a sitter. I would never do that. I know you're the one who gave it to me."

"What? Gave you what?"

"You gave me the Ford Explorer." She swung around and pointed at the SUV in his driveway, "That one, right there." She lifted an eyebrow. "Don't deny it."

He dropped his head. "I won't."

"I came by to thank you, and I made you brownies. It's my secret recipe," her chin quivered, "How did you know the red Ford Explorer was my dream car?"

Franklin looked heavenward. It had to have been Jesus' plan. "Sue, please come in. It's freezing out there."

When she stepped inside, she took off her snow boots. Standing in white stocking feet, her eyes were red and swollen.

"May I take your jacket for you?"

"No, thank you, I can't stay long. My friend's teenaged daughter is watching the kids. I promised I wouldn't be long."

"I understand, but please allow me to at least make you a cup of tea."

"That does sound good. I can use something to warm me up."

"So, is that a yes?"

"It's a yes, thank you."

Franklin hung her jacket on the coat rack.

She scanned the room as she walked along side him. "You have a beautiful home. It's very cozy."

"Thank you," he pulled a chair out for her, "Please Sue, have a seat."

"If I had a kitchen like this, I'd bake everyday," she placed the container on the table top.

He helped her scoot in. "You like to bake?"

"Yes, it's relaxing. It's like therapy for me," she hung her purse on the back of the chair, "and the kids love it when I make them goodies."

"I bet they do." He put the teakettle on the fire.

"I've been baking ever since I was little girl. My father passed away when I was twelve. My little brother, Larry, he was only eight. I watched my little brother for my mom, so she could go to work at the factory. She worked second shift. So, I had to cook dinner for me and him."

It amazed Franklin how talkative and friendly she was. From his previous encounters with her, he had pegged her as an insecure introvert.

"We didn't have much food, but it taught me how to create recipes and how to substitute items for other items. I'd experiment with different ingredients to create meals. I wish he didn't live so far away. I really miss him."

He leaned against the counter with his arms across his chest. "Where does he live?"

"He lives near Branson, Missouri. He and his wife go to some mega church there. He preaches to me a lot, but I don't mind. He's my brother, and I love him. When I told him about the car, he said it was from God. The man that delivered it to me told me the same thing. He told me that Jesus loved me too. He had quite a story about his own experience with Jesus.

I think God could have something to do with it, because nothing good like that ever happened to me before. But I know that you're the one who gave it to me."

The kettle whistle blew. Harry moseyed into the kitchen.

"Is that your dog?"

"Yes, his name is Harry."

As though the dog would understand her better, she exaggerated her voice like a little girl's. "Hello Harry. You're such a pretty puppy," she threw him kisses, "Yes, you're so pretty."

That voice went through him like a piece of chalk screeching against a black-board.

"Come over here. Come on."

Harry looked at her, turned around, moseyed back to his bed, and conked out.

"He passed out fast. He must have been tuckered out."

"Yes he must have." He placed a mug of brewing tea and a dessert plate in front of her.

Before he sat down, Franklin lifted the lid off the Tupperware container. "These brownies look like a professional baked them."

"Thank you. I'm very detailed."

"I can tell," he picked one up and examined it, "Wow, look at all the pecans in there, and they look fudgy." He picked at it. "You put chocolate chips in there too?"

"Yes, I did."

When he sat down, he wiped the crumbs off his fingertips. "How did you know I gave you the Explorer?"

"Frank, your name was on the title. I assume Dr. B. Francis Franklyn is your legal name, correct?"

For a plain woman, she had a sweet smile.

"The Lord did lay it on my heart to give it to you."

Swallowing down a sip of tea, she looked him in the eye. "But its two years old. It only had forty-three miles on it. Why is it still brand new?"

Lord, help me.

Sue set the mug down. "I'm so sorry. I—um—you have a lot of pain in your face. You don't have to answer that."

"Don't be sorry, it's okay. I bought it for my wife two years ago for a Christmas present three days before she had passed away."

She sucked in her breath as she placed her hand over her mouth. "I'm so very sorry. I shouldn't have pried."

"You did not pry. You asked a perfectly normal question."

It struck Franklin. Since Sue had come by, she had made eye contact with him. He rubbed his lips. "I would like to ask you a question. It's a nosey one. That is, if you don't mind?"

"A nosey one," she giggled, "No, I don't mind."

"Until tonight, you never made eye contact with me. Why not?"

Her smile fell off her face. "Sometimes it takes me a while to feel comfortable around someone. Well—and—you're a wealthy, highly educated man. I'm just ordinary Sue. I'm nothing to write home about."

Franklin never thought himself more special than others, in fact, quite the contrary. But she had such low expectations of herself. That seemed odd.

"Sue, Jesus loves you." Without much thought, the words flowed out of his mouth. "He loves you so much that He laid it on my heart to give you the Explorer. When I bought it, I parked it in my brother-in-law's garage to hide it, and it has sat idle in there ever since."

Sniffling, she pressed the back of her hand against her mouth.

"Sue, think about it. The Lord didn't just give you a vehicle. He gave you your dream vehicle. How could I have known that? I bought it for my Katie. But God held it for you. Just think about that. You're special in Jesus' eyes. He loves you." Franklin found it remarkable that he sounded like Pastor Mark.

Silent tears rolled down Sue's cheeks. "In all my fifty-seven years, I have never had anyone make me feel special. I never felt loved, either."

It fascinated him how the words kept flowing out of his mouth like a river flowing over a waterfall. "Yes. God loves you so much that He picked me to help you get your dream vehicle. Think about it, nobody else came by when you were broke down in the ditch before I did. And then I met Charlie's nephew, Tommy, and Charlie happened to have his wrecker at Tommy's house. That's not all coincidence.

I'm about to tell you something that you may not have known. I parked in front of your Subaru at Christmas Town, and that was the only available parking space in the parking lot. Maggie prayed that we would meet up with you, and God told her that we would before the end of the day. We did, didn't we? It was all part of His plan."

She cried.

"Sue, the moment I gave my life to Jesus, it was like a veil was lifted off my eyes. It was something spiritual that I can't explain, but I see things now, like never before."

"But how could I ever thank God?"

He responded, "All you have to do is repent, and ask Jesus into your heart."

Sniffling, she asked, "Can you help me?"

Uh-oh! Now what do I do?

With droopy eyes, Sue stared into Franklin's. "Well, can you?"

Lord, help me do this. "Yes. I will."

She bowed her head and folded her hands in front of her.

"Repeat after me, Father in the name of Jesus, I repent for all my sins. I ask you to come into my heart. Amen!"

The prayer seemed too short, but he hoped it was good enough.

Her head popped up. "Am I a Christian now?"

"Yes, you're a Christian."

"I understand what you meant by the veil. I can see Jesus is real, now. It feels so good, I can't stop crying."

It's a beautiful feeling, isn't it?"

She nodded, "It is."

Exuberant, he bit into a brownie. The delectable flavor burst into his taste buds. "Sue, this is fantastic! It's the best brownie I've ever had."

"Thank you," she blushed.

"I'm serious. If you sold these, you'd be a millionaire."

"I've been told that I should open a bakery, but I don't know how to do that."

He had no right to advice her. For years, his insecurities kept him from opening a diner. Only because of Katie's encouragement, that he had considered doing so. "You know how to bake, right?"

"Yes, but I don't have a clue how to run a business."

"The community college offers continuing education courses to help you start a business, or you can take a course or two online."

"I can't right now. I have to juggle my time between work and the kids. I just don't have the time."

She had a point, but it was a shame she had a talent that she couldn't utilize, especially when she needed the money.

"Frank, I need to get home. I can't thank you enough for all you have done for me."

"No problem. Thank you for these fantastic brownies. I'll get your jacket for you."

As he helped her slip on her jacket, she asked, "Do you like Hermit cookies? I've developed a recipe for those."

"Hermit cookies are my favorite."

"Sometime I'll make you a batch."

"Thank you, Sue. I'd appreciate that."

Franklin walked her to the car. After she drove away, he raised his arms heavenward. With the snow hitting him in the face, he hollered out, "Jesus, being used by you was the best thing that ever happened to me. Let's do this more often."

He bounced up the porch steps. He grabbed the doorknob. The reality hit him. "Kitty is coming home tomorrow." He closed the door, and leaned his forehead against it. "Lord, what am I going to do when they leave?"

CHAPTER 25

Kitty and Jake Return with a Surprise

WITH MAGGIE'S FINGER TIPS clinging to the windowsill, she hopped up and down on her toes, as she hollered, "They're here, they're here." She spun around. "Grampy, they're here. Can I go out to them?"

"Of course." Franklin sprung out of his chair as she rushed out the door.

Franklin stepped onto the porch. The overnight storm left its breathtaking footprint on the neighborhood.

Maggie ran down the long walkway, shouting, "Mom—Daddy," as Kitty and Jake emerged from the white Pathfinder. She leaped into her mother's arms, nearly knocking her off her feet.

Standing on the porch, Franklin stayed back to allow his daughter's little family to reunite. Meanwhile, his eyes admired God's majestic artwork on the landscape.

Snow crystals arrayed naked branches on the hardwoods. Fresh-wet snow overlaid the conifers. The trees stood tall against the backdrop of the sun rays soaring through the bluish-gray stratus clouds. The smoke bellowing from Mark's stone chimney augmented the picturesque wintry postcard scene.

After a few moments in her mother's arms, Maggie reached for her father. Jake took her, and he carried her with her legs wrapped around his waist. While they moved up the walkway, Maggie pointed out the different lawn ornaments.

Kitty walked briskly towards Franklin. "Daddy, I got some great news for you."

He hurried off the steps and started down his long walkway. He flung his arms open. "I got some great news for you, too."

Kitty ran into his arms. "I love you, Daddy."

"I love you too." Out of the corner of his eye, he noticed Jake, with Maggie, rush passed them. Franklin cuffed his hands around Kitty's face. "My precious cinnamon bun, before we go in, I got something to tell you."

"What is it, Daddy."

"I gave my life to Jesus."

Wearing a radiant smile, tears dropped from her eyes, one after another, until a steady stream flowed down her cheeks. She tilted her head upward. "Praise God," she screamed. With her arms straight up, she broke into a dance. "Hallelujah! My Daddy got saved. Thank you, Jesus. Hallelujah!"

Catching her breath, she grabbed his arms. "Daddy, God answered my prayers. I can't tell you how happy I am. Sometimes I thought it would never happen. But Maggie always said, 'it will happen.' Her faith is unmoving."

He chortled, "She made that clear to me too."

"She did? That's my little girl."

He touched her face. "Kitty, I have something I would like to say."

"Yes, Daddy."

"Our family has suffered a lot of pain. I'm sorry for all the added pain I have caused you, and our family. All I want now is for our family to heal."

She stepped back. "Daddy, the moment you told me you got saved, the healing process began."

"But I have one more thing I would like to say. It won't do any good, but I would like to let you know how I feel."

Her eyebrows arched up. "What's that?"

"I don't want you to go to Thailand." For a brief moment, he turned his face away. "It'll be difficult to be separated from my family again."

"I understand, Daddy. But you don't have to worry. We're not going there."

"You're not?"

"No. God steered us into a different direction when we were down there."

Without a doubt, Franklin could have leaped for joy, but he waited to hear, like Paul Harvey had always said, 'the rest of the story.' "So, what's the different direction part?" He braced himself for the worse case scenario.

"Daddy, I can't tell you until we're all together."

"Well, let's go inside, so we can all have a nice talk together."

She pressed her hand against his shoulder. "Hold on. I got some great news I'd like to tell you."

"Well, I can use a dose of great news."

"Good. We can stay for Christmas."

In a monotone voice, Franklin replied, "That is great news."

Her eyes twinkled and her dimples appeared on her cheeks. "Just think Daddy. We can have an old fashion family Christmas like old times."

But without Katie, it couldn't be the same. Nevertheless, though he wasn't sure if he was up to it, it was time to make new memories with the beautiful family he still had. "Yes we can."

"I'm so excited."

He needed to find out that different direction she had mentioned. "So am I. But I think we should go inside. It's bitter cold out here."

"Yes. Let's."

While walking up the walkway, he laid his arm around her shoulders. "I remember when Jake asked me for your hand in marriage. We were hunting up north in Moose Alley."

"Daddy, what made you think of that."

"I don't know. I've been thinking about my family, lately. I had dropped a huge bull. When we were gutting it, I told him that I would do the same to him if he ever hurt you."

Raising her upper lip, she stopped short. "You didn't?"

"I did. You should have seen his face."

"He must have been terrified. That was mean."

"Has he ever hurt you?"

The two started up the porch steps.

"Really Daddy. Come on. Jake? Of course not."

"Good. Then I did my job."

She busted out laughing. "You're so funny." Standing near the front door, she commented, "By the way, I was hoping that I could get you to make me your famous meatloaf, maybe for dinner tonight. I've been craving it for a while now."

He clicked his tongue. "Not tonight. My little princess kept me very active and on my toes while you were gone. It's not that I'm complaining. I loved having her, but I need a break. So, I was hoping that you and Jake could treat me to Donati's tonight."

Taking hold of the door knob, Franklin moved aside to let her in.

"Of course, Daddy, we'd love to." She walked through the doorway.

Maggie was knelling in front of Harry nose to nose when Franklin and Kitty came through the door. Squatted in front of the fireplace, Jake turned his head their way. Kitty hung her jacket onto the coat rack.

Harry snatched a dog biscuit out of Maggie's hand, and he took off. When she chased him, the two sounded like a couple of horses running through the house.

Shoving her gloves into the pockets of her jacket, Kitty glimpsed over her shoulder just as Maggie disappeared into the kitchen with Harry.

With his elbow on the banister, Jake had his eyes on Kitty.

She took energetic steps toward him. "Jake, Daddy got saved!"

Maggie chased behind Harry back into the room.

Jake replied, "I know. Maggie told me. Praise the Lord."

Maggie halted. "Grampy, you told me not to say anything to my mom. I didn't."

Jake glanced at Franklin before he snapped his head toward his daughter. "Did Grampy tell you not to tell us?"

Franklin stepped closer to Jake. "Please, hold on. Let me explain. I told her not to tell Kitty because I believed that was my place to tell her, not hers. But I never told her not to tell you. I did presume she understood I meant the both of you. But I didn't think of spelling it out to her."

"I see." Hunching over, Jake placed a hand on Maggie's shoulder. "Didn't you understand that Grampy meant me too?"

She swayed her head. She looked over at Franklin. "Grampy, I'm very sorry."

"Princess, you just didn't understand. No apologies needed."

A smile popped on her face. "Thank you, Grampy."

Giving Franklin a half hug, Jake commented, "Dad, welcome to the family of God. Jesus is faithful."

Harry nudged Maggie, and woofed.

"You got a Husky." Kitty knelt and sat back on her heels. She took hold of Harry's neck. "He's beautiful. When did you get him?"

Before Franklin could answer, Maggie interjected, "His name is Harry." She draped her arms around the dog's neck.

"Hello Harry." Kitty tilted her head toward Franklin. "Why did you get a Siberian husky? I thought you didn't like purebreds."

"Who told you that?"

"You did! Remember when my friend's dog had puppies? They were purebred Pulis? I was in high school? Do you remember?"

"Huh? Oh yes. Are you talking about that ugly dog that looked like a black Cousin It from The Adam's Family?"

She rolled her eyes. "You never let me get the Puli because you thought she was ugly?"

"Yes. But can you both please sit down. I would like to discuss something right now." While Franklin adjusted his sweater vest, his eyes fell on Maggie, his little bundle of joy. "Would you like to sit next to me on Nana's old chair?"

"Really?"

"Yes really." Franklin sat down.

"Thank you." When she sat in it, she rubbed her hands along the arm rests.

"Are you comfortable?"

She answered, "Yes. Nana's chair is so comfortable."

"Good, then it's your chair from now on."

"Really, it's mine?"

"Yes. Whenever you come and visit, you sit there."

"Thank you." She wiggled her toes.

Kitty had her hands folded on her lap.

Jake stretched his arm behind his wife. "So, Dad, what would you like to discuss."

"Your different plan on where you're going."

"Oh, you heard about the new plan." Jake turned his attention on Kitty. "Do you want to tell him?"

"It's okay. You can."

Jake tapped her on the shoulder. "Are you sure?"

"I don't mind. I was going to tell him, but you can tell him."

Frustrated by their unbelievable conversation of over who would tell him, Franklin jumped in, "Would one of you please tell me?"

"Grampy, I go through this all the time. It's like when you explain your name."

Franklin held a finger against his lips. "Shh, be nice." He looked over toward the couch. "So please tell me, what's the plan?"

"Let me explain," Jake responded.

"Explain."

Without hesitation, Jake began his narration. "Well, Sam and Jennifer Buckland were the missionaries we went to meet. Jennifer's parents, Alan and Ava Smyth, stayed at the same hotel that we stayed at. They lived in Fairbanks for the past twenty-five years or so. This past fall they moved back to Flagstaff, Arizona. That's where they're originally from. They had a diner in Fairbanks. But now that they're in their seventies, they closed the diner. There's a church on their property as well."

"A church? You would think they'd have a house," Franklin commented.

Jake sat forward, and he dangled his folded hands between his legs. "There's a seven room and two bath apartment above the diner."

"So, they lived in the apartment?" Franklin inquired.

"I don't know. I didn't ask."

He didn't ask? He didn't ask a perfectly normal question?

"They needed more parking spaces. At the time, the property was only on a half an acre."

Why couldn't Jake have just spelled out their plans without adding all that unnecessary information?

"When they bought the extra acreage to expand, an old vacant church building came with it. Over the years, they rented it out for weddings and such . . ."

Franklin interrupted, "Why are you telling me all this? Did you buy it?"

"Nope, but we had a miracle."

Kitty touched Jake's knee. "I would like to tell him about it."

"Sure honey, go ahead."

Kitty climbed around Jake, and she squatted near Franklin with one hand resting on the arm of the chair. Her entire face sparkled. "Daddy, God had laid it on the Smyths' hearts to give us the church for our ministry."

"What do you mean, give? Like for free? The diner too?"

"Not the diner, but yes on the church. Daddy, this is so exciting."

"Does that mean you're moving to Alaska?"

"Yes."

"Praise the Lord! You're not leaving the country. Kitty, you just made me a very happy man."

"Thank you, Daddy, but there's more good news."

God is so good. In anticipation, Franklin listened.

"Now, hear me out before you say anything."

When she forewarned him like that, Franklin had no doubt that her good news wasn't good. "Just spit it out."

"Okay. They're prepared to sell the diner for a mere twenty thousand dollars. That includes the apartment."

Franklin sat upright and rigid like an army colonel about to scold his men. "Why are you telling me this?"

"Daddy, wait before you jump, please. I know you no longer want a diner, but just think of it this way. If you bought the diner, we can help you realize your dream, and Maggie can grow up around you."

Maggie leaped out of the chair. Stretching her arms heavenward, she shouted, "Praise the Lord!" She danced around the living room, shouting, "We can live near Grampy! I'm growing up with Grampy!"

Franklin barked, "Kitty, you know I won't open a diner without your mother. Why are you bringing this up?"

Maggie halted, standing in front of Franklin and her mother.

Kitty flinched. She pleaded, "Don't you see that this is from God?"

"That's farcical!"

"But Daddy, it's not a farce. God doesn't want you to rot away in this house grieving over mom, any longer. It's His will for you to start living again. This type of grief you're hanging on to is not only affecting you, but us too."

With his jaw clenched, he upbraided, "I am working with moving on with my life, but I refuse to open a diner without your mother. Why can't you respect my wishes? It's not going to happen, period."

"What kind of Grampy are you?" Maggie hollered with her eyes filled with tears.

Franklin gaped at her like he had just seen an alien. "What do you mean?"

Weeping, she ran to her father. Jake lifted her on his lap. Clinging unto him, she cried, "Why don't you want to live near us? I thought you loved us." She turned her face into her father's chest, and sobbed.

Slack-jawed, Franklin ran his hand through his hair. "Maggie, I'm sorry. Please don't think I don't love you. I love you very much, and your mom and your daddy too."

Maggie turned her head. "I love you too. But don't you want me to grow up near you? I wanted you to teach me to be a chef like you."

Her watery and droopy eyes grabbed Franklin's heart. "Yes, I want you to grow up around me. But I can't open a diner."

She whined, "Why?"

Kitty chimed in, "Yes Daddy, why?"

Franklin exploded out of the chair. He stomped off to his den, slamming the door behind him.

CHAPTER 26

Franklin's Revelation

FRANKLIN PLOPPED DOWN ON his office chair, and wiped his eyes with the back of his hand. Mucus oozed out of his nose and down onto his upper lip. Without thinking, he rolled his lips inward bursting the salty water-works into his mouth.

Sitting back in his chair, he mulled over the time he had with Maggie. Setting up the Christmas tree with Maggie, being reunited with Bob Lapierre, building trust in Pastor Mark, letting down his guard with Jesse, and helping Sue and the kids.

"Wait a minute. I've been moving on with my life. I've even changed. How did that happen without me realizing it?" Tears dripped off his chin. "But how can I do the diner without my baby?"

He grabbed his head. "My family is closing in on me. How can I explain it to them? How do I work this out in my own mind? Wait a minute. I still have my beautiful family."

When his fingertips touched the box of Kleenex, it jounced from his hand. Before it fell off the desk, he caught it. While wiping his face, he noticed Katie's bible still on his desk. He must have forgotten to put it back into the safe, but he felt drawn to open it. His hand trembled as he reached for it. He snatched her bible up.

After he laid it down in front of him, he slid his thumb along the small bloodstain on the bible case. "That's all I have left of my baby. Her blood drop." Blubbering like a baby, he realized he was making himself totally miserable. "I can't keep doing this." He unzipped the bible cover.

Tucked inside the slip pocket, he found Maggie's Christmas play's program from the night of the accident." He turned it around. "There it is." While reading it, he mumbled. "Philippians 3:13-14=Frank's high calling: the dream diner."

"Frank's high calling? What? The scripture!"

He frantically slid his finger down the bible's table of contents. "There's Philippians," he flipped through the pages. "Verse 13, where is it?" he found it.

> "This one thing I do, forgetting those things which are behind, and reaching forth unto those things which are before, I press toward the mark for the prize of the high calling of God in Christ Jesus."

He laid his head down on top of his crossed arms. He sobbed. No matter how many times he wiped away the tears, their flow seemed endless.

While he reread the verse through his blurred vision, it all became clearer for him.

Then from within him, he heard, "The past cannot see the future."

"Jesus, you spoke to me," he shoved his finger against his chest, "and I heard it. Just like Katie had described it."

Flashbacks from over the past five days swirled through his mind. While he pondered on each event, he envisioned the divine design of God's tapestry that Pastor Mark had talked about. "Yes. My family, my beautiful family."

Franklin rose to his feet. Standing at attention, he snapped a salute to the Lord. "Sir, I am ready. Give me my marching orders."

CHAPTER 27

Moving Forward without Katie

As Franklin meandered through the house, he heard laughter. He followed it. When he reached the kitchen, he stayed back to observe his beautiful family.

He eased his back against the pine molding that edged the ornate-log archway. He crossed one foot over the other and crossed his arms against his chest.

With her eyes crossed, Maggie had a piece of peanut butter and jelly sandwich hanging from her tongue. A string of drool latched from her tongue down to her chin.

With her face twisted, Kitty squeezed her eyes tight. "Ew', that's disgusting."

Jake chuckled, "Okay, that's enough. You're grossing out your mother. Just eat it."

She wiggled her tongue before she slurped the morsel into her mouth.

Franklin ambled into the kitchen. "Did anybody make me something? I'm starved."

Wearing a milk mustache, Maggie waved her hand. "I did. I made you a peanut butter and jelly sandwich. Do you want it?"

"Daddy," Kitty shrieked. "Are you alright?"

"I'm just fine. Well, where's my sandwich?"

"I'll get it," Maggie hurried off.

With her forehead puckered, Kitty questioned, "Are you sure you're okay? The way you took off concerned me."

Jake, sat across the table, and he kept his eyes focused on Kitty and Franklin.

"I do apologize for running out like that. Can my family forgive me?"

"Grampy, here's your sandwich," she placed it down, "I forgive you."

"Thank you, princess." Franklin added, "I needed to be alone. I hope you understand."

Jake nodded, as he responded, "No problem. I understand."

"Daddy, of course we understand. I'm so sorry for pressuring you. I just want to know that you're okay."

"Yes, I'm doing just fine. I had some time with Jesus." Franklin lifted the top slice of rye bread in search for the peanut butter layer.

"Grampy, what are looking for?"

"This is quite a master piece." He bit into the sandwich. The taste of strawberry preserves melded with caraway seeds bursted across his taste buds. "Maggie, this sandwich is quite unique. I never had peanut butter and jelly on Jewish rye before. It makes it interesting."

She blushed, "Thank you. Mom wanted to put it on the wheat bread like ours, but I told her your favorite bread is rye. But she told me that she couldn't make it with rye bread. I told her I could, so I got to make your sandwich for you."

"Well princess, you did a great job."

"Opps, I forgot your milk. I made you chocolate milk. It's in the refrigerator. I'll go get it."

He glanced over at Kitty and then Jake. He mouthed, "Chocolate milk?"

Grins appeared on both their faces as they nodded in sync.

"Daddy, I'm sorry for upsetting you."

"You did not upset me. I upset myself."

"Here you go, Grampy."

Franklin looked down into the glass filled with mud-like chocolate milk.

Maggie hovered over him. "I tasted it like you taught me. You're going to love it. It tastes like chocolate pudding."

He took a gulp, and he clinched a fist as he forced it down his throat. "I've never had anything like this before."

"Mom, I told you he'd like it," Maggie declared as she skipped back to her seat.

Jake remarked, "By the look on your face, I imagine you have never tasted anything like it."

"No, not quite, but she has the creative potential to work with me in my diner."

Jake froze with a coffee mug in mid-air.

Kitty's jaw dropped. "You're going to move to Fairbanks?"

"I am. Since working a diner is my high calling in life, I thought I should follow God's lead."

"Praise the Lord!" Jake hollered out."

Kitty and Maggie jumped out of their chairs, and they both threw their arms around Franklin.

"Daddy, I love you so much."

"I love you too Grampy. I get to grow up around you." Maggie put her face into his. "So, I get to work with you, really?"

Franklin padded Maggie on the arm. "Well, since I'm naming it Maggie's Diner, I think you need to."

Maggie hoped around the kitchen. "A diner named after me! I can't believe this is happening."

Wearing a smile from ear to ear, Kitty squatted down next to Franklin. "Daddy, does this mean you're going to resign from the university?"

"I already did."

Kitty stood up. "You resigned?"

"Yes."

She placed her hands on her hips. "What were you planning on doing for the rest of your life?"

"Become a Wal-Mart greeter."

Jake cracked-up.

Maggie bellowed, "I like Wal-Mart greeters! They give you a basket and they say hello and they're really. . ."

"Maggie!" Kitty called out, "Grampy is joking."

Maggie shrugged, "I still like them."

"Daddy, would you please tell us what were you planning on doing?"

"I wasn't sure what I was going to do. But I thought about moving up to Alaska."

Kitty threw her hands upward. "So you planned to move to Alaska all along. Why didn't you just tell us?"

"We were discussing the diner, not where I thought about moving."

Recollection dawned on Maggie's face with her finger pointed upward. "Grampy, I told you that God told me the diner wasn't the picture. He was giving you a real diner, remember?"

"Hold on," Jake blurted, as he reached down toward the floor near him. He sat the shopping bag that Mark had given Franklin on the table, and he pulled out the picture. "Maggie told us that your new Pastor gave you this."

"Yes he did, yesterday."

"Grampy, I told Mommy and Daddy about Mr. Jesse and Mrs. Hamilton and Lucas and McKenzie, and I showed them the picture. I even told them the story you told me at breakfast, this morning."

He scratched the itch in the palm of his hand. "What story?"

"How you led Mrs. Hamilton to the Lord last night when I was asleep, and how good her brownies were. You said they were the best brownies you ever had in your life."

"That's true, they were delicious. You liked them too. But I haven't seen the diner your parents are talking about, and I can't make a decision until I see it."

"Daddy, wait a minute. I'm confused. Please clarify this for me. So, you're not going to decide whether or not you're going to move to Fairbanks unless you like the diner?"

"No. I'm going to move to Fairbanks. But if I don't like that diner, I'll find another one."

Wearing a huge smile, Maggie sat down. "You're going to like the diner my parents found. Jesus just told me, 'That's your diner.'"

Because every time Maggie had said that Jesus had said so it came to pass, Franklin wasn't about to argue with her, but he still had to see if for himself.

Kitty scooted her chair in. "I have a gut feeling about this too, Daddy."

Could that have been Franklin's confirmation? No doubt, he liked the price. Maybe that diner was exactly what he had dreamed about. The more he thought about it, the happier he felt about it. He busted out laughing.

With her head tilted, Kitty asked. "Daddy, what's so funny?"

"I don't know. I just feel like laughing."

On Christmas day, the family gathered around the dinner table for their traditional yuletide feast, along with Franklin and Maggie's new friends: Pastor Mark and Grace, Jesse, and Sue and her grandchildren. For the first time in his life, Franklin prayed the blessings over the meal.

One could taste the love in their feast of a standing rib-roast accompanied with sides of roasted potatoes and tender-maple-glazed carrots.

Maggie, Lucas, and McKenzie helped serve the warm sweet and savory Indian pudding topped with a scoop of homemade French vanilla ice cream for desert.

With a silver spoon in hand, Franklin recalled the man with the white hair at the mall. "Jesse, the day I met you there was a man with white hair who helped me hold you. Did you see where he disappeared to?"

Jesse's forehead crinkled. "What man with white hair?"

"The tall brawny guy, he had white hair. Don't you remember? He was the one who helped me constrain you."

Biting down on his lower lip, Jesse swayed his head. "No." He let out a hearty laugh. "I get it! You're joking. Frank, you had me for a moment. You're good."

A lopsided grin appeared on Maggie's face. She waggled her eyebrows. "I told you he was an angel. Grampy, like the bible says, watch out because you may entertain an angel in unawares."

Franklin conceded, "No two," referring to the strange man he had met at Christmas Town.

www.ingramcontent.com/pod-product-compliance
Lightning Source LLC
Chambersburg PA
CBHW070222030726
47505CB00006B/1774